The author was born in Sutton Coldfield, England. He studied at Ellesmere College, Shropshire, leaving to take up a position in his father's watch component manufacturing business in Birmingham. Later the company was sold to an international group based in the Far East. With his father's business incorporated into a larger organisation it resulted in the author gaining experience in the group's facilities in the East. Retired now, the author has returned to live in the region.

For Da Pengsawang

Michael Bishton

THE ISLAND

A CIP catalogue record for this title is available from the British Library.

ISBN 978 178455 046 2

www.austinmacauley.com

First Published (2014)
Austin Macauley Publishers Ltd.
25 Canada Square
Canary Wharf
London
E14 5LB

Printed and bound in Great Britain

1

As he remembered it from his boyhood years, so had it made itself known to him in that first burst of impressions he got stepping from the car. Nor had the demands of the journey southwards from Bangkok altered to any marked extent. To reach this spot on the Gulf of Thailand remained a drive of some three hours or more, this four people they made, not including the drivers, divided between a pair of limousines. Honestly stated, to call the location a resort was to stretch the reality of the situation. No length to it to speak of, the distinctly obscure slab of beach that to all appearances made for this out-of-the-way place in its every slant bore so austere a character, the scene in some essence felt like an earlier dawn of man. To make a print in the sand with your foot, as it struck you, was to join with a candour and plainness of purpose hardly to be guessed at.

The beach was like a gaunt, wasted man, lost to the illumination which by rights should be in a shoreline. That it was home to a fishing village was not on some days entirely obvious to anyone making a first acquaintance with this section of the coast. With the settlement's dwellings hidden from view, it was the pattern of life that the boats departed in the evening and it wasn't the odd occasion that they shunned returning at dawn the next day, preferring instead to stay out on the ocean for a second night. The village encampment itself enjoyed the protection of the wooded terrain that at the rear bounded the belt of white sand down its full length, ensuring that the circles of rough village abodes stayed out of sight. With his earlier experience of the area, merged as it was with a definite if reluctant intimacy with the people, the man, the Eastern industrialist, Pracha Wantana, couldn't doubt that once the village was found, once he set eyes on it again, an atmosphere and shape would yet be revealed that in its essential rawness would remain a perfect fit with the primal nature of the beach, provided a person was to disregard the many television aerials standing erect from the thatched roofing of the dwellings, in some sense an unlikely crop still, but one that could only have proliferated in the intervening time.

But it was the seclusion that he and his colleagues had come for. Only in a single place did the isolated, lonely stretch of sand produce a construction in keeping with the habits of men steeped in the wider civilization indicated by a city like Bangkok. Shabby in appearance as the restaurant was, it was the exemplary simpleness of the villagers' lives rather than any especial economic shackles that held them back from bringing their custom to its door. Not until the two cars began approaching the beach had it dawned on Wantana that the restaurant might well no longer stand. It had been a moment seeing him blush violently on his inside, for what would he then do with his guests. Again, a constant in his life, he cursed his own blind impetuosity. He had thought of the beach, he had remembered the restaurant, and thinking the thought the great charge of intention overtaking him had swept aside the possibility that something may have changed. He had wanted something from the beach; it would give it to him.

The single access road to this enclave by the sea reached up to the side of the restaurant's simple timber structure and could be interpreted as dividing the beach into two halves. Some way along the sand on the leftward direction, there stood a chain of private beach chalets, their darkened ancient wood like a sort of coal. Each of the five properties in question was built on stilts. Outwardly they sustained the uncultivated cast of the site. Inside these 'cottages', though, was laid out a marked gesture to twentieth century material solace. Wantana knew enough to be confident of the upkeep of the five chalets on their interiors. The Bidaya family had kept faith with this stern coastal outpost. At intervals it allowed a release from Bangkok. Even if for many of its elite families the city was compulsive. The properties down near the water's edge were theirs, as was the entire stretch of the territory forming this shoreline; as was what stood on this territory; the fishing village, everything, one family ruled; the Bidaya family, as feudal in their instincts as some Eastern militaries.

The portion of the beach going off to the left marched on beyond the last of the holiday shacks. As far as it went, it yielded a scene that one might term as featureless in the extreme in that here the works of undisturbed nature continued to reign unopposed. Of the territory adjoining the beach at that farthest quarter there was nothing but timeless raw forest to reckon with. With little conical mounds of sand heaped around their bases, the trees set out along the periphery of the sand, and which formed the first line of the forest, were meshed together so tightly it left the onlooker facing an impenetrable wall. At a glance the gaps between the trees felt no wider than would take your hand, all of it unyielding shadow seething with otherness, with nature like a scar, dread and ill-omened. The worlds that Wantana and his three guests inhabited and moved in for the great part weren't of this variety.

During the time of his boyhood it had been the habit of the villagers to warn Wantana away from the part of the beach continuing past the chain of holiday properties. In masterly fashion their tales angled for everything that was a boy's imagination, planting the idea of the forest as home to primitive types unconstrained in their impulses, and never without large knives, their instinct more attuned to dispose of a stranger than to find a word with which to address him. On vacation he had listened to the village people and it didn't matter the distances a significant industrialist had travelled in the years since, he still listened, still paid attention, and not like a man on a charge to build a business empire, but like the boy he had been. He was caught in something. They had done it, the fishing folk. So much the forest was other, at this place as well as elsewhere in Thailand.

His early years had instilled him with another factor embedded with this one beach. It was why, inside the chalet he had chosen for himself, he had from the first morning washed and showered with some haste, his mind focused on getting back to the room in which he had passed the night, giving as it did an unobstructed view of the ocean.

Now it was the third morning of their visit, but his ardour to witness the coming of the boats hadn't lessened. With a towel tied around his waist, he stood at the bare rectangular opening in the front wall that served as a window to the room (and also an entrance if you were inclined to step through it from the wood cabin's simple veranda), his wide oriental bulkiness planted down with the resolve and presumption of ten men, the square set with which he was braced on his feet producing a quintessential image of the thirst some men betray for securing an unadulterated dominance over their fellows. Even alone as he was, his innate despotism sparked off his body like a roll of drums. So it was that he watched for the fishing boats, and so it was that he also waited again for the Englishman in the party, whose habit it was, going by the previous mornings, to stalk down to the water's edge indecently early, dawn just starting to show, the tentative light an image of famine, no more with a centre to it than last week's drunk on his unsteady legs.

Pracha Wantana was in possession of an intelligence that was more than capable of indulging itself by way of the abstract. In fact, the fanciful of mind was a distinct bent of his. But at this time his thinking was condensed into an altogether harder focus. The issues he was concentrated on related to his career, and to his ambitions for that career. The question of the Englishman was large amongst these concerns. Wantana was deeply confused, for having known Richard Marshall for a considerable quantity of years he was being forced to confront someone he barely recognized. There had been a kind of revolution even in physical terms. Marshall had never been a markedly tall man, but this new representation, this new human individual, carried himself as if he were. The faultless grooming seemed an unmovable thing. It took off from the hair, which was worn much shorter than before. With the uncompromising look of it, it shot at Wantana as indicating a devoutly abstemiousness person, something Marshall had never been. Brown in shade and keeping to an exceptional flatness overall, the hair in its style of cut gave off without doubt a distinct air of the military. Garlanded at the summit by such unwavering precision, it came about that this precision carried to the rest of the man as if it was a kind of oil flowing over his parts. However the re-girded man was dressed a silken orderliness breathed through the image he presented. He held himself so protectively of this, and of so much more. To Wantana's perception it was someone oozing with consciousness of his glamour, an air never apparent to Marshall before, and firm in a self-satisfaction that smirked without favour at the society about him. And most especially at what that society might choose to condemn in him as a man. Where society forced its rules at this figure, Wantana saw a precocious grin of mutiny curling off a man's features. The exceptional strangeness in the person was that every movement of his body was played out as if it was a secret pact with his own self. This was Richard Marshall, one of his long-established serving executives? He doubted his very eyes still, as he had from the moment of Marshall's sudden appearance in his office in Hong Kong days before.

Reaching the beach on the first evening his rancour was high. He despised himself for the jam he was in with Richard Marshall. Under his breath he swore, all of it for himself. The person he was tried to his bone to give an explanation of was the man he had been when the link to Marshall had taken root. A crucial relationship had had a beginning. He, Wantana, was responsible. And then, as the hours had unfolded at the beach, everything had come to a head. He was in a sort of daze from it. Richard Marshall had astonished him. He had astonished himself. Never mind, he was about to go one better. It wasn't over yet.

In fact, within minutes of their two cars pulling up at the beach, Pracha Wantana had been beset by all manner of misgivings. As was his habit, he had conceived of the idea of a short break from his office in a sudden flourish. With equal impetuosity he had acted on it. But once the four of them began to extract themselves from the cars, he had been overcome by a feeling of foolishness. Knots of apprehension had whirled about his insides. Why had he picked this place? Too often when there was a visitor from the West standing in his Hong Kong office he was spurred into abrupt changes in his routine. A titan of industry, at moments he was also an instinctive host with a very real need to play the part, and never less than with grandeur, with extravagance. Perhaps his readiness to take himself to a place of isolation was a reflection of the impossibility of the business step he was meditating on. When contemplating a major advance for his organization, it was his way to put his ideas to an assortment of confidantes and advisors, more than a little captivated as to the reaction he would get; but not necessarily the band comprising his established inner circle of senior executives; nor to a collection of outside men wearing the stripes of major financial organizations. He was as likely to go out of his way to avoid such people.

Not infrequently in the course of a day he would in a sudden burst put together these little groups from the most random and unpromising of sources within his organization, even resorting to the lowliest amongst his workers; for what he sought as much as the counsel was the opportunity to gaze at the emotion showing in the faces of those he employed called suddenly to his presence not to be given orders but to be treated as human beings deserving of simple respect. It was an exchange: he was enhanced by the magical confirmation of his figure he couldn't mistake in the faces, the eyes glowing as they did on the other side of the desk from the definite impact he made on these men; they were enhanced by the mere fact that they were even in his office, by the revelation that they were in fact known to him at all.

But there was this other factor. Goading himself to a moment of far-reaching decision, often at such times his inclination indeed was to shun sagacious professional advice. The larger the impending decision, the more it seemed he sought to lighten the load by the apparent amateurishness of those against whom he might test out his provisional plans. But just how should he go about entering into a discourse with others on the subject of his newest idea? It outreached anything he had ever conceived of. Such was its scale that he was brought to a covetousness so personal he had retreated from the smallest word on the subject. Secrecy was necessary as a strategy, but secrecy was also urged as a form of emotional barricade for he went in terror of provoking a universal derision at the preposterousness of the idea. At this instant he was debating whether to pursue a controlling interest in the largest American watch company in existence. The international oil and gas company holding the shares in question was looking to offload them having tired of the value of their investment. In truth this debate he had entered into with himself as to whether to proceed with the exotic business raid was what he was living to the exclusion of everything else. Just as had been the case when over a matter of weeks he first decided upon and then realised the flotation of his company on the newly inaugurated Hong Kong stock exchange.

Now it was the prospect of America filling his eyes. Unknown to his father he had initiated the first moves in the hunt to acquire the shares, that unknown to the family owning the historic American watch enterprise, were being toted around with a certain wantonness. He could not say precisely that his quest represented the attempt at an epic commercial takeover since the shareholding in question did not constitute a majority stake. Still, the percentage involved undoubtedly represented a controlling interest and with the pain of his pursuit of these shares it was he himself who had been taken over. It was a state of grace. Nothing could be as enriching. Once again he burned with vitality. Once again he thrilled to an immense eagerness for life. The strangulation at his interior regions was one of expectation, for himself, for his organization. He was drunk with a single idea, but this one was terrible in the audacity of it. Wanting to believe, he could not believe. Hope and desolation alternated by the hour. In the course of a day his emotions swung back and forth through to his depths. But waking at dawn he thrilled to a feeling of newness. He would not, could not, stand down from it.

He had achieved much, but he had forgotten all of it. It was the idea of America giving his legs their purpose. He could no longer maintain his silence on the matter, neither professionally or privately. But before he made it known fully in the public domain, he was driven to set out his plans to a small circle he could perceive as intimates of a sort. Thinking of who to speak to, he had chosen in haste, but not without thought. What interested him above all was that he be comfortable with the persons he selected, what interested him was to be certain of them in human terms, so that even as he would implore them to be objective and impartial in their answers to his questions, he could be confident their responses to him would never fail to observe an essential caution that finally in sum would bolster his desperate devotion to the project.

But the one exceptional person who on any interpretation stood out as closest to him in both the personal and business sense, he just could not find it in himself to take into his confidence. If at this early stage he exposed his ideas to his father's inspection, he suspected that that would be the end of the venture. To lead his father to where he intended to go with this project, at some point he would effectively have to lift him up onto his back and carry him.

Bound to his father, constantly he mediated for him. And that was to mediate on his own behalf. There were moments when he saw himself as forced to inhabit a kind of no man's land existing between two determined irreconcilable extremes. How could he begin to convey to the circle of western business contacts he was developing, the sheer depth of his father's removal from their world? It was because of his father's simple persistence in the matter that he, Pracha Wantana, otherwise, Daniel T.K. Bai, had reaped a western education. But as to reaching for even a tentative, experimental sense of the countries those transactions pointed to, his father declined. He might send his mind into speculation of the cosmos with more certainty. And more relish. From first to last he bent to insuperable gravitational forces of belonging. But was the man less complicated because of this? And hadn't he journeyed like the most courageous of the footsore? A land mass without precedent was behind him. His origins in Chaozhu, Guangdong Province, he had cast off those beginnings. He had found his way out of a country whose distances flayed the soul, a country in store to land and numbers of people on a scale its own. A country in which ancestral distance was so resolutely a sort of blood bound up with the grain of the air, it seemed to offer up the march of the preceding ages as a graspable presence that lived on still. But here simmered the paradox of the man. For all that the facts named him as a migrant, he hadn't ever believed in a journey that would genuinely revolutionise the streets. He crossed boundaries but he did not jettison an entire distinct region. Yes, at length he had found his way to Thailand, to a city, Bangkok, and therein was embodied a language and mores resolutely not his own. But to aspire to territory that another universe of man had fashioned: No! Upheaval of that magnitude was impossible. So, born to a place, he had moved on. In fact, his wanderings had turned around a well of rootedness. And that was the East really, Wantana told himself. Somewhere that was the East.

Already, yes, it was the morning of the third day at the beach, and as he waited for the trawlers to materialise on the water before him, Pracha Wantana, despite the mad challenge that waited for him on this penultimate day – from nowhere, in extraordinary fashion, Richard Marshall had put down this massive taunt, this massive dare, openly mocking Wantana, the man he took orders from – felt less deterred in his doubts, both with regard to his historic business quest and, somewhat remarkably, given the naked physical test he must take on during the next hour, in respect of the place he had brought his guests to. This would be their last full day at the beach. The next morning it was arranged for the cars to return to collect his party, in its grey civility the cortege of two automobiles so coloured with the city Wantana saw it as trailing the city along behind it, setting some aspect of the urban confabulation down beside the cheerless coastal outpost.

But as he started to anticipate the cars coming, their image threw a sceptical glance at him. Truly, his excursion to this place had taken a turn he could never have foreseen. In fact, on this morning of the third day at the base physical level he trembled, his eyes going to the island lying some two and half thousand meters offshore, a wide climbing concentrated circle of rock, isolated and proud at the centre of the bay.

Everywhere he went now Pracha Wantana mesmerised people. Yet who purred like he did out of awareness of the natural appeal he enjoyed? One might say, in fact, here was the boundlessly sensitive man. Was it simply a devilish charm that he possessed? He did not know. But beginning a new day a part of his mind was to be found hypnotised: what might these mysterious powers of his bring him in the coming hours? Too often on meeting him it was as though people exploded to a sense that finally they were on the verge of discovering the purpose to their lives. And the purpose was exactly to be noticed by this Thai-Chinese businessman whose path they had crossed unexpectedly. Wantana was urged to divide the world accordingly: there were those, the vast featureless majority, who were desperately seeking from they knew not where a look or a touch that constituted a blessing, or some form of anointment, and there were the one or two, the true anointed ones if you like, who were possessed of the magnetisms that qualified them to dispense these sanctifications upon their fellows. The common herd, consciously or not, was doomed to this search. In his position of authority faces passed in front of him one hour to the next and repeatedly he saw in these faces a desperate plea for some form of ultimate recognition. The plea settled on him. He was to understand that the man in front of him believed himself more than worthy to be taken up and take him Wantana must, please! This occurred even as a person drew in his first breath after being introduced to him. To live now was to gain Wantana's eye. But once Wantana had recognized the adulation surging out of the poor wretch's own eyes, he would spin away in cold derision. None amongst his fellow men did he turn on more contemptuously than the very ones compelled to throw themselves down at his feet as though he were a living deity. Yet did the savagery of his rejection deter them? Not a bit of it. Their determination to stay near was as if redoubled. Perhaps that was another reason he had sought out this haven from his childhood. The Bidaya family used the beach to get away briefly from Bangkok. Well, he needed a release. Rarely had he felt such pressure to escape his office in Hong Kong. It mortified him to see the obstinate prostration of the adherents he drew in. But it terrified him as well. He could not shake them off.

And yet: simply, he could not do without them. It was noted that his innermost circle would, invariably, be composed of exactly this breed of person. His was a composure lacking a manful mastery, revealing instead this dreadful dependence on a regular show of cravenness from those who accompanied him and did his bidding. However brash and confident he could appear in his bearing, he had still to come to the inner confidence required if a man is to surround himself with the strongest personalities. Possessed of massive ambition, he it was who consistently disrupted whatever were the chances of this ambition succeeding to the heights that could satisfy him, and for the very reason that the people he set to work to help him realise these aims so often were shown to be seriously flawed in their professional abilities. To have the ambition that he had but without the courage for the kind of individual necessary to the ambition was a handicap that never spared him. Free to choose whomsoever he wished as his closest lieutenants, he went in fear of selecting the best and ablest. Men in his employment pleased him by their competence and efficiency, but they pleased him more by their flattery and general servility, their overt desperation to ingratiate themselves with him.

Wantana had wearied of simply serving the great watch companies of the world in the role of component supplier. He had his factories in Hong Kong and China. To complement these he had seized numerous manufacturing operations throughout Switzerland. He was one of the world's principal suppliers to the global watch industry. The international watch houses of the world depended on him. Their illustrious resonant labels adorned objects that could not be but for the parts he provided. But it was the recognition attached to the organizations massed beneath these trademarks that he had started to crave. It was their celebrity that he now aspired to, their richness and density of being as commercial entities, their brilliant worth and glamour, their indomitability, their primacy, their 'statehood'. His plan was to get there in a single move. Certainly he had built an impressive commercial grouping. He was going to reinvent it in the space of weeks.

He Wantana – forthwith know that word he signed himself with as synonymous with one of the great international watch enterprises of the world. Not for another day would he remain a simple unheralded manufacturer of items that the watch companies of the world screwed together to realise the famous object making their collections. And nor for him would there be the long trial of building a new brand name stage by stage, year by year. That didn't interest him. Truly, he would transform his organization overnight. In a manoeuvre like a card sharp's producer of parts for watches to international watch marque of the big name. This was what he wanted now. This was the dream that had snatched him up.

And it would leave him in direct competition with his father. Since in his capacity as a commercial distributor, his father was acting for one of the international goliaths in the watch business, representing exclusively across the nations of the Pacific Basin a Japanese watch label whose name had proceeded to burst onto the world scene in a matter of years; and not least as regards this arrangement that they had entered into with Narong Wantana covering the markets of the Pacific Rim, laying the foundations of the accelerating wealth of the Wantana family.

But the son intended to astonish the father. The son's modest manufacturing organization would be reborn as this very thing, a watch concern of global significance, no matter that it might compromise the father's relations with the Japanese giant in question, no matter that the son would find himself going head to head with his father in many markets. No, Pracha Wantana could not be put off. With the conclusion of the negotiations that had yet to properly begin, he would, by this simple exercise, establish himself as one of the preeminent, legendary watch concerns standing astride the globe. And he wanted America. He wanted it as the first Chinese industrialist to gain control of a major American corporation.

More than conscious of each other, Wantana watched from the beach chalet, Richard Marshall watched from down near the water, in all their sea-going mass the boats emerging from the wall of haze on either side of the natural object the locals venerated as an island, creeping slowly forward until they began to fan out along the centremost section of the beach. Eighteen trawlers in all and once it was firm and straight the line that they formed had the boats pointed directly at the curve of white sand, the series of rugged prows nosing the sand like deer cocking their heads at a scent of danger. The return of the boats had been soundless, but where there is a timeless community like this, a body of people straddling the meeting of land and sea, a village in a blood-clasp with nature, bound by the deepest instinct to the lapping of the waves, reared in its pores to the repeated stealthy approach of vessels bearing its own, is it not possible to believe that some invisible force or thread of tension goes forward to cross the waves ahead of the boats, then to inveigle itself into the alert sleep of the people? What is beyond doubt is that as soon as the shapes did edge gently out of the mist a little army of sturdy village girls trailed forward across the sand, their brown vests and short workaday brown skirts like a uniform.

As a single body, and even if with their express lack of hurriedness, the girls never veered in their march towards the water. Insignificant against the sweep of the ocean, once the sea was at their feet the young females commenced to wade out towards the boats as if with the sureness of grown men. The teasing distance that the boats stood off from the shore seemed almost like a malicious test that the deckhands on the trawlers had deliberately laid down for these solid sisters of theirs. In no time the young women were submerged almost up to their chests and though their legs were hidden, none watching could be misled as to the innate power of their lower limbs, all of this might pitched at the dragging weight of water. By turning their palms outwards some of the girls used their hands to assist them, their arms swinging away from their bodies in a motion describing a slow, dreamy arc, which drawn out languid stroke was repeated on and on. However it was that their legs called on simple muscle power, with this movement of their arms, it was the grace, femininity and merriment of the girls that was eventually so telling to the eye, as if these were things hung from a taut string that was stretched out across the low waves.

When the girls reached the boats, sharing themselves out between them, the water was swilling at their shoulders. Now all the strength and power in the image transferred to the sea itself and to the climbing hulls of the boats. To someone like Pracha Wantana looking on at these things from the shore the village girls milling at the bases of the trawlers' sides were nothing but a clutch of tiny heads bobbing like sea buoys above the surface. Should some nameless force suddenly take hold of the boats, twisting the hulls uncontrollably on their anchor lines, it seemed all these little skulls would be crushed like glass.

Still no sound reached back to the beach. With the girls still and waiting, it was as though a dance of mime was being executed just out from the shore. The girls had their elbows angled out over the water as if with intentional exaggeration, so that it appeared almost a calculated display. You thought of a person resting his arm on the wall of some country lane in a great show of personal insouciance. Soon the mime went to its next design. As if in step with each other the girls, like gymnasts, pushed their arms straight up and held them there unwavering. It was then that the men on the boats leant over the sides to hand down the baskets filled with the catch from the night hours. On the journey back the troupe of girls did struggle, as proud as they were. The whole way they had to keep the baskets balanced above their heads. They waded forward like prisoners trudging towards the worst. Deep as laundry baskets but broader, there wasn't a girl whose own basket didn't spill over with the work of the boats. Gaining the beach the girls immediately sank down under their loads, their sodden clothes pasted against their bodies. But just as they themselves had appeared so mysteriously on the beach at the moment the boats came into view, so now they looked up to find other villagers, men, boys, mothers, descending over the sand to help them.

Pracha Wantana turned away, at a loss to give a proper account of the events he had just watched, which in truth added up to nothing more than a simple undying ritual in the life of one of the nation's villages. With the splendid office he inhabited in Hong Kong, it was a staple of his life to be witness to the comings and goings of larger kinds of vessels; so many of the working ships of the oceans were dark and monstrous apparitions, as impenetrable in their industrialization as the great mining installations of old. They entered the bay of Hong Kong, they departed it. In between, and for all their pitiless steeled factory hugeness, they stood off from the shore in a slightly wretched slovenly fashion, slumbering at their isolated anchorages like unkempt outcasts, their demeanour on the water at once aggressive and wary, this wariness driven seemingly by the nearness of the land, the nearness of one of the world's great cities, a place that ran on ceaselessly in Wantana's mind, ran on curse and heaven one, ran on as perhaps a desert will stare at you if it is to be crossed and your flagon is dry.

Hong Kong was the city to which on a day in the past his father had moved his young family wholesale, judging it impractical for him to remain in Bangkok. The tensions between the Bidaya family and the Wantana family had become insupportable. It was the city he, Pracha Wantana, his father's eldest child, had made his way back to after a prolonged hiatus in Europe, paid for by his father, having the end of endowing him with a rather exalted formal education. And which place on the night of his return from Europe he had retreated from violently as the car ferried him from Kai Tak airport to the house in Yau Yat Tsuen, darkness gripping the eastern city, darkness in the low gaze he sent at it.

Not looking anywhere particularly he had found himself counting off a somewhat anguished inventory of a famed metropolis, the fairground of a displaced mind riding the fairground that was one city's maze of thoroughfares. He did know these streets, after all. In some, once dawn took over, especially near the water, you were free to tread a path out in the open, the avenues broad and patient with it, the day writ clear and simple in the unobstructed space, the city at these points no less simple. But further in where a city thickened chunk on chunk, you entered tight streets little short of catacombs no matter that technically the high-built street frontages brought about a shape like a ravine, no matter that the sky was visible where these the walls of the ravines peaked. It was the pavements, the floor of the canyons, that had the feel of a subterranean world, the spirit of daylight absent.

Then there were enclosed city channels where the buildings sat lower, squatter. Exhaustingly fetid, in touch, in smell, in vision, in clutch, and no less resistant to daylight, the city regions they comprised sweltered, not so much from the heat as from the density of construction sandwiched between the runs of the backed-up narrow lanes. Narrow, but when walking the rag-bag facades had a way of stealing closer, then closer still. With your advance it was the jaws of a vice groping at your shoulders, a ratchet tighter with every ten steps. At places the skyscrapers had their roots in the quagmire. Where the city kept to lines of low-set roofs, where it sprawled in ad hoc shapeless fashion, the slovenly domestic warrens and sinister commercial lean-tos could be laced one to the other with such remorselessness the morass appeared the fruit of generations of drunken minds.

In the rear of the car that night, he had quickly wilted, a tyranny at his throat, the tyranny of boxed living spaces growing outwards in great seamless gluts. No, on the night of his return from Europe, he hadn't had the inclination to look, but it had flooded into the car anyway; closing his eyes the leprous conglomeration of concrete forced in on him with increased ferocity.

And, of course, a man breathed in, he breathed out. His lungs sucked in oxygen and in Hong Kong that opened him to the reek. Be it harbour, be it city, in its odorous weight and dissolute quality air lay about as a kind of vagrancy against the senses. Yes, Hong Kong: harbour, city, with its clammy grip the air could seem a thing to unravel, like matted unwashed hair. Harbour, city, on some days the rankness went to stench. And with an effort to render it meaningfully it could play tricks. One day's impression of the ponderous fragrance was not the sensation pursuing you the next. At an earlier time in his life, before he had left for the western colleges, on some street or other of the city, or maybe it was while out on a boat in the harbour, that stale dull to the water seen on metal left to languish, a moment had been when he had caught a tang strongly evocative of sodden towelling stagnating in an airless room.

Hong Kong: with his father's fateful decision it had become his home. It was the city in which he did his work and endlessly that work would have him addressing tables of figures. The cleverest executives felt threatened by his instinct for numbers. He could decipher and extract the essentials of a balance sheet in the time that a marksman will aim his rifle. His hands shot to such documents with a rare passion. In moments these same hands discarded the papers with utter disdain and apathy. Called on to make a presentation to a line of bankers, he became irresistible. At such moments he was a man supremely in touch with himself. A man absolved of personal doubt. A man standing where he knew absolutely he should. Someone who would be polite with bankers, but someone whose eyes let out that he placed himself above them. As he gave voice to reams of figures it was a flute that he was playing and he was this flute.

Hearing the step of a tall man on the short stairway to the chalet's veranda, Pracha Wantana swung himself into a beach gown and made ready to go out to greet one of the three persons, this one French by origin, he had invited on this somewhat bizarre excursion back to his roots. He had decided on it after a disturbed night. The previous day Richard Marshall, the chief of his English operation, had appeared unexpectedly in Hong Kong. Richard Marshall standing in front of his desk, Richard Marshall this exorbitant human issue he was facing, a matter he had avoided for months, perhaps for years, he had known he couldn't delay any longer. He had to resolve the thing. He didn't like these matters. He wasn't comfortable with them. He had confessed his discomfort to the man from France, that rare beast in his life; someone close at the human level rather than just one more on his payroll.

And after the Englishman Marshall had left that day, he had gone to his habit following all significant business meetings, of pacing alone back and forth across that office of his in Hong Kong. Leaving aside the matter of Marshall, he had a love of the meetings that were the bread and butter of an industrialist's days. The smallest of such conferences could leave him impaled on the flood in his head. He kept on seeing the faces and what had been exposed on them. His mind replayed the threads of speeches, of arguments, of inspired perceptions. These were his own words he was hearing as well as those of the men he had been seated with. And then it would be the eyes in isolation that kept on pushing at him. It was when he got back to the eyes after the event that he intercepted their repeated click of calculation, their lethal emotional distance. Almost invariably at the conclusion of a meeting he was overcome by the feeling that he had missed something crucial. But, of course, he hadn't missed anything. All of it came to him in time. And often, with the last man exiting his office, it needed not a minute more. The helpless eruptions of recall followed one upon the other, stampeding through his mind as if without a care for his sanity. So it was that to disentangle the avalanche he paced back and forth alone across his office. He paced like a convict in his cell. He loved the sudden solitude, the seclusion, after the throes of battle. He was on a quest of construction outside the range of most men.

The aircraft that he observed from the masterful windows of his Hong Kong office as they manoeuvred on the tight spaces at Kai Tak were now carrying so many western personages to the door of that office. There were eminent industrialists like him, like him the definitive power in their organizations; but also his door saw a stream of business executives positioned lower than board level, sales representatives principally, the majority of course with posts in the international watch trade or related industries. But as well lawyers, the odd architect; and as his powers to invest had started to expand so fabulously, so governments had commenced to show an interest in establishing a dialogue with him, despatching their officials to join the others in the cue outside his office. And if a man rises like this, there will be journalists hovering nearby from one month to the next in order to record the event. Yes, the story, it is everything. And nowhere more so than when it the story is a man, one man.

Time: it was how the day advanced, appointment to appointment. It was the most banal word in the human lexicon. But also it told of one family's terrible romance. Watches, timepieces by another name – starting with his father, the Wantanas, amongst Southeast Asia's most powerful industrial dynasties, they were absorbed, obsessed.

Routinely Pracha Wantana – though in his life in Hong Kong, being of a Thai-Chinese family, he reverted to his Chinese name, Daniel T.K. Bai – found himself in his father's office in Star House in Kowloon. The sight offered by his father's desk these days Wantana accepted as a signal indicating something of the point the man had reached in his life. He didn't dirty his hands anymore. That he had consigned to his offspring. The immaculacy inseparable from his father's desk resounded like a hard vision of power. In any case the wood was to shine, so was the purity, the absence of object. His father operated behind a desk that was like a piece in a showroom. Whoever came to the far side of his desk was regarded over a sea of perfection. Bare was the plateau, vestal was the plateau. Almost, that is. Something was allowed in. Something was permitted a place. Too true a watch, and invariably a sparkling steel model seeing the watch case integrated with a handsome muscular steel bracelet. On any day, there it was laid out flat; and always, rigidly, just the lone example.

Languishing as it did without interference amidst an area otherwise pristine, it was heightened, brought to bear, both in its presence and for the thing it was. Day to day it wasn't the same watch. It was his father's pleasure to swap things around, picking at will from the vast collection his distribution agreement with the Japanese manufacturer was founded on. Watches, this was his father's business. But it was also, beyond his family, the man's avenue of connection to the world.

His father's desk: there you had it these days, a bare space but for the one item, positioned so as to be in reach of his father, there for his idling, for his communion. In conversation with the person seated opposite, his father's eyes would keep flicking to the spot, and, inevitably, his hand would soon follow. It was so much more than an animal's fur that he was caressing, so much more than the texture of any living thing that was the magnet for his hand.

A desk maintained as a virgin space, but Wantana's father was some kind of warrior with his watches, and somehow desperately defensive with his commercial success, desperately protective of it, even with the man who was the most senior of his offspring, the one he had allowed this western education. At moments they were father and son, but at others they competed with terrible passion. In the relationship of these two men seemed the ambiguity of Cain.

And on the evening in question, the night the young college graduate had become reacquainted with Hong Kong, his father, ruddy swollen features, the marvellous hood to the face the two small eyes that seemed to gaze outward with historic patience, hadn't been indifferent. Behind the superstructures of the house in Yau Yat Tsuen he had exemplified the image of a man waiting, and to the extent of retreating to his study, to the extent of seating himself there in exceptional stillness, altogether a man maintaining a very real vigil with himself.

Bai Khe Wah, otherwise Narong Wantana, had been at pains to count the years. Having a number before him would help him to go back to that time when he had become filled with the determination to send his eldest away for his education, away to the unparalleled West. Where had he been standing when first he drew out this line of possibility and thereafter tentatively followed it with his eyes? Certainly it had been Bangkok, but not at a spot in the city readily associable with such imaginings. With his concentration that evening, a car coming closer, the first son soon to appear, it was a multitude of corridors the eminent personage passed down. Located on one was the village in China he had set out from years previously. His fingers played on the desk. It felt to him as though with this nervousness he was prodding a mound of blessings. It was done now. He was holding this crib of completion. He could use it to cosset his head for the years of toil at a variety of workplaces, the first a common street trader's stall in Bangkok. He could use it to laugh at the memory of how this absurd experiment with destiny could leave him in a cold sweat. To have permitted his son all of this had been the purest gamble with himself. And the gamble would continue, for now he would have to take on someone with a fearsome trail at his back however young this person was in years. There in the figure of his son images he himself recoiled from speculating about. He could name the terrible distances his son had crossed, but he wasn't about to try to pencil in the spectres which were the great vaulted halls, the hushed coliseums of study, the ideas he bore for all he could say just so much unmitigated nonsense in his head.

And let it be nonsense. It had no bearing. The days he passed were oblivious of it. To all intents, only one imprint of the West leaked to his mental world: the watches grown in Switzerland.

Yet on that night also, the night he had kicked his heels in anticipation of the reappearance of the eldest of his tribe, he experienced the powerful sense he too somehow was on a march of return. He was being restored to himself. From everywhere he was starting to gather in countless shattered fragments of a man, pieces torn away, a kind of wreckage no less. But with the son coming back at last was the feeling he could piece together an essential wholeness that had been taken from him as if by force. Building a significant business enterprise, simultaneously in the palm of that other thing a man went at, a family of his own, truly, he had been so miscellaneous and spread apart as a man. So much of himself had sheared off to lie scattered all about, meaningless splinters that the city hordes trod underfoot in their charge down the pavements. It was the unremitting exertion of providing for a family with a dimension in constant mutation; it was the unreality of where the eldest had gone to; of what this son of his had been engaging with; it was the unreality of having encouraged these decisions in himself; the unreality of making traffic with forbidden deities. Then there was the fact of his other young. Would he be able to grant to them what he had made available to their brother?

But on the night his concern was more. With the eldest returning exceptional fear existed as well. Sending him away, what had he made his first son into? Had something formed that would have him eternally embarrassed, mortified at himself; something, someone, in possession of depths of knowledge that would open a gulf between them, he this simple soul from the fields.

But equally wasn't it for him to offer pity to his son? It would be a man he would welcome in the next minutes, and enshrined in this new adult would be a desperate pointedness, for nowhere was the eldest son the eldest in quite the way he was when the family was Chinese; when the line of offspring wore the dye that was apartness, history on its own, rule on its own: China. It would be a deluge that went to the boy, a deluge that flew back off him; and yes, a flood his son could flaunt if he wished, but which nevertheless would haunt him, persecute him.

So while waiting, as if to free his soul in the interim, Bai Khe Wah, Narong Wantana, had felt compelled to turn to what he knew. What he wanted to turn to anyway; his corporate affairs. In this he and his eldest could correspond. For so long what he had wished for most was not simply a man to share these matters with but also an intimate, a confessor. Hadn't he yearned for a church in which to unburden himself of the challenges in his affairs and a church in which to plan their enlargement?

And in a sense, waiting on that night, his family came to him differently, because now two would be leading all the many young forward, and flanking one another he and the first could target horizons that confined with himself he would never ever have found the courage to take on. Just fleetingly the idea of this beginning, the idea of it slowly embracing his family, had been Narong Wantana's trance.

And at a point in the next years the young man had stood in front of the resplendent chairman's desk to urge his father to renounce his increasing conservatism in business matters and help him finance what he intended would be the most palatial manufacturing building that had ever been erected in Hong Kong; a plant conceived to advance his own particular business enterprise, that of watch component manufacturer. How he, Pracha Wantana, otherwise Daniel T.K. Bai, had talked addressing his father.

He had begun by reminding his father that metal watch bracelets had been the earliest of the products of the manufacturing enterprise he had started going on his return to Hong Kong from the western schools, the initial funding of course a gift from his parents. Nor had it ever been anticipated that he would have but the single customer. His own father no less! But before long he had added the fabrication of stainless steel watch cases. Soon too had come watch dials. Largely this had occurred because of spontaneous enquiries he had received. He had been responding to events. And some of the enquiries originated in Europe. But if you have an operation centred on the creation of such things, Europe was effectively one country: Switzerland. He had his dream now. He intended to become the world's foremost supplier of components to the great watch organizations of Switzerland. Should he tell his father their names? But whatever for? Like no other man, his father knew these names. It was his very heart they had always carried to, his very heart that formed the words. In fact, before he, the first son, had ever set out to the western academies he had learnt theses names directly from his own father. Simply, his father loved to speak the words. In his father's eyes the words were meteors, the business enterprises behind them were meteors. The meteors of Switzerland! His father was dazzled. He had always been dazzled.

The building shown in the plans he had placed on his father's desk would in external appearance be like no other industrial building that had ever been constructed in the territory. And it would be necessary if he was to convince those he must convince. The good citizens of Switzerland, his father would have to accept what he explained about them. Too true this was one of the countries his father had sent him off to acquire an official education. His senior child let it be the best education in his father's means. Except at the time his father hadn't had the means. He had had to borrow the money. What was a technocrat? Well, when you engaged with the Swiss, you understood the term. The Swiss had faces as we all have faces. But bound up with theirs were these imperishable curtains, layer on layer; the scepticism, the monasticism. This is what he had to break down. It was the gravest aloofness that you could encounter in the Swiss, their souls a convent where method was venerated. How was he to achieve the initial break through; an opening that would have such people inspired? That this unknown Chinese businessman was capable of rising to their scientific standards – what should he do to lodge the prospect in their heads so that they started to believe? Well, the answer was on his father's desk. You want a sign of the man, well what accomplishes that like a building owed to his vision? Were the Swiss heading these famous watch firms to meet just another Chinese businessman in just another drab Hong Kong factory unit, he wouldn't have a chance. As his father had been moved to point out at his first inspection of the plans, his own building on the outside would appear more a modernistic hotel than an industrial edifice. It was a fabulous look the architects had created. Corner to corner something chiselled like a nugget of ore, its outside surfaces deep bronze. Bronze was the colour of meditation. But the architects had married that to a vision of technicality that those arriving at Kai Tak would be able take in as their planes tracked towards the terminal. In their seats, not knowing what this edifice was, they would be startled. As was also surely evident to his father as he took in the drawings, the factory would rise to thirteen floors. An office would be permanently set aside for his father on the topmost floor. It would lie adjacent to his. In their rooms they could stare out at the airport. Alone in their rooms they could watch the glinting airliners climb up into the sky, as if the suitors for a kind of cosmic blessing…

And abruptly, the son had been unable to continue, his voice giving out. To the older man it was this indescribable voice calling on him to follow, and incredibly bearing a sound that he knew from the dinner table in his actual home. The simple migrant struggles for years to establish a foothold that might gradually calm the anxieties provoked by the naked exploration he took on abandoning his roots, and then with the realization of a son he finds that the wildest shores of exploration still await him. This is what we can do, this where we can go, the voice pleads. You must believe it. And behind his mighty desk Bai Kai Wah had heard the summons, he heard because this was the house that he had built.

Appealing to his father that day Pracha Wantana had though, all of a sudden, been overcome with a terrible sense of futility, believing none of his words were getting through. In despair he had turned from his father's desk and gone to stand at the large window in the office. With his back to his father he had scanned the harbour, this pulsing valley amid the cityscape. Taking off from the surface of the water on that day was the image of a mellow pond out where you could follow the pinpoints of the boats. The various smaller craft crisscrossed in all gravity, their motors visibly reined in. The traffic of port, harbour, bay, this mix of vessels cutting their sundry missions, was as everlasting as the cycle of the days was everlasting. At their retarded velocities the more glamorous private boats propelled themselves along in a placid slipping motion, tenderness in the glide of raking hull, but an edge too of suspicion. In contrast, the working boats, the tugs, unhurried or not, they ploughed a furrow. Their movement was peremptory, like that of men on production lines. And wasn't it always inevitable to look again for the first kind, at once boat and scimitar, which chapter and verse with the crush of such a city as backdrop invoked those never to possess such things as much as the blessed ones enjoying the means; until your eyes like metal to a magnet found the best and sleekest of the motor yachts, and once finding holding on the sight, the boat's advance not a little hypnotic, engines terribly cut back, awful grace in the shape of the craft, grace in its obedient slink over the water, and behind a long, long ribbon of white turbulence extending away from the stern that made you think of the human spine, and of some of the products brought into existence every day inside these dens of manufacturing that at the time were so much the basis of Hong Kong, and so famously his own first motley plant amongst them.

Of course, finally, his father had agreed. The factory building unlike any other had been built. And now his father was older, and so was he. The problem with his father was that he interested him like no other man. He sensed that much of his emerging business career was centred on achieving a kind of ultimate victory over his father. To his eternal vexation his father was a man who achieved his victories merely by his presence. He required nothing beyond. Innately physical to the man was a peace as if born of the centuries. Now at the end of his fifties the lack of agitation in his father was like a forest. But, of course, his father's supreme achievement was his family who could not escape him. Even he, Pracha Wantana, otherwise Daniel T.K. Bai – every day he thrust off to outdo his father, every day he clung to him.

It sometimes seemed to Pracha Wantana that following his final homecoming from the academic years in Europe, not a day had visited him that hadn't at some stage seen him closeted privately with this man who was the patriarch of an overarching Thai-Chinese family, that had acquired the fame now of being amongst the most significant industrial families of the East. As solidly as an ox treks up and down a field, so the habit was enshrined in his routine, so it resided in his father's. But it hadn't to be imagined that throughout the day the secretaries of these two men stalked them like vultures. That an hour in the day had been ordained that were they to forego it for whatever reason would have these faithful ladies foaming with anxiety. Their arrangement attended through the very absence of planning. For all the regularity with which they met, no science told them when to convene, or when to break off. As their separate working days unfolded, the moment would converge on them arbitrarily. To Wantana's mind, it was as if out of sight of them a splendid barge was kept rigorously oiled and polished, ready at a moment's notice to drop anchor, its regal decks sacred because they were maintained solely for the one pair of noble confidantes. Two figures he kept seeing in his imagination, himself, his father, there suddenly in their business attire marching along some remote, mist-clad jetty. Stepping aboard, it was noticeable how they barely cast a single glance at the pole-man in the rear, or at each other. With a twist of the man's oar, the barge would move off into the waters of some secluded lake. The shore receding, a womb of strategic discussion would close about the two associates the lake all silence all peace.

But as Wantana never ceased asking himself: Was this in fact father and son? It just did not reach to him like that. The sense he had of these interludes was of two men who originally, at a certain mysterious moment in their pasts, had come upon each other by accident, and thereafter had continued to meet, each having discovered something exceptionally favourable in the other. Parting finally, another day's meeting concluded, they did so with an air that said each was to travel far from the other, the worlds they were returning to utterly unrelated, yet each sending back a last look to assure that somehow they would sit down again, whatever it took, even if neither entertained hopes that this could be soon.

Meanwhile, the next day, the next week, or the succeeding month, father, son, they would look out of their windows, or down on to some document, and floating into view would be the material effect of where they had gone one day with their talks. It was how a business, many interrelated businesses, made their way.

But at the onset of his business career the first factory building he had occupied with his watch parts manufacturing firm, and which it had been necessary to return to after one of those meetings with his father, too quickly he had just hated.

His earliest industrial premises had been wholly unspectacular, just something desperately plain; plain in its scheme as a standardized, sheer-sided quadrilateral industrial structure, plain in its smooth white-coated stucco walls, plain in the provision of its four stories, plain in the building's profound sameness with the neighbouring manufacturing units. In the image presented was the look of a district: that of the industrial quarter in Hong Kong called San Po Kong.

Others had been in the building before him, other organizations, all with their concentrations of obsessive doing; all with the point in time when they were, and that time too, inevitably, the forerunner of the time when they would no longer be, the building passed along like a baton. Even on the days when he did not leave the spruce administration floor he could grow listless at the demoralising mediocrity of those early walls of his. Too swiftly his first ever industrial unit he had born with grimacing heart.

But the sound was there, the sound of a factory. It resided above him it travelled up from below, where in the great hangars at ground level the heaviest pressing operations were effected. Massive sliding doors characterised these fearsome shops opening to the street. It was the pattern too with the other manufacturing premises continuing on along the narrow industrial thoroughfares of San Po Kong. The habit of a street saw these great access points standing open through the day, the towering doors drawn back so that street and industrial shop lapped against each other without release, in some streets a kind of native oneness developing from the embrace.

Be it his own men down there at street level, or those of the neighbouring enterprises, routinely they of these booming industrial barns worked in their vests, clothing streaked and soiled like the superstructures of the overarching presses the men tended. At break-time small gangs of these eminences, those working as press and machine setters, thick-set patronising men, would drift out through the great breaches in the walls, sauntering forth onto the sidewalk to let their presence be known to the world, to allow the world to take them in in their full scope as men. In their sundry boots, dungarees and vests, it was their way to assume idling nonchalant cavalier poses, all of it a heavy rite of factory man. As they stood about, some with oily rags dangling from their hands, the street took on an aspect comparable to the sprawling deck of one those cargo-hauling colossuses anchored out in Hong Kong's bay. Didn't it? At moments Wantana played with the idea that the men of his most uncompromising factory holds, these grim 'engine-room' regions of a factory, were as much a race apart as that breed having the distinction of actual working seamen. With the sound reaching him in his office came such spurts of intrepid simple-hearted imagination; in the sound was the street, all the streets, San Po Kong a beehive of manufacturing.

But before all else in the sound was the muted blast of his one plant, his start-out industrial unit. The jangle never left his ears, the daily whirl of a factory, of making a product, of despatching it on time. And if the premises were without any vestige of the majesty, the swank, he had begun to conceive of and wish for, the echo, the boom, the hum, the murmur of the floors under his control, by itself was a story, a story he was more and more urgent for.

Yes, back then his young heart had been full of radiance for the act of manufacturing, for steel alive with an industrial texture, for blocks of the stuff under intricate attack within the clutches of a miraculous state-of-the-art milling machine, there at the work station, with its flashing cutters and rainstorm of lubricants, a carnival of sorts. But it wasn't any lone machine tool that could satisfy his passion. His heart had hungered for the image of lines of machines receding ever into the distance, for the sight of three hundred girls curved over a single monumental workbench in an attitude of assiduous concentration, every one of the girls identically clothed in the blue of the company uniform, every one of the girls cloaked to the ends of time with these straight black tresses of theirs. Hong Kong was China even then. He was China. And he had wanted many more factories.

But for that he needed to impress; and not his kind, but the other kind, they with their western backgrounds.

Reaching San Po Kong each morning, the car having moments before passed by Kai Tak airport, he would watch his driver, Sim, cut back in a stroke their charged spurt through the city. Executing the exit from the highway it always felt to him that with this twist of the wheel what Sim was asking of the car was that it actually contract in size in readiness for the tight passages it would have to negotiate in order to make its way through to the heart of San Po Kong, so much a warren at its centre.

But the oppression of the area didn't materialise while you stayed next to the highway. To that part of the district there was a different shape to San Po Kong. Against the highway immediately on the inside the industrial units were large, standing edge-on to the road, the line of them stretched out in parade ground fashion, the road used as a gauging point. Down the line portions of daylight showed between the buildings.

On the other side, the harbour side of the highway, the land was not built up in the least as it ran forward quickly, no distance at all in fact, as it ran forward in the matter-of-fact way that neglected land often does, to the perimeter reached where it went up against the bowl of the illustrious harbour, the water pure expanse, but a spirit to the surface ripples not in the one circuit they were locked to.

In amongst the file of industrial units abutting the highway was found a building no less rectangular, no less unexciting, no less matched in height with the factories, but in its use not of the industrial fold at all. Eight storeys high, there were outside walkways at every height. On those walkways intermittently was seen the young. San Po Kong was industrial, yet San Po Kong had a school. White like the erections performing a manufacturing purpose, its white was somehow of a different ilk. White true to white, you might say, white unvisited by corruption, as devoid of tarnish as the glaring white the boys and girls were dressed in head to foot who populated the building. With its so virtuously-clad young filtering forth at the different levels the school was a white universe. It was an impeccable universe that the community that was Hong Kong had every right to view with pride.

For a whole year the turn off the highway that Sim made from instinct had allowed Wantana a darting glance of deep communion, his gaze striking off to the vacant industrial plot he had acquired. The prestigious parcel of land, the envy of any of his kind, had stood one building along from the school. The original construction resting on the site had suffered the fate that waited for many larger buildings in a city. It had been battered to nothing at the hands of the great cranes, merciless in the time that they stayed. Wantana had acted, perhaps paying more than he should have.

And for the next year, whatever his day was comprised of, wherever these matters had taken him, however he had proceeded to throw himself into these matters, a great part of him had dwelt in that vacant area between the buildings. In his meditation with his ideas for the plot, with his visions for the plot, a figure still and mordant like Geronimo. It had been the future he was addressing; his, the organisation's. But, of course, wasn't it one and the same?

And then suddenly the building that had appeared endlessly in his imagination was a living thing. But the mornings with Sim remained what they always had. The car executed the turn off the highway, and as it did he, Pracha Wantana, Daniel T.K. Bai, industrialist, businessman, took note in long familiarity, in long comprehension. Outside the factories were the pavements, at the early hour winding passages pulsing with the eternal migration to the factories, some of the younger factory girls having tied handkerchiefs around the bottom halves of their faces, the care they had administered leaving hardly more than their eyes exposed.

Thus had he brought into being the most beautiful manufacturing plant Hong Kong had ever seen. It was where his principal office was still.

But achieving the dream of inhabiting a superlative structure that as a manufacturing plant astonished, his sympathies had begun to alter; he had started to retreat from the world of factories. His passion for the finished product that was a watch didn't lessen, it was the inclination to plan the nuts and bolts of their creation which he was losing, the inclination to go where the machines stood. The realm which was industrial fabrication increasingly he couldn't be bothered with, and even if the things coming off the machines were recognizably the fundamentals of the hallowed object his family observed like pieties. What went on in factories purely he didn't want to address anymore; more and more his pleasure was to offload all of that. He employed men, numbers and numbers of them. Let them do it.

The person who had arrived on the balcony of his beach chalet, an architect by profession, was also amongst the visitors he opened his office door to in the course of a month, but Wantana no longer included him with those he saw out of professional duty. In middle age Jacot-Descombes, his marriage in France at an end, had sought and accepted a position in Hong Kong. Working intermittently on projects for Pracha Wantana, a friendship had developed between the two of them somewhat to their mutual amazement. Jacot-Descombes lived in a room at the Hong Kong YMCA. Wantana had his pavilions and his fortresses. No matter the core activity that your company was about, if you were a businessman in Hong Kong at this time, you felt a certain obligation to set up an offshoot devoted to some property development, however limited its ambitions. Wantana had followed the practice. At the beginning he had done so almost feeling that it was necessary as a kind of rite of passage for an emerging man of affairs in the territory. But anyway, throwing himself into the design and construction of his own imposing industrial headquarters had stirred an interest to go further in this sphere of activity.

'Marcel!' Wantana exclaimed.

'What?' Jacot-Descombes said.

'I am looking at your face!' Wantana said. 'I agree, this place is far worse than I remember.'

'It's not that,' Jacot-Descombes said.

'But please,' Wantana said, 'tomorrow it's Hong Kong. We'll be back there.'

'And the small matter which is today?'

'I am thinking of nothing else.'

'You intend to go through with this?'

'I have no choice.'

'Of course you do,' Jacot-Descombes said. 'Simply decline. It will cost you nothing.'

'How can you say that?'

'You are who you are. It allows you to place yourself above such things.'

'You think I should put out a gracious smile and say that it's just not for me.'

'Why not?'

'He has challenged me.'

'That's absurd. You are elevating it to something it is not. Which sadly men are in the habit of, and always it ends in trapping them. You are just giving him an importance he doesn't deserve. Besides, how can you challenge the man you work for?'

'By doing exactly what he has done.'

'Pracha, look!' Jacot-Descombes said. 'Cast your eyes out there!'

'Believe me, I have been looking nowhere else.'

'To reach the island is a swim of two thousand metres,' Jacot-Descombes said.

'Two and half thousand, my good friend. I won't allow you to short change me.'

'It will turn into a race.'

'Race, no. That I do refuse.'

'I am not questioning your courage.'

'You should. At the physical level I am a devout coward. The thought of driving a car in Hong Kong terrifies me. Richard Marshall! I watched his kind in the time I was at the colleges in the West. Think of this overweight Chinese boy sitting on the steps of various pavilions. One after the other they passed before his eyes. With bat and ball not a single one who wasn't a master. Who was I beside that?'

'At thirty-five with no training behind you it is an insane test. Pracha, give it up.'

'No,' Wantana said.

'I am going to speak to Marshall,' Jacot-Decombes said. 'Someone has to put him right.'

'Stay out of it. This is my problem.'

'Is that an order?'

'Marcel!' Wantana protested. 'When have I ever imagined I could do that?'

'You're not about to trust anyone you're not free to order.'

'Except you.'

'Except me?'

'And aren't we so many children to you.'

'What?'

'It's this manner you have, sometimes.'

'Why haven't you said?'

'I'm telling you now.'

'So give me an order.'

'Like one of my lackeys?'

'Why not?'

'Then get in the dingy. Go out to the fishing boat. But see to it they give us room.'

'What is this about?' Jacot-Descombes said. 'I still do not fully understand. You are contemplating an incalculable advance for your organization. Before you go public on this idea you wanted to consult with a few close associates. You invited the three of us here to gain the benefit of our wisdom, such as it is. But in fact more lay behind your invitation. Let me put it to you. With each of us in turn you were seeking an answer to a particular question, a different question in each case.'

'The three of you,' Wantana said, 'you are not anyone. I needed these answers.'

'And myself? Have you achieved your aim?

'I don't think I have to reply to that.'

'Yes, but Richard Marshall? This I can't get to grips with.'

'You know enough.'

'Do I?

'His father has died. He believes I am considering closing my operation in England and dispensing with him.'

'And is he right?'

'You ask that a man cower in a corner without issuing sound or movement,' Wantana said. 'The poor wretches. All the powerless. Just how should they fight back? Too often it's a choice between the comic and murder. You employ men you learn about them. There isn't a better way.'

'So the truth is you invited him here so as to put him up against a wall. There he stands while you decide his fate.'

'Perhaps,' Wantana said. 'But the justice of that interpretation only extends so far. Need I even bother, in fact? I could get someone to give him the news and have nothing more to do with it.'

'But you can't do that,' Jacot-Descombes said, 'not with him.'

'No, I can't.'

'What is it?'

'What is it?

'Yes.'

'Marcel, I don't know. I DON'T KNOW.'

'This isn't just anyone.'

'I will tell you something. There was a time when I talked of Richard Marshall as more my brother than my actual brothers.'

'He thinks you have taken the decision.'

'Before he is forced out, he wants blood on the floor. My blood!'

'You were keen to have his word on the massive step you are considering for your organization, but at the same time he was here to convince you he's worth keeping.'

'That's just the position I occupy. I accept it. I'm not betraying anyone.'

'But bringing him here – wasn't it just making things worse for yourself?'

'Of course. But he had made something clear.'

'What?'

'That he wasn't going to let me forget.'

'Forget…'

'That once I named him as like a brother.'

‘But you haven’t forgotten.’

‘In the end, how famous is a man with his kin?’

‘But Marshall...?’

‘He is someone facing humiliation,’ Wantana said. ‘I’m not blind to it. He must return to his family half a man. Look around: the humiliated of the earth – they fill the cities, they fill my factories. There but for the grace of God you might say. Which is it to be for oneself, the armies of the mute set-upon, or that master clown who always has a part at the circus? Never see him hang his head.’

It was just Wantana. On impulse he fired off these overblown statements apparently reflective of wide unsparing meditations. Some of it you took seriously, but a large part you couldn’t. Seen against one’s experience of Wantana across the full span of a day it didn’t hold sway. A quirk more than a tic, but not ever so much. Minute to minute the man’s great human hum was the market-place, sleeves rolled up in anticipation. You couldn’t think otherwise.

‘In fact,’ Wantana said, ‘everything I have just described to you amounts to yesterday.’

‘What?’

‘I am sorry,’ Wantana said. ‘I’ve been holding back. Richard Marshall has resigned his position. He has taken the decision on himself. He is bidding farewell, like a man. I’m almost proud of him.’

‘Then…’

‘Somehow he has discovered the courage to live without me. Overdue, but he has got there.’

‘So you *can* call it off,’ Jacot-Descombes said.

‘Think of it,’ Wantana said, ‘never to set eyes on each other again. The two of us, done and ended. It happened here, at this beach.’

‘Why didn’t you say?’ Jacot-Descombes said. ‘It wasn’t my wish to watch you go into the water.’

‘Another half hour and you will.’

‘But Why!’ Jacot-Descombes said. ‘I don’t understand.’

‘See it!’ Wantana said, pointing to the island. ‘Two families exist who can’t escape it. Can’t rid their bodies of it.

The damned island. If only he knew it but today isn't about Richard Marshall. It hasn't got anything to do with him. It goes back to a time when there wasn't anyone named Richard Marshall. So one day I would meet him. Tell me about that. I have a sense of his face, and he mine. But more? At this minute I would question that. My father's family, any family here – he imagines he knows one single thing! No, today is about Joti Bidaya. It's about the Bidayas one and all.'

'I appeal for you to call it off.'

'Where is the great risk?' Wantana said. 'A boat will accompany us. You will be on the boat. We arranged this at your suggestion, remember? Aren't you here to keep watch over all of us? In this region you go to places I would never think of going. And which of us was the one born in the East?

'Can you swim? I mean to this standard.'

'I can swim. He is in for a surprise, old-boy athlete he might be.'

'Do you really want to do this?'

'Frankly, no. The prospect appals me.'

'Then turn your back! That's the authority you have.'

'Bidaya. This is a name you have heard the past days. The Wantanas and the Bidayas: I should give you the whole story. Finally, it's a story that will mark the East. It has already.'

'Sadly, I have somewhere to go, remember,' Jacot-Descombes said. 'The next two hours I am the guardian angel.'

'When it is finished then,' Wantana said.

2

On the evening of their arrival at the beach Wantana was the first to make his way over to the restaurant. Sauntering across from the line of beach properties, the shorts roomy, the sports shirt only partially buttoned, sandals less than handsome, even in his vacation dress an air to his squat figure like a jailer with his stick, he had balked at the sight his eyes threw at him, the restaurant's coarseness biting into his mind hard and luridly. From the moment of lifting himself from the car not five straight minutes had gone by when he didn't give thanks that Andrew Camondo, the head of the historic American watch company, couldn't see him. Of course, his idea was insane anyway. An anonymous Chinese businessman and this most grand of American corporations, the march of the American cosmos, of American exception, crossed with its name – wasn't he inviting something far crueller than mere laughter? He had been buoyed in spirits leaving the beach chalet, some thirty yards away, but before he had reached the restaurant table he was lost to all of that elation, the sudden flood of demoralization like a vicious attack of cramp.

But once seated at an outside table, his mind rebounded, went to questioning, and with force: was it so far-fetched? Why should he think himself ridiculous? He was imaging doing, achieving, what he knew he could do, could achieve. If you were in touch with anything it was with the innate sense of what it was you were capable of taking on. Being true to every part of that was the journey you set out on in life. He questioned, and questioning he demanded that he believe. America! He could do it.

And then this beach! Let him embrace it. Were it the case that Andrew Camondo was amongst those in his party, this singularly uncomplicated location, this artless stretch of sand, could through its very eccentric nature have proved critical to

Camondo overcoming his prejudices to the idea of Wantana gaining control of his great company. And what prejudice there would be when Camondo did get to learn of Wantana's intentions! As a businessman Wantana had learnt early on in his career that some of the most far-reaching discussions he entered into never occurred inside his office following pre-arranged meetings, but rather flared up spontaneously within the boundaries of some random social setting. Restaurant, clean or foul, hotel bar, hotel suite, there wasn't end to the settings that against all odds could work for you in your deal-forging, or in which the spark of the great idea first appeared to two men. No, an insignificant beach resort from his childhood that he had long forgotten hadn't to be fled in embarrassment seen against the improbable status he was aiming to build for himself. It just didn't matter. Corporate chieftains discovered conviviality in no end of places, and often precisely through the situation's unlikelihood. Once found that conviviality could reorder the world. And in the eventuality of some historic commercial agreement, it was likely that the two leader's interest in the formal documents that followed from the understanding would be limited at best. They had met as two men and what had been said they would honour. If the setting for the talks had helped them find their way towards each other, then that was to their good fortune. It was a relief anyway to have escaped their offices.

All the restaurant's outside tables enjoyed the benefit of a parasol, awnings old and bitter in their bedraggled look. That initial evening while waiting for his guests he chose a front table straddling the line of the sand. Seating himself he immediately felt the touch of a dog about his chins. Where first there was just a single stray, soon others descended. Their relentless pacing around the feet of the chairs developed a kind of geometry, every angle of which seethed with pitiful supplication. Back and forth they slunk, their persistence coaxed from the quarries of dreadfully emaciated frames. Their lifeless coats were entirely shrivelled away in parts, and their eyes told of the distance of their spiritual injuries. But though he spoke of eyes, of something such as sight, the black holes he stared into were revolting to him, and exactly for the affliction, the death in life he discovered there.

In any case, the premises he looked at, timber, rudimentary, scruffy, he was entitled to class as a restaurant, and that had him acknowledging the significance that these establishments in all their forms had in his life. In his professional affairs the time he gave in his mind to the labour and intricacies of seduction. Though not all these assignments once embarked on proved that much of a test. If the purpose he was about was to secure in men an absolute obedience to his own objectives, if it was to gain from them an utterly resounding acquiescence, and, furthermore, if it was to disarm and overwhelm like this without the full extent of their submission before him ever properly occurring to them, then, sadly, he also knew that with many it asked but little of him. People, even the ones he admired in his way, did frustrate him by the obvious lure he had for them; but in the situations where to get his way with someone it demanded all of his powers as a man, so often it was in a restaurant that he began. So often, there was nowhere else. He took to a table and set his sights on securing what it was that he wanted from the man seated opposite. What he wanted so that he could proceed on to the next man. Each in turn, they would bow to him. He just needed the time, and once he could assure himself that another had fallen to him he could bask in the knowledge he had advanced a further step in his aims for his organization; one then another, as individuals forgotten soon enough but not the thing it had been necessary to get from the man.

Also, restaurants were revealing themselves to be an unrepeatable backdrop against which to consolidate both the largest and smallest of his victories. After he had constructed his glamorous watch component factory in Hong Kong, his ideas had started to develop in keeping with the majestic outlook from his office. But his expanding ideas for his business had circled back at him as mocking taunts. Watch parts! That the Swiss would think of with high opinion. Sadly the manufacturing skills existing in the colony didn't match with the idea. In visualizing the stainless steel watch cases, the sweet-faced watch dials, the striking bracelets, he could be as bold as he liked in the scale of manufacturing excellence he dreamt up for his organization. To realize though these levels of competence and know-how across his manufacturing floors would demand teachers. To that end he had despatched emissaries to the likeliest regions. Since the context was the watch industry, his people were straightaway poking about Switzerland. Wantana never hesitated to employ the ablest technical specialists. This was human proficiency he was never challenged by in his insecurities. If the production engineers weren't the best, he couldn't proceed anywhere. In that matter his eyes had been open from the start.

His days as a student had left Wantana sensitive towards the Swiss. How should he appeal to men who in applying themselves to their work sought perfection not only of the product they were helping create, but also of the manner of their own individual application to the work? Sainthood was found though method. See the Swiss and see method taut as a bow. That aspect could lead to the impression that the Swiss, not a little, scoffed at the universes lying beyond the borders of their nation. In fact, knowing what he did about the Swiss, Wantana never doubted for a moment that as many as he wanted would be his for the asking. Instinctively he knew the lever and the lever was at his fingertips. What had he discovered at the engineering school in Switzerland? Nothing less than that the land-locked dreamed. Dream a dream the Swiss most certainly did: escape. Not forever, just for a period. But the fulfilment of the dream wasn't to be had in the mere physical act of putting their borders behind them, it could only be accomplished if the path out brought them into contact with the sea. In their hearts the image of escape and the image of the sea were one and the same. If the sweetener you had to offer was one of the world's great maritime cities, then the Swiss as individuals were as open to being bought off as the next man. He had only to make true this interlude in their lives they craved.

So it was that as soon as some worthy candidates had been unearthed Wantana's message went out to them without delay:

cast off home and habit and take your chances in the East. In economic terms, at the very least, you will be rewarded for your trouble. Each floor in his headline plant now enjoyed its complement of these professionally pious men. Wantana had divined the importance his own figure would have for them. Bereft of some minimal contact with the organization's monarch, this Chinese man they had overthrown their lives for, their sense of security would suffer in time.

Thus it was that once a month he gave himself the duty of entertaining the foreign technicians and their wives. In fact, these evenings had become a ritual in the life of his emerging organization. Since it was Hong Kong, he could vary the locations of these dinners as it came to him. Restaurants littered the city. Effectively, he held court on those evenings. In accordance with who he was, in accordance with the place they were, the tables were circular. But with the numbers needing to be accommodated the tables echoed with the dimension and one shape they carried. On any night the largest in the place, this great round the tables had said but China.

The demand on Wantana on these evenings was that he never lose sight of the performance that was asked of him. On such evenings the wives of those men newly arrived in the colony were liable to become engrossed with their host. They were seen to marvel at the grace and diligence with which he bore down on each of his guests in turn. The conversation of the uncommon individual before them wheeled around the table with such apparent observance. First one European tongue lay on his lips then another; someone with revolutions of being at his call. Every circuit he made of the table with his talk was an unashamed demonstration of his gifts and self-belief. That their own men had the pride of vast technical competence didn't lessen the impact of their obvious limitation when measured by the Chinese person everyone was focused on at the table; jolly and extravagant, but serious in his responsibilities, and seriously a man in his absolute willingness for these responsibilities, in his comfort with them; and always on those evenings so keen to spark the laughter of his guests. As the European ladies continued to observe their host, most were reconciled to the exotic place their husbands had led them off to so impetuously. But, without fail, it was always the case that a few were not. Wantana knew it.

And let it be known that following his insistence that men pull up stakes with their families, sometimes a chain of events was set going, never to be foreseen by man, woman or child, that resulted in the cruel rupturing of their families. For Hong Kong, the East, was temptation, was opportunity. But none of that was his responsibility. He did what he did to build his empire. He couldn't say what it would mean for others.

His developing itinerary was taking him to other cities, some far from his industrial base in Hong Kong. But a city reached was really little different to the city discarded the day before, off floating in your wake somewhere. And always there followed the rotation of restaurants. Travelling overseas often the people he was expecting as he waited inside a restaurant remained his own, in these circumstances the senior executives of the offshoots he was establishing in various countries. Those like Richard Marshall. Alone at a table, his gaze was liable to idle around the doorways to the salons. In one restaurant after another it felt as if without moving from his chair he was able to cross the whole wide spectrum of human physical diversity, so regularly in those places did the entrance of one type in the human mix precede its complete antithesis. But, of course, there was nothing in that. By noting it he was merely highlighting a routine formula in the life of a great city. Still, confronted by the procession, he took bearings from it.

Away on a trip it was when he breakfasted alone in a hotel that he became watchful of the wider world. He became conscious of how for the lone traveller breakfast in a hotel restaurant became a solitary séance of sorts. He saw the single diners just down from their rooms, asking himself where was the place on their journey they had set out from, where was it they going. But then his eyes would alight on the tables where the breakfast interlude stood as something altogether different. Wherever was the hotel he happened to be ensconced in, it was at breakfast that so often he found himself witness to a miniature conference at some neighbouring table. Observing these various gatherings on different occasions, invariably a single figure swiftly emerged to view. As the meeting or get-together progressed, this individual was always accentuated by the proceedings. It was very the essence of these conclaves that a dominating personality existed, that everything bent to him or her. The circle of people seated at the table had apparently assembled in response to a summons, and once in place were to be observed straining for an expression and posture that the mighty one with power over the gathering could be convinced of. However far his own table was located from that of the cluster of strangers in conference, Wantana was able to understand that the lives of the people meeting like this were under sentence to be significantly altered on the whim of the individual so visibly controlling the discussion. And, of course, every time his eyes settled on one of these commanding figures, he was effectively seeing himself.

Absolutely, he too, sometimes, favoured a public place for a conference with his people. He too despatched word where the table was to be found, who was to attend. He would dress in his hotel room in high anticipation of these tables. Like nothing else they played to the significance that he wanted for himself, that simply he saw himself as born to. It was on occasions like this that his men set about perfecting the gentle tilt of their obsequiousness. Soaking up this homage to his own person, why should he not be especially satisfied? That a few of the arrivals might be fresh to the organization, that as individuals these gatherings might furnish them with rare opportunity to meet with their more experienced colleagues, being based as executives in different sectors of the globe, none of this could prevent their swift immersion into the protocols of life in his employment. He had no hand in this. As far as he was concerned the proprieties arrived in their ears as if by some process of magic. All that was evident to him was that when finally they stood before him, they did so in obedience to the organization's expectations of them.

There he would be, his elbows planted on the table, his fingers extended vertically each side of his nose, inspecting like this the ring of men lodged at the table. Creeping around the points of his fingers, his eyes would at first be pensive and wary. Already he had taken himself far. At times it had led him to a breed of person little could have prepared him for. But somewhere he had discovered the assurance to engage with the most unappetising and deadly in the corporate melange, those who for all that they manage to carry off a perfectly conventional human appearance across their outward physical form, strike one on closer inspection as born to the habits and cunning and want of consideration of a lower universe in the chain of existence. What rapacious creatures could lurk behind the formal business get-up of shirt and tie. So much assurance had he come by, it was in fact these wonderful specimens who should perhaps have been in terror of him. Once he had been an unremarkable adolescent who had occasionally accepted invitations into the homes of the few who had befriended him at the western colleges. Blessed be they who are in ignorance of what they shape beneath their wing. Out in the world now, he could meet like with like. And with such effectiveness that it was being asked whether he should ever presume to distinguish himself from the worst of the primitives masquerading in a plaid suit. Like had a way of finding like, had it not? So it was being whispered amongst a few he had offended.

But as he sat in those restaurants attending to his work, he told himself that all of it was meant to be. He was meant to be. The figure he presented to the world sang with the work of forging his own version of an empire, and yes, never more so than when he was surrounded by those who waited on his word, who acted on his word, who couldn't do without his word, who lived his word. Those strangers nearby observing him presiding over a public meeting with his men would see a man talking. But in fact what did this say? Did it begin to communicate the first sense of the image beheld? For a start the man was never not arched forward in his chair, for a start he was never not impassioned, for start he was never not insisting, never not arguing, never not appealing, urging, cajoling, educating, never not reprimanding, never not pacifying, never not by his rapt speech laying the foundations of glorious plans, never not impressing this lustre a rare few have, a human face but by some mystery a way to it so much a coin of exception. Single-minded industrialist, yes, but on those occasions he was also philosopher, eminence grise, worldly savant, archaeological student, social scientist, psycho-analyst, professional sports coach, political theorist. He was the humorous dandy, the aloof dignitary, the colleague in arms, the awesome linguist. Yes, let it be repeated, where he held court he was building. Where he held court he thrived.

And finally, exemplifying the image of a man becoming attuned to a whirlwind of travel, he would rise in some haste from the table, explaining that his schedule demanded he proceed directly to the airport without delay. Leaving a restaurant in these circumstances, we can confirm that it was inevitably a city he was departing and inevitably a city of rank. One by one he was placing down the stones of the trajectory that would be his life. Already he was journeying between Hong Kong and Switzerland with some regularity. He had built and acquired significant industrial interests in each of these locations. But he was finding that he could only gather in these early successes as mere encouragement.

It hadn't begun like that. Back in Hong Kong after the years in Europe to come by an education, back in the sphere of his father, at his wellsprings had been caution, quiet. Of course, there were business horizons, as there had to be, but the ones he was inclined to see distinction in didn't leave a man's consciousness hostage. He would proceed equably. No, for him Hong Kong hadn't looked out especially.

But then one day, as if overnight, it had. Suddenly he was burning with ambition; ambition this crazed rider-less horse loose in the street. His many brothers, his many sisters: his ambition had swiftly become a curse on them, the exploding need of his for self-promotion a madness of sorts, the conviction of his own exception no less. Suddenly he had had a keenness to drape his life in all manner of glinting conceptions. Excessively grandiose in desire and intention, they tumbled out of his imagination one after the other, the flood of them telling of his accelerating passion for himself.

The Wantanas, one of the great industrial families of the East, but with the scale of ambition that had suddenly overtaken the eldest son an immense tension had been inserted into the family. Pursuing simultaneously an existence in the East and another in Europe was satisfactory if this was accepted as a beginning. But something additional was required; something of an altogether different scale. The whole point of the business success he now craved was that in some ultimately extravagant fashion it would consolidate his name, yes, specifically before a western audience, but more crucial still, before the highest of those audiences. When he had learned of the plight of the great American watch company and seen the opportunity it offered, right before his eyes he had known the way, he had known the land.

Amongst other things were not a man's doings and achievements a kind of mirror only the one looked into; a mirror of sacrament before which his presence in the world took on a celebratory aspect. A man possessed a basic label of identity, the simple name he carried, legitimizing his existence in the eyes of his fellow beings. But at the personal level the issue was how exactly that name bore down on the man in question. In a man's identification with his name there developed a kind of rite. But such were the overtones generated by this rite it turned into one that sent him in search of some peerless, galvanising feat, his life's-work no less, by which to appease the deliciousness and cruelty of the rite.

Yet surely the notion that he could succeed in his American objective was outlandish to a degree unheard of. Could Hong Kong, the East itself, be anything more than passing diversion to the men installed in the imposing building in New York representing the headquarters of the Camondo family and its famed watch business? To deliver control of an historic American corporation to an unknown Thai-Chinese industrialist – wasn't he, Pracha Wantana, floating in the realm of fantasy? Yet he did not deceive himself. Outright control of this organization was what he was determined on.

But then, the weight of all of this torturing his mind, on impulse he had fled his office.

And where had he come to? It was the truth that he had entered a country that at an ulterior level, every day of his life, he was urged to distance himself from. He had wanted to believe he would never see this remote coastal resort ever again; in any case, a location from his childhood so grey and unbelievable to the adult man. He had made his way to the beach conscious of the personal trial he was forcing upon himself. He didn't question that others in the family, those nearest to him in age, born in Bangkok like himself, were equally afflicted.

A tide had built up in him that if it returned once it kept on returning. A man, their father, had long before departed his country. His uncertain investigations of the road had carried him to Thailand, the migrant in him, the migrant he was, in search of a cradle for his hopes even as he was abandoning a cradle. This particular voyager had quickly put his faith in the city of Bangkok. Narong Wantana, otherwise Bai Khe Wah, had decided to go no further. Meeting a woman of Chinese origin, the city had played host to the birth of the earliest of his children. And in time, as sprawling as the city was, the day occurred when the family had required of the city a much greater physical magnitude still. In their hearts they pushed at the limits of the city out of the cry that a broader, kinder space would open as a kind of appendage to the city.

For the Wantana family Bangkok had developed into an environment of profound shadow in that nowhere in it, or the nation, could they discover a place that did not taunt them with the sense that their whole existence was grievously subordinate to that of another family domiciled in the city; in fact, a Thai family of expressly noble extraction. An onerous shade had proceeded to form over the heads of the Wantana brood that was fated to strengthen by the day, one dawn then the next filtering to city and man alike. A nation-state encompassing borders along which entire armies might be lost and they could not find any place whatsoever where they could breathe in the simple uncomplicated way that breath was meant to come. Had Pracha Wantana to question himself about this? Had he fallen to distorting or misconstruing these early experiences and the stench it had left?

No, he did not believe so. How could he mislead himself in the matter? It was what he had lived. He thought of it as his own discovery: that there were private oppressions that reduced the largest nation to the length of a single street; a street that a person could not free himself from wherever he might travel to inside this one land. Certain spiritual persecutions that if in their coming together it resulted in a load taking hold synonymous with the very air over a man's head, and the air was his native air, or what passed most closely for it, then, truly, the simple act of drawing breath evolved into a contest that drained the strength from a man. But leave the land behind, a single step sufficed, and the sense of release was magical. A single step outside, no matter the direction, the sense of release was profound.

Of the ideas that Wantana regularly constructed of his father, all without exemption seemed far-removed from the self-flagellation of a city gymnasium. But back in the beginning, as the lowly watchmaker from China experimented with the universe of his new city, it had been his decision to visit one of the city's gyms with some frequency. As an establishment, according to family legend anyway, the gym was to be seen as a den of anonymity. He, Pracha Wantana, his father's son, liked to think of society's glib emblems of rank and standing, be they of dress or demeanour, being given up at the door simply through being insupportable inside that particular door. Though he could only suppose that most of those who arrived at that one entrance on a consistent basis never for a moment presumed to any such hierarchical airs. It had to have been nothing more than a decidedly second rate venue, the majority of its devotees surely a class of minor citizen. Amongst the regular crowd, certain faces had gradually begun to stand out for his father. One especially had been prominent. Finally, it was the stranger who made the effort to speak. Perhaps this man had dug out a timepiece from his pocket in serious need of refurbishment; as objects watches ancient and modern possessed personalities that willingly had a man dropping his guard. The new face was let in, just a fraction. An object in a man's hand bearing the virtue of steel, of the masculine, the technical, it could be that between the men human congress stirred, and seemingly painlessly. Anyway, the gymnasium had ensured that these two were fated to continue to meet, like it or not. In fact, with their initial contact, they had become resolved to pursue the association, each markedly disposed towards the other.

Of course, a session at an end and the fitness centre departed society was liable to rebuild itself in an instant. Narong Wantana was quickly forced into a revolution in his thinking as regards his new acquaintance. In the case of the somewhat unfathomable man from the gymnasium, the venue's murky anonymity was the very attraction it had for him, constituting the cloak he sought. For an interval he could go as someone else. He was exposed as a man the moment the walls of the somewhat tawdry gym lay at his back.

Out on the street the evidence hit one in the face and first was a man's stride, its haunting lightness and fluidity the clearest signal of certain things: of breeding, of achievement, of position. With this story in his head of his father's historic encounter in the Bangkok fitness centre Pracha Wantana saw in the stranger from the gym traits akin to the stubborn pride of certain aristocratic Chinese whom he had always been aware of on the streets of Hong Kong, the base the Wantana family came to ultimately in the search to get free of their immersion with the Bidaya family, if only at the physical level.

Yes, with his life now centred on Hong Kong, the great maritime city, he, Pracha Wantana, otherwise known as Daniel T.K.Bai, did take note of a certain type he picked out almost routinely on his jaunts through the metropolis. Ostracised and made destitute following unmentionable political upheaval, these exiles were forever washing up in the colony, years after the event it might be. Forced into some dismal occupation simply in order to live, they were to be seen flirting with a variety of common trades, but in such a stately, summary manner it never appeared in some critical sense to be the actual man himself who was the silhouette witnessed shuffling across the floor bent over with guilt and shame, but somehow a shape to be taken as like fate refused, a shape representative solely of a job of work, and that the former high-born one succeeded in dominating to his salvation. Of course, the man was there in front of you, but some telling trait innate to him allowed him yet to stand clear of the worst of his shame. It was as if two figures appeared to your eyes. A note in the man, mysterious, compelling, transcended the wretchedness he was being forced to live. Vested with this force, this genius, his disgrace was transfigured to the point where, amazingly, it succeeded in expanding and reinforcing the mists of a privileged bearing, despite everything. Assuredly, the souls of these men were in touch with the stigma that had collected over their lives, but stored somewhere was a fearsome recalcitrance, impregnability and denial. Thus was the poison driven back and nullified. Thus was it that indeed two went forward, the indomitable prince of a man and this other who, crouched, misshapen, was doomed to drag himself in the wake of the master. It was this lurking apparition, this foul half person that became the indigent appealing for the hand-out. In the evenings the erstwhile 'royal' made his way back to the squalid quarters that had become his home. And it came about that though this man entered the dwelling, his beggarliness did not. At the door the lord of the house rediscovered himself with even greater defiance. Rising up in all his former 'colours', he continued on as if serenely oblivious of the untouchable at his back, until that is, there appeared this little disdainful flick of the fingers indicating that the degenerate should seek out whatever shelter was available in the gullies down around the base of the home. In the sound of the door closing was an incomparable echo. The incomparable indifference it told of, bequeathed only to those of kingly origin, and then to but a few of this caste, thrown at all men and their works. Of course, on the inside the rooms were shrunken and threadbare. But the master was blind to it. More was he suddenly deaf; should some sickly wailing rise up from the outside, the door stayed barred, whatever was the cold of the nights.

With his chance encounter at the Bangkok city gym, Wantana's father, Narong Wantana, had been entitled to think of himself as rubbing up against a Bangkok opposed in kind to any he recognized. A Bangkok significant for the sheer range of its immunities, even if in this mixed-up city that failed to strike out every one of the gutter-black alleys; a Bangkok free of the interminable bidding wars of the streets; a Bangkok of a certain schooling; a Bangkok, let it be said, of fragrance of the soul. Which exactly was Thailand, wasn't it?

The evocative environment that could be in the figure of a man; there he stood, his father's new friend, and truly the cloth was resonant. Think of a man's sheer breeding in the way of those tall reeds a river bank was home to swaying against a light river breeze; to the hilt, the carriage of the high-born, the effortless vanities of the high-born, the separation and fatefulness of the high-born. Yet this was someone who from dawn to dusk didn't spare himself from a harsh regime of single-minded industrial endeavour. He reigned over engineering interests, manufacturing interests, broader commercial interests. A swan dripping iron, as Pracha Wantana sometimes mused to himself.

But what had been his father's reaction as his knowledge of the man from the gymnasium had expanded? There was a scale here, in regard to what the man from the gym had responsibility for that had surely exploded onto Narong Wantana's brain. Even now, years later, he, Pracha Wantana, a corporate chieftain himself, he was carried away at the impossibility of it. And how was he to forget the former impoverishment of his humble immigrant father? Sometimes, learning things about a man, it is the comparison with your own circumstances at the time which is the deafening factor in your mind. There must have been a moment when his father had gone rigid in his parts at the realization of what his new friend encompassed. And now? Now he, Pracha Wantana, had it in his head as a kind of prospectus, which indubitably was his way. Often, nothing conveyed ethos and superstructure like a common list. Not to him anyway. The stranger's business was the servicing of a nation and its armies, no less:

Aviation Division: Supply of aircraft. Supply of engine parts, tools and instruments for both fixed and rotor wings, as well as the airframe in isolation, and special tools and chemicals. Supply of airfield pulling trucks, airfield crash trucks, airfield runway sweeping trucks. Supply of spare parts for gas turbine and steam turbine generators.

Chemical Division: Supply of industrial chemicals and related equipment.

Engineering Division: Supply of general machines such as drilling machines, milling machines, testing machines, lathes, boilers high pressure cleaners, pumps and various kinds of material handling equipment. Marine Division: Supply of marine products, namely tug boats, patrol boats, fishing boats, dredgers. Supply of marine spare parts including engines and propellers. Supply of oil pollution sweeping arms. Medical Division: Supply of general medical equipment and scientific apparatus such as bedside and general monitors, blood pressure monitoring equipment, X-ray scanners, infant incubators, microscopes, spectrophotometers, ultrasonic cleaners and dehumidifiers, etc. Telecom Division: Telecommunication and electronics equipment, such as EPABX telephone sets, computers, radio transceivers, VHF/UHF and colour TV transmitters, frequency monitoring equipment, domestic earth satellite equipment, electronic warfare and guided missile equipment, etc.

In considering the man to whom his father had effectively become joined, it was simple instinct for Wantana to tote up in a cold commercial way the facts of the businesses this individual had controlled, as they had anyway existed at the time when he and his father had been drawn to each other in the Bangkok fitness centre, forming what was destined to be a lasting friendship, as well as an incalculable one. Who was it who could properly explain human bonds like these? In reminding himself of the extent of what the stranger had once ruled over, it was as though Pracha Wantana was gauging himself against this list and its tally. But not simply as a measure for the appetites he too was possessed by. Today, at every step, mankind went about erecting this history of organizations. There they were beyond number as a man peered over his shoulder. The smell of their eventual and seemingly inevitable ruin permeated every texture of existence. And hadn't each of these organizations been blessed with a name as well? But at the moment one was removed, another sprang forward. And if he told himself that with this history a shadow had formed on the planet that had remade the planet, then he had to accept that alongside all the other persons implicated, he was speaking of things that he had done and would go on doing. It was why he had returned to Thailand. Wasn't he there to meditate on the next stage of his life's journey? For him the idea of this journey was meaningless unless it reflected his business ambitions; to lead his organization on; on and on to ideas ever more arresting. It was who was, wasn't it?

But as to that, the essential person he was, it had all begun in Thailand and Thailand for the Wantanas had been Suthin Bidaya, the man his father had met in the Bangkok gym and who finally by his magnetisms and achievements and powerful patronage of the Wantanas, had so hung over the Wantana family, his father had become determined to change cities. And that decision had enabled the Wantanas in due course to come into their own.

Hong Kong and Bangkok; hear these names clearly: two cities, one family, at last with pride of independence, the Wantana family. To view the family it was necessary to take your mental tents and pitch them firmly in each of these places. As travelled internationally as some in the fold were, and none more so than he the most senior of his father's offspring, in the story of this renowned Eastern industrial family every other great metropolis was but maid to this Eastern duo; in the theatre where these two cities resided the Wantana clan was amongst the most notable of such families in the area. It was a family destined to leave its mark like few others. Hong Kong and Bangkok would be evidence to it. And by mark he meant commercial undertakings reaching as far as ground-breaking infrastructure projects, letting the people ease the burden of their lives. As to the more usual ventures, well, gladly he could run down it item by item: significant manufacturing enterprises, hotels, condominiums, towering office structures, stores, shop chains. It was endless, and all in the planning. Everything that is axiomatic to a great city and indispensable if a city was to be made manifest on a scale that would send its name out far and wide across the globe.

In the Hong Kong of the day, the Hong Kong Pracha Wantana had departed forty-eight hours previously so as to rediscover the beach from his early years, a curiosity was the pilgrimage that occurred on Sundays. On this day the workers and their families decamped from their garrets in tower, tenement or outlying village and invaded the spaces of the operatic lobbies of the luxury hotels. They might have crossed the seas to nuzzle at these distinctive walls. What it was to be seated for an hour at one of those marble-faced intersections created to serve the whims and compulsions of the decorous classes. Their outing was penance and frolic. They ordered food, they observed the foreign visitors. The children slid like eels around the leather sofas. But how long would the high end hotels tolerate this?

Pracha Wantana could recall the period in Bangkok when for the Wantana family, Sunday grew to be associated with its own very particular excursion. A city was to be crossed, the objective; that district where the new friend of the family maintained his principal residence. This was not invitation or summons or challenge, just a very singular alliance flowering in spurts, the hesitation with which the Wantanas set out on those days a product perhaps of the gulfs being confronted: Thai and Chinese, wealth and sparseness of means, to name but two. The start of a friendship, and, not seen by his father then, the unfolding of a feeling of soul-breaking oppression, the face he looked at in the mirror, his own, an image of human surrender, human chains. Hadn't they all been attendants at court, and hadn't this subordination gained a momentum that threatened to corrupt their blood forever, leaving them, like a people suffering an endless occupation of their country, mortally handicapped as human beings? He himself, Pracha Wantana, was on the verge of a decision that would leave Richard Marshall, the head of his English offshoot, on a rack of humiliation. Yet the Wantanas themselves, they knew humiliation, and had right from the beginning.

And as to himself, the eldest child in a large Chinese family, who was he now, who was this person he had taken in hand and led in a hot-headed moment to a beach from his family's past? Wasn't it the blood of a Suthin Bidaya that he, Pracha Wantana, relied on, lived out, in all the wealth of its special corruptions? The blood of a Suthin Bidaya: his veins crawled with a like concoction. He was more than keen to think they did. He recognized things about himself that Bidaya might have instructed him in. How irresistible it became for a man to impose himself on those who saw themselves as profoundly in his debt. If a man was inclined to revisit one of his own past acts of singular generosity through constantly accepting the invitations of the very persons he had given exceptional assistance to, then it was here that he could bathe as he had never bathed before. It wasn't water but a deluge of caresses that flooded over him. The hands were many and there was never any let-up in their attendance to the figure of the white knight. Could anything be more gratifying for a man than to witness the beneficiaries of his sweeping munificence reeling at his feet in everlasting gratitude for the outstanding purity he had once displayed towards them? Wantana knew himself to be a connoisseur of this kind of prostration; certainly where these prayers whimpered in homage to him alone. Amongst the kingdoms of man, few were sweet like this.

Had Suthin Bidaya, the illustrious czar who liked to hide away in unsung city haunts, ever been brought up short at the thought that his championing of the Chinese immigrant might evolve into a grievous form of tyranny for that man and his family? At Bidaya's prompting, Bidaya the backer, Wantana's father had been persuaded to cast aside his watchmaker's tools. Workroom gave way to spruce office suite. From there Narong Wantana resolved to build a business that was far more than a repair shop. The plan was for a distribution enterprise, the product a significant collection of timepieces. He wasn't going to renege on his friend, nor on the opportunity that had been presented. Would any sane man have refused? Besides, he had an ache, a zeal for watches that was life-consuming.

Employing his standing in the business world, the cultivated tycoon had approached one of the smaller Swiss watch companies, though with a long history and a name on their products as exclusive as it got, and synonymous with a price bracket that didn't kid about. Would this firm like to see their timepieces on offer in Thailand through an exclusive arrangement? Choosing to diversify his portfolio into the marketing of luxury watches was surely distraction, sport to the enigmatic industrial baron. But it had been nothing like that to Wantana's father. And it would be this experience that eventually led to his gaining the attention of the emerging Japanese giant that he was destined to act for across the entire region; which in turn was to furnish him with the spurs that empowered his ultimate independence from the man he had encountered in the Bangkok gym.

Switzerland was this great church of private sanctums that from the mountain tops practised the rites of a divine separateness; across its cloistered vales the tap, tap of the mechanical heralded intractable codes and messianic application. Stricture arched over and along its avenues and equally this template glistened in the eyes of many of the people. But though Bidaya came from the fetid and chaotic, when these self-enraptured perfectionists discovered who this man was who was sending out such careful overtures, their moats collapsed in a paroxysm of enthusiasm.

Some years later Suthin Bidaya and Narong Wantana, comrades in arms still, had been compelled to confront a worsening situation. Growing tyrannies were baying at their relationship, incalculable poison wedging between two families. The decision was for one of the families to decamp. It wasn't to be conceived of as a parting. Nevertheless something precipitous had grown up. No more was it a question of two men, but so much, yes, of two families. The emotional conflicts that had arisen in the entanglement of two clans were eating away at child at woman at man. The poison was nowhere to be rationalized. For one of the families the matter was how to breathe.

Now from his offices in Hong Kong, Narong Wantana was deep into his relationship with the burgeoning Japanese conglomerate, a group on course to establish itself as a true global giant in the watch industry. But what was any eastern nation in comparison with America? Such was the susceptibility that had taken over Pracha Wantana, Narong Wantana's eldest.

It was their first evening at the beach and already a part of Wantana's mind was restive for Hong Kong. He hadn't been away much more than a day. Did that mean anything? Not with him. His head lifted, he was helpless not to covet the promise in the air that said soon he would be back in the territory, returned to his regular daily round which, not to be forgotten, came first with its inveterate commerce with but a single figure. And once given back to his routine, would it be three months or less before he was able to march up to his father's door emboldened by a triumph his father could never have imagined? How would he go about eliciting the words as he stood before his father's royal desk? How would he proceed to fashion the announcement? Despite his secrecy in the affair, he didn't doubt that his father had his suspicions. But still, it would be shocking in its way; both the news of the achievement and the confirmation of his father's exclusion from the planning.

No, he wasn't going to bring his father into it. This had been the grit he sought, the strength of mind he had forced on himself. And wasn't that revolutionary. It was a publically quoted company he was running, building up, had ultimate power over, but the principal shareholding made the pledge of family, and did it with an affirmation evoking the one heritage, the one human identity: China. If he breathed, then the consequences and meaning of where he stood, what he represented in his figure, he bore like gangrene. He, Pracha Wantana, Daniel T.K. Bai, he was his father's son, the eldest of the offspring. He was that firstborn echoing like legend; the leading son in a house of many sons, many daughters, and the family China to a day. Only here did this portent resound, did such a burden of responsibility descend on a man, was a man trapped to a path of exception, was a man answerable on a different scale. However he chose to act, in whatever direction, it let fly a cost to his father, to his existence; whether it amounted to endless applause or merciless denigration, whether arriving as flood or remorseless trickle, something immovable would be unleashed against the father's name. As two men, he and his father were bound inextricably. Whatever the first's shame, it behoved his father to accept it as his own. Of course, what he was describing was China in earlier periods. But really, had any of it receded. The merits and achievements of the eldest son were ascribed to the father at the moment of the senior man's flight into eternity. Conversely, while the father lived, he must take responsibility for the crimes of his children. It was a morass a man like Narong Wantana, otherwise Bai Khe Wah, knew for his home. The unknowable outputs lying latent within his sons and daughters were more the perfume his breath stored than the actual faces.

For Wantana to have denied his father admission to his ideas for the future of his organization filled him with silence. He couldn't foresee his father's reaction. But the day when he did allow his father into the secret he craved like little else. He looked out to see a day, a tiny portion of it, under lights. The moment pounded at his heart, thundered the name he bore. Whatever his father had expected of his first son, surely it had fallen short of this. And when he did finally speak, would his father ever be able to understand from what depths these words came? From what depths his eldest son's sense of vindication travelled. They met every day, but they had never met like this. He was consumed gluttonously for those seconds in a day when he would lay it before his father. An emotion had hold of him like few he had experienced. A man went forward every day not knowing exactly how finally it would be given to him to express himself, but sensing nevertheless that some ultimate shrine of recognition awaited him, and finally it wasn't believable that a man could be denied. He would be delivered to this threshold, he would be known before the world and not without glory. In anticipation, he kept poring over the scene in his father's office. A thousand versions existed in his head. In all, he delayed, he kept the words back, the delicious agony on his inside like some octopus he was wrestling. This was the longest moment he would live and only he could ensure that it was. Of course, in the end he wouldn't be able to contain himself, though it wouldn't be an explosion because finally it didn't ask for anything but that one should open one's mouth. It would be a man speaking and as quietly as he could. It was done, he would say. He had succeeded. America was his.

With one of the dogs menacing his legs, Wantana strained to keep to these emotional heights, to hold the line with a critical part of himself, the effort some great balancing act, the heart in its desperate hopes never not a tension ready to turn tail, never not a provenance where all the counter-arguments, the discomfort, the ridicule at self, got a free ride. And it did start up, as it always started up, the doubt ushering in, driving in, the doubt soon strangling him. Why had he let himself be taken in? His impulsiveness was the greatest curse of man.

His mind in a spell, his hopes at a climax, suddenly it was that belief deserted him. It was as if the blood in his veins abandoned him. The thing which was the heart still operated somewhere but solely as a conduit for the terrible sense of futility and self-disgust that a man could be prey to in but a moment, even a man as determined and colossal in his imaginings as Pracha Wantana. It wouldn't ever be. His ideas were just impossible. Somehow he would have to see out these four days amidst these people he had brought to act as a sounding board. In the coming weeks there would be no triumph with which to seek out his father. The project was not based on reason. He was ahead of himself to a foolish extent.

How had he ever convinced himself that this was his rightful level?

Which of his three guests would emerge first? Having established that the four beach properties survived, and more were serviceable, he had requested the presence of these people. On the rudimentary level it had been necessary to bring along some bed linen that was all. Quaintly rustic, the four structures were propped in his view as he looked over from the restaurant, to their exteriors this aspect like tree-houses.

He had to make his mind up about all three of these persons he had brought with him. The questions were most critical in the case of Richard Marshall. In fact, if it was three and a dilemma with each, in truth the difficulties with Richard Marshall were not to be compared. He, Pracha Wantana: where was the legendary decisiveness that everyone looked to him for? Faced with the Marshall question, he was this beggar with his cap hung out.

Allowing his commercial dependence on certain of them, was it surprising that very occasionally Wantana should give himself up to some idle speculation about these western individuals who gravitated to the East? A quantity of these men were now at work on the floors beneath his office. But with established lives in the colony he classed them separately from the fleeting visitors. His mature idea of those who passed through Hong Kong in days had formed in the first year of his returning to the colony, student no more.

Thinking back to those times he could never do so without seeing this flashy oversized American motor slipping along at a snail's pace between the rows of buildings, so much the sole vehicle at large on the street, the two men seated on the inside with set faces, their heavy concentration directed at unearthing the lone quarry amongst the frontages lining the pavements, facades greyed over like bone in the weak light. Invariably the streets the car followed belonged to an unceremonious district of the city, its innate desultoriness made worse by the callow period of intermission that occurs as night revolves into day, against the lingering wall of shadow the first light of dawn in the sky an invasion like the flowering of a pollutant. Or akin to the swirling action of a detergent as it enters water. The occupants of the car would have to strain to read the business signs, even where the glow from an electric bulb showed behind the windows of the various premises. Mostly on these occasions it was the one at the wheel who started in triumph, his little shriek of discovery striking a discordant note next to the fraternal silence that had developed and thickened through the cabin of the vehicle.

A man and his driver: Sim Eng Chiang was intimate with many of the lesser secrets of the young dignitary seated in the rear. Do not think though that this narrowed the distance between them. No matter, some miserable eating den found, that by a miracle stood open for business at the ungodly hour, Sim was never allowed to remain in the car. He was under orders, if tacitly, to share the table with the young master. 'Sim, what have you chosen here? We will need all our strength and more to enter this lice-infested slaughter-house.' Reaching the door of the restaurant, the street a faded, lifeless corridor but for this one site of dim, idle illumination, faithfully Sim would step aside for Wantana, both of them fully expecting a nauseous gust at their nostrils with their first step inside.

Impressively on these occasions – a nightclub not long exited after a very long night – he, Wantana, was up for a challenge. Wanting food, his daredevilry centred on the restaurants. Had he the courage he could plumb the depths. Hong Kong possessed its charms. In fact, the fantastical night scenes gone to nothing more than a mix of glass stains on a nightclub table, he had the city before him as some great oddity to be investigated, to be experimented with, to be confronted as a test of character. He had his car, he had his driver, and, given the early hour, nowhere in this place that wasn't minutes away. What was it the lower city provinces were made of? What was he made of in response to them? After all, he gave work to their inhabitants. At this juncture, not an enormous number of them, but that might change. A night-time of relish, of extravagance, concluded, daybreak picking its tired way, often he was suddenly in the grip of various appetites, including the most basic; and feasts were to be found in Hong Kong in the unlikeliest of haunts, at the unlikeliest of times, in the worst of localities. So, yes, why not: let him, just briefly, slum it with the working classes. Let him go incognito, like Suthin Bidaya. Dawn's light at the harbour gates, a long night of play survived and packed away, at these moments he was split from his world, nothing more than a man in his clothes. It was just him and good old Sim. And alone like that he was alone with the city, alone and forgotten by the city, he with this rank of his, a rank of wealth, of education, of power, of feudal privilege, in this strange moment of nothingness in the city, half-formed light filtering in, taken down to his rightful size before the onslaught of the towering chill street canyons, the concrete of a city silent and all-powerful.

Thirty minutes before Sim would have brought the car as close as he could to the entrance of a nightclub in Kowloon's Tsim Sha Sui district, there to wait and observe, as was his practise, as largely was his life. In Tsim Sha Sui at night the neon took over the streets. To the eye it could appear an impassable swamp. Sometimes, sitting in solitude inside the car, watching from some spot he had found against a curb deep inside the notorious area of entertainment, wasn't Sim helpless not to let his eyes follow a few of the western strays as they traipsed along the pavements. All with a nose for the most suspect of the neon, how many of these men found the lights of Hong Kong at night a singular field of play, tripping some of the darkest lights in their imaginations? Given the kind of employer Sim had, many of the routes he was asked to follow in the city wore the colours of these foreign men. But, of course, this was Hong Kong. Such people did not just visit the city, in part they were the city.

It was when he, Wantana, at last stood in the entrance of a night club, his figure enlarged somehow by the wreath of garish lighting invariably built into all the doorways of this kind, one such entry so interchangeable with the next, that would fetch Sim out of his meditations. At these moments it was for his driver to act smartly, which often involved sending the car across the street in a vertiginous dive. With some such classic manoeuvre achieved Sim was asked only to sit out the succeeding seconds as the one possessed of decisiveness and elation in his movement flung up to the side of the car in something like two strides, had, of course, Sim done his job. When it was just the two of them off and about in the city Sim hadn't to think beyond the duties of simple wheelman. He didn't have to coddle the young gentleman. Once appraised of where he, Sim, was with the car, it would be Wantana who opened the rear door of the vehicle, and, after dropping his head like a soldier going through a gap in the wall in the midst of a furious street battle, Wantana who closed the door. It was a time when certain creeds of a city's street-universe featured in his life in some depth, so much was he the twenty-three year old, twenty-four year old single man not infrequently at play in the city, and of a night-time so much did he carry his complicity with the city like so much treasure. This till of exotic currency that as often as he rang out the draw was strangely able to replenish itself at will. So it had been on some mornings in the time before he married: from the nightclub straight off to his office, pausing only for breakfast. Sim had known how to do that.

And yes, like his driver, he would make out the grizzly western men on the pavements in the early hours, his eyes as unsympathetic as his driver's.

The least of his generosity was for the commercial buyers who arrived to spend just the week in the city, the power they had to spend having Hong Kong's businessmen on their best behaviour while the week lasted. Some of the buyers of course got into his office. Even back when he was a young upstart businessman he wouldn't deny that he saw them as small, that he held them in contempt, though in his role as a manufacturer he would go to any lengths to get their orders for his products. Did these people live out the months in trepidation that at the last moment their superiors would turn into assassins? To receive a memo rescinding the journey to foreign regions was everywhere the dread of all employees of a commercial organization. How many podiums did these people ascend in their lives? The oriental destination, cupping as it did this proposition of the orgiastic, had to be one of them. Did their tiny hearts quiver in expectation of the hotel room overlooking the harbour? Or were they deceiving themselves to a monstrous degree? Was this ostensible lust for the enchantments of the eastern regions that they made such a noise about amongst the circle of their colleagues in fact a desperate attempt to recover their ebbing powers as men? Paradoxically, was a man ever so in touch with himself as in the conscious understanding of the mounting deadness of his own interior? God, the years some of these buyers had held down their bloodless posts. There as they stood, they were dying inside their suits.

The foreign commercial buyers were the last people he drew a line from in his estimations of his friend Jacot-Descombes. A better human guide was the contingent of Swiss technicians he had succeeded in populating his beauteous factory with. For a few of these men their initiation into Hong Kong was a time of severe stress. Instances had occurred in which it appeared they could not bear to lose sight of him. Had they been aware of the apathy and irritation he could feel towards them, they would have been utterly undone. His aides having informed him that the search for properly qualified production engineers had at length proved fruitful, to the extent anyway that a number of likely candidates were ready to join the organization, he might sanction their transfer to his employment while disdaining taking any final decision as to the precise spot where to slot them in. He needed these men, their skills, why hang about?

Thereon, of course, an interval descended. Often an applicant had to extricate himself from his existing employment and then complete the obligatory travel arrangements. With the eventual appearance of a batch of the technicians in Hong Kong, it frequently appeared the case that he, Wantana, would require a reminder from one of his immediate acolytes for him to properly comprehend who these people were and what they were doing in his building. Faced suddenly by the newest of the arrivals, he might even display mild surprise that he had ever issued any sort of invitation to them, men who had uprooted their families at his calling. Once he had been convinced that he it was who had sent out the orders, he could respond to the effect that well, since you are here, we'll have to find work for you then.

Anyway, as it was reasonable to suggest that they might benefit from a period of convalescence following the rigours of their journey, he would instruct them to involve themselves in their domestic arrangements while he put himself to considering things. He could be confident that no one went far in Hong Kong.

Amazingly though, as he deliberated on the options, he would open his office door to discover one or more of the most recent newcomers skulking mere yards away. The fact was during the month following their arrival he was like father and mother to them. Did he exaggerate? There could be times when exaggeration came quicker to his tongue than anything, but not in this. On the days when he received his father into his sterling Hong Kong industrial facility, he had known the esteemed gentleman to look at him in consternation. Was it really necessary for them to be host to this experience? Did they really require these people? Wantana had to stress that it was necessary. They did need them. Of course, his father knew that. Besides, Narong Wantana could also be somewhat amused by these specimens from the far shores who whenever he approached twisted about in a most unbelievable fashion in the hope of capturing in their bodies a pose of consummate deference. Their veins bulged in an agony to please. Man was comical in his slavish compulsions. And when it was western man, there just wasn't entertainment to match.

As he waited next to the beach, the mangy ill-nourished dogs going round and back like wolves, Wantana was cognizant of the sun that would appear on high the next morning. In this country you accepted it for what it was. At spots it broke the back of the earth. It could do the same to luckless man. Which, let him remember, was where it had travelled from. In times gone by, chains on your ankles, pick-axe commended to the two hands you owned; the sun in the sky became a vision of the iniquity of forced labour.

And the point was it had been the genius of the human system to reinvent the test where the sun couldn't reach. It wasn't unknown for the fodder of the assembly line to protest their lot with a noise like the raucous chanting of wide-skirted washerwomen. Bound to tasks they named as insulting, the roots the factory operatives and their families put down in the cities incidentally shook a fist at the world. A wage passed across as recompense for their torture excused nothing. But with the obscenities and hollers of the common herd reaching their ears, there were others who were informed of the dissimulation in all of it. To be one of the few empowered to see through the falsity had its responsibilities. Pracha Wantana accepted the responsibility. He had only to look hard at many that he employed to comprehend the breadth of how men deceived themselves. Had these people not found him, he could not say what would have happened to them. Docile to the last, they just killed time between commands. To be conducted to the next task, all was found in that. Without the direction he brought to their lives they would have circled about themselves in utter bemusement in the effort to understand their place in the scheme of things. They might curse his name, but know it for what it was: a curse of blessings.

He became aware of a young woman standing at the side of the table. She was heavily pregnant. A peerless halo, godly and ascendant, was in her eyes and on her skin. She was of it and it was of her. Her beatitude was crimson. It was a cascade she carried with her. Frozen like stone, the furtive lizards might have been gaping at her. He explained that he would not order until his guests made their appearance. She sent down a smile absolved of the possibility of the vaguest poison. She seemed removed from everything. Taking up her resplendent weight, all of it at once trenchant and ghostly, she shuffled back a few feet before turning. Where there appeared to be no channel between the tables, suddenly a pathway opened. And where she passed who was it who would dare claim it wasn't a hand of anointment extending out from her, a hand of anointment flowing back to her.

Could any idea reverberate so limitlessly as the simple conception of a woman and her child? He felt uncomfortable with a thought like that and mystified as to what he was trying to express. After all, he was an industrialist. He always had been. The term itself was a touchstone. Business purpose was the firmest ground. To his comprehension where he belonged. He hadn't even to consider this. But the place he belonged? Not this country. The country where his origins were mortified him. He had his home now. It was Hong Kong.

Yet he was still to break out from the oppression of the Bidayas. Nearing Thailand he was assailed by a vision of serenity. It was all in the figure of one man, Joti Bidaya, the eldest son of Suthin Bidaya. Gauged against Joti Bidaya didn't his almost gun-toting materialism get its comeuppance? So much two families; young, he had lived next to Joti Bidaya. Something was fixed in him: Joti Bidaya was the superior man. The idea had started when each was a child. This face of a man reaching at him, his concentration on his job fizzled out like fuse wire broken from the explosive.

And Thailand! The very air posted secret, inviolability; twenty-four hours in a day; why, why, get into a lather; naturally, a man was allowed the idea of promise, but with promise the thing was not to get ahead of it.

Well he did and never would he apologise for the fact.

There had been a phase where he was almost inclined to give himself up to conception of himself that went so far as to conflict with the facts of his parentage. Released from the European academies, he had not known quite who he was. This difficulty had persisted. In any case, for countless years, Bangkok, Thailand had represented grievous calumny upon his name. That he now possessed the courage to flirt with this abyss was one of the triumphs of his life. His discontent with the land had been vast, a wound on his spirit. But in fact the anger, the restlessness hounded him still. An element waged in him which was remorseless. What was eternal in his life was the deepest uncertainty as to where to erect a front door he could take as conclusive, which he could accept as right. Every day he searched his brain, a pure plea to know. It was like the lethal contest he was locked in with Marshall, except in the strain to understand where lay his proper place on the planet, piteously it was his own person he kept circling. Hong Kong was fabulous for the energy, the unquenchable immediacy. The word now, and everything in that now, enshrined as your mascot. The people, they collided with the moment as slaves of the moment. But, though his imagination was in great part in store to it, to its image, to the ways of its interactions, to its fashion of dormitory, Hong Kong was mere settlement or jurisdiction. It bequeathed a house to live in but failed to attach a cast-iron name to the house.

And to reflect on his American intentions he had come to an Eastern land that did properly bear a name, that had the empowerment of a credible identity, but sadly this was the one location he was convinced he should do everything to banish from his life. If country, nation it was, it was more a mood, and it lay in wait for you. Dampened hearts came forward, accosted, inveigled, went to endangering certainty of purpose, drew a question somehow against those national territories hogging the light in the pantheon of nations. Behold a Thai person's smile and often you could be struck by the lugubrious fatalism of the smile. Strangely, this was most explicit in the faces of the very young. On some days during that earlier period in Thailand so compelling had been the feeling that an underlying spiritual cosmos was sprinkled everywhere as an active manifestation of sorts, one indicative of an immense otherworldly dispassion, even apathy, the fuse for which was some unfathomable ingredient alive in so many of the people, that often he had been ready to discover before him a very real mist hugging the footings of man and building alike. Of course, he realized that he might have been confusing this with that funereal haziness that at certain hours could cling like icing to the country's major river-flows. This was the country his father had come to and made his home. This was a country where historically the fact of a journey, within its borders or to places beyond, led a man to entrust himself to the river. This was the country that the earliest of his father's offspring, despite everything, were urged to honour as crucible, as the star enfolding their beginnings in life. But did it meet for him personally a certitude that he picked up from others, amongst whom was Richard Marshall, when he was assailed by a sense of their overpowering strength of being owed to certainty of cloth; a strength that outshone the passing anxieties of their lives, however traumatic. That somewhere there should be some definitive place that in your grazing against it ordered the planet and ordered you. Tribally to your depths, whether you resisted or not, to be meshed with a specific collection of streets and the parish that bounded them. Were those without this in the most compelling sense fated at some level to be both hunters and the hunted?

But in his heart he knew the cloth: China. But in his case it didn't come with China and couldn't.

Between him and Marshall, who served who!? Who was it shadowing who? He levelled the question straight at this den of apathy which was the hated beach. In this silent war between the two of them, in the dragging punishment of it, an idea kept striking at him: that sometimes, in some circumstances, unspoken things occurred between men more binding in their minds than anything a man might formally vow to a woman. Did he feel trapped like that? Let him do the deed. Let him draw a line through a man. He wanted no strength like this. Let him betray, if betrayal it be. He had to get free. He wanted no freedom like it. He had reached the end with Richard Marshall. The fatigue blocked his soul, the fatigue which was Richard Marshall.

At the restaurant table he was directly in line with the verandas of the four beach dwellings. Jacot-Descombes it was who materialised before so much as a sign of the others. This licking height he had; it bore greater accent still for the trouncing leanness of his body. Harpoon walked. The gangly didn't exist. What pride the man was encased in. In one thing Jacot-Descombes exasperated him. At days end, someone not without material means, his preference as living quarters, as a base wherein to fold up his long frame, was a room at the

Hong Kong YMCA. As essential domicile, he possessed nothing more. In the machinations of his mental world someone who put down plans for whole buildings, whole streets, but regarding himself at this point in his life his interest was for no more than a peg for his coat. A quality to the French architect was the mirror of the beach. Wantana wasn't brought up for a second to speculate what lay at the back of the Swiss technicians he had imported into his Eastern plants, no more than he would do with the thousand-fold girls lining the monster assembly benches. He gave passing thought to Jacot-Descombes though.

Standing at the front of the veranda, the aging European who had appeared placed both his hands on the uppermost bar of the balustrade, his arms like stays. Looking from the beach what you saw was this little Matterhorn jutting up from the sea some two and a half thousands metres out from the shore, its belly broad where it was arranged on the sea's surface. It held your attention but you couldn't say why. Though substantial enough to be described with its own shore, a circle at places adequate to take a dingy, the craggy island was colourless, stark like a primitive idol, chiselled like that too, a rugged cone of rock that peaked, a rugged cone of rock to do nothing with, a cone of rock that no one saw, no one remembered. Except that you did see, you did remember. Wherever they went the Wantana family remembered, the Bidaya family no less. He, Pracha Wantana, should he succeed in his American plans, should he go ahead in the next months, as he envisaged, and buy a house in New York, he understood he wouldn't stand in that house and not find his thought on odd days, for quick seconds, swinging back to a beach in Thailand and the lustreless island that lay off from the beach. Mysteriously, it had been like that for years. His father uprooting the family to Hong Kong hadn't stilled this thing in his brain. And finally, hadn't he, on impulse, come back to the beach? But it wasn't the beach. It was the island. The island inhabited him.

The man on the veranda, fifty-six years old, was concentrated in his gaze over the sea. The man on the veranda had for Wantana developed to a friend, when by this definition of human ways he saw himself as separate, fated to follow a cruel path grown from the difference of his destiny. He employed people, the vastness of the number now testifying to his role as creator propping up civilisations – there was no false modesty to Wantana – continuously he spoke to people, but friends? At the earliest of their meetings he had allowed Jacot-Descombes time. With most he just didn't. Of course the Frenchman had enjoyed a head start on others. It was something he couldn't properly explain. Architects were singled out for him. Architect, as it called off the profession, was a hallowed word to him. Joti Bidaya, Suthin Bidaya's son, had trained as an architect.

He had never travelled with Jacot-Descombes before and that was significant. He had made a journey of two persons once, with his newly wed wife for his honeymoon in Hawaii, and in three days cut short by himself out of homesickness for his office. Beyond that to go somewhere was to seat himself with an entourage. He didn't deceive himself into thinking Jacot-Descombes could be treated like that. He would never think to anyway. In this man's company an experience had started to unfold without precedent. Next to this man he wasn't in himself pitched into a contest of strength as to their standing and merits as men. With this man it did not matter to him how his star should fare when reflected against someone else's. Measured against Jacot-Descombes he hadn't the smallest need to see his star gain new proof of its pre-eminence.

A new day, a new coronation, Wantana's weakness for this was unparalleled. Where were there coronets for your head like the ones you extracted from the blood of your fellow beings? Each new encounter was a new challenge, but then it wasn't, because he always made the assumption of his 'victory'. Where he saw that this would not materialise, he turned away, determined on ignoring the person. But with Jacot-Descombes he had turned back. And soon had settled a composure he couldn't recognize as his own. It inferred a security different in kind to the fickle confidences a posse of his underlings infused him with. Certainly, the architect represented his release from the terrible oppressiveness that descended on him in time in the company of the feckless galley slaves he was so addicted to. Wasn't he this leader of men who could not lead without he inserted between him and the thousands he commanded, and also the world at large, a little tribe of near flunkies, men who made a show of hanging on his every word. But, need or addiction, or both, from time to time it was necessary to escape these people. Whatever this thing was in himself, sometimes the greater need was to rise above it. In the company of the French architect, he achieved this liberation from the sycophants he operated through, and from himself. The realization that in meeting the gaze of another human being your eyes had suddenly discovered the secret of deference, well, it was like being given new eyes. He could take pleasure in them, for a time.

And with respect to this journey to the beach, there was something else: more than any professional advisor, more than any executive on his payroll, regarding the mammoth business move he was contemplating he was ready to hear the Frenchman, ready to listen hard. Beyond the competencies he enshrined, the world was in this man. The compass had gone round until it was weary of the circle. There was human seeing there that didn't reach your sight any other way. It was that he was interested in from the architect, not the figures. For his fear of America wasn't in the mechanics of taking on another business, however large. He, Wantana, had an identity which couldn't be escaped, which surely wasn't going to make anything easy. Not when you considered the power that would abide in his person, the power he would wield over people, American people, over a great American commercial enterprise. But what he couldn't do with Jacot-Descombes, in any critical sense, was discuss the issue of Richard Marshall. What he couldn't do was disburden himself of the torment. And was there another word? To no one could he turn in the matter.

But in fact wasn't he overstating the Frenchman? So, as to America, he could draw on Jacot-Descombes' worldly common sense. So?! Ultimately, with the position he held, he shared nothing. The numbers depending on him removed the possibility the very considerable business grouping he was building precluded it. One occasion in Switzerland he had been on the point of signing documents sealing the transfer of a renowned watchcase making firm to his ownership, when he received word that the man he intended to bring in to run the show once it became his had undergone a change of heart. In a second he had gone back on his own decision: that of acquiring the company. Thirty-five years old, he had his instinct. Look around for wisdom better qualified? Sooner believe in fairies.

Once again he followed where the Frenchman had his eyes trained and suddenly, indeed thirty-five years old, Wantana knew: if one day his ashes were to be scattered somewhere his instruction would be this vision of cold rock anchored off from the shore of his childhood, against the water of the bay a curve that showed like a frayed sleeve. The idea hit him and he accepted it. It was right. There it lay. There it would be. The island!

In Hong Kong his youngest sister just took to staring at Jacot-Descombes, hopelessness in her face, devotion in her face. It mattered not where she was or whomsoever she accompanied, she went off to something. In this action of regarding the one figure of a man a silence visited his sister whose like was outside his experience, the notes of living flesh, of a life-form, lowering, arresting, and the person herself ecstatic in her suspension. This man somewhere left or right of her, her head turned and stayed.

Time was in the lank brown hair, in the regular crossways lay it had, in its holding fullness, in its dying lustre, in a man's carelessness for what he wore. The beach's rawness, even at twilight, somehow left a man in his frame conspicuous against it. The effort at absorbing the architect often entangled Wantana in a strange dichotomy. Bringing a face into focus, were the tones reflective of northern European man or was there a score not of fasting, rather of the sensualities bound with sunlight. Making an assessment of Jacot-Descombes should he decide the witness of a face in fact pointed southwards? In the presentation of a man Jacot-Descombes appeared multiple. A long oval for a face, the features were like a representation of muscle sinew, the narrow shape at the centre of the face quite imaginable as some tendon risen to the surface. If any face incarnated oaths of discipline, of restraint, it was this one. But then in a moment it didn't. All of a sudden the references were loser, spiriting your gaze towards Latin marshes, Latin ardours, nothing so much as Mediterranean dissipations. But why was this? Even placed directly in front of you it was a face that just kept off, as if your own eyes refused to focus properly, some fog intervening.

On his arrival in the East, it was a fog of impenetrable diffidence that had trailed off the architect, someone at least a head above most others out on the streets of Hong Kong. It was a strange detachment, so determined on succeeding in something even as it signalled an unqualified human remoteness. The facts suggested that this might be someone on a quest to break out from arrangements that had formed his whole existence. The manner confirmed it, so that in some way he appeared a man who was out of step with himself. Nevertheless, an invasion of differentness had seemed so welcome to him. It was where he was in his life, Wantana decided. With his speculations about Jacot-Descombes the thought always came to him of a man newly installed in civilian life after a lifetime in the military. Case in hand, the old life locking shut behind him, the street he faced something else, you wagered your blood that here was someone not about to retreat. Because a proportion did take fright at the first contact.

The gaze was a tall man's gaze, calm but it didn't let you off. And that as well was a trait of soldiers wasn't it, those with stripes. Not unkindly, but you got the once-over. Somehow, initially, a tall man's gaze did a job on you. And it was your own eyes that caught and stored the sense of assault, of summary assessment. Jacot-Descombes inspection of him at their first meeting still rankled.

Watching him cross towards the restaurant, Wantana revisited the figure of the Frenchman, the unquantifiable elements jostling against the things that by now were unmistakeable about him. Wherever the extended frame ranged in its parts, so an ornate languor spilled out. But that was conflict too, for in temperament he wasn't a languorous man. Whether intercepted in its northern articulation or its Mediterranean one, the face was a spare ascetic object. It did wear its flesh like bone. As did the whole of him. The years building in his skin, the addition seemed to hone away at him. Someone expert with a military-style knife, Wantana had watched him pare down a stake. It was the image of how age held him fast. But the product wasn't emaciation, or an aura of sickness, just the sternest of figures. In physical terms he was a precipice of a man. Though to muted effect, you got from the face a shadow of the aquiline grandeur found in the features of ancient Spanish conquerors; tantalising persons not to be separated from their stallions, every one of which allowed a man to set his saddle to the height that his will demanded. And the will was for a throne and as it turned out the noblest throne a man ever realised for himself was in the discovery of such animals. From this station in life the conqueror's eyes constructed a gaze that swept over the natives like a sword.

But, of course, Jacot-Descombes was merely a working architect of the twentieth century, even if blessed with an appearance that might have invited notice in any time. Wantana thought of Lincoln with his jaded, tutorial height, that air of removal of his – what else did the black and white photographs say - as if an actual leafage about his head.

Once this man appeared in his office, Wantana had started to circle his prey. He always had scope for this. There was safety of distance in the position that he occupied. Held off as he was by the curtain of power he lived behind, no one could really see what his intentions were. He could calculate to his heart's delight. In the company of this Frenchman his gaze was being altered and the company was interesting to him for its own sake. With an office like his, high-up, all its cuffs glass and more glass, a city like Hong Kong protruded like Titanic. There wasn't discrimination to it, or selection, it was barrage. But then a man arrived in your office whose talk framed a city in unimaginable ways. Whose talk let you into the secret of space, space as it was described where a city's construction hadn't joined up, for that was space purely different. Whose talk laid the idea that amongst a man's possibilities an undertaking was there that was separate: architect

Wantana was a man drawn to the work of shaping some vast commercial organization, but somewhere in all of that the simple things that were buildings were taking on a magnification that absorbed him in isolation of the value of these constructions as mere propositions of business. Weren't these four-sided creations structures that looked to nothing else, a product of man not to be compared with his other outputs? His family had a passion for watches, as he did. This one item, manufactured, traded had powered the family to a fortune. But this wasn't wherein a man worked, wherein he made his home, wherein he came to a dialogue with his fellows, wherein a street was formed, wherein a town or city struck up from the earth. Buildings stood on soil, but communion with such emplacements could be a kind of soil itself. The godly act of creation architects were sunk with wouldn't be known to him. But he could be the impresario, the hands-to-the-deck instigator.

Watching the French architect draw back one of the iron chairs, Wantana realized once more that this was a man who already in his short time in the East had looked on things that would forever lie outside his own experience of the area. Strangely, he was taking to Jacot-Descombes out of a readiness to be treated as an ordinary mortal of sorts; out of an acceptance, almost, that beside the Frenchman he actually was ordinary. It was bewildering in the extreme. In fact, he was confounded by this passivity in himself. After all, the person in question was a western individual. Casting his mind towards those far coastlines, wasn't this increasingly a species he was driven to humble, notwithstanding that he was absorbed by their example.

As it was, despite the harshness of the beach, in the case of Jacot-Descombes he didn't have any fears regarding where he had led the Frenchman to. Rather, if he was to hold the architect's interest, wouldn't he need to 'vary the diet'? This particular European allowed you range for that. Equally, he could take him deep into the city, he could take him to where nature was like the gaps in a person's mouth where two teeth have been lost. They had come to such a place. Down on the sand near to the water's edge was the rotting carcass of a large row-boat. Beyond that it was beach it was thickets of undergrowth, one of those parcels of time where time wasn't.

'I talked of a resort,' Wantana said, 'but I dare say you didn't imagine anything quite like this.'

'It was here the family took holidays? Years ago.'

'Now I am looking at it, I am surprised too.'

'I can't imagine you will rush to invite Andrew Camondo to this place.'

'Believe it!'

'Of course, I don't know him,' Jacot-Descombes said.

'So tell me seriously,' Wantana said, 'what will his reaction be? Not the beach. Me! If I succeed in acquiring these shares I intend to take a role in the firm. More than that, in fact'

'And you think he will resist you.'

'We have met. He is a customer of mine. He gets watch components from more than one source in Hong Kong. All the watch companies do. But this is something else. When the news breaks I think it will come to him like a kick in the teeth.'

'Effectively, you will have control of the organization.'

'Absolutely.'

'You think this is when he will see you for the first time.'

'To have this great American corporation associated with an anonymous Chinese businessman from Hong Kong – I want your ideas on it! A great American company, but more crucially, it's a great American family that lies behind it. The company stretches back, the generations of this one family with it. Think of the classical heritage in Camondo's keeping. To hand all of that over to…I mean, some ant-heap in the East where the people such as they are exist on rice! To take that decision!'

'You aren't any anonymous businessman.'

'I am now! Now my target is the Camondo family. I'm nobody because…Look at my face! The Camondos?!'

'I cannot advise you.'

'You are always advising me. You might not know it, but it's the case. It's a different conversation with you.'

'Then forget your dream.'

'Come, you must do better than that.'

'The only person here qualified to speak to you on this subject you are thinking of firing.'

'You like him? Richard Marshall?

'I haven't the first idea about him. Two days ago all of us were in your office. That's when I was introduced to him.'

'I can call in legions of my executives, consultants, lawyers, and when we get back I will do. But at this minute that's not what I want.'

'Your sister is barely out of university.'

'She is not here as counsel. But don't forget she was educated in America.'

'So use it. When it's time to meet Camondo face to face, you could do worse than take her with you.'

'You are suggesting that I use my sister to divert the American!? Who is the person who would accuse me of an idea like that?'

'I haven't said anything of the sort,' Jacot-Descombes protested, suddenly fearful of this powerful man, and suddenly understanding that the boundaries to their friendship came about as you talked. Everyday asked a new start. The difficulty was increased because you could never be sure when Wantana was being playful and when he was not. It really did constitute an immense problem, one peculiar to Wantana.

'This is a family!' Wantana said, reaching for an expressly sober note. 'The Wantanas – business is something of a fist in our veins. It just doesn't retreat in any of us. I will do many things. If I am honest, there is little that is sacrosanct. But I couldn't even conceive of a thing like that. This you will learn about me.'

Brought up hard, reckoning in his brain like fate, Jacot-Descombes saw that he would never learn anything; for all that he could sit within touching distance of this man, for all that he could receive his conversation and return his own, some reality wider and denser than a city held Wantana away from him, something as unalterable as it was impregnable, something unutterably closed-off and unseeable. In all of this was the Chinese industrialist hidden away. The severity of it was daunting.

'And anyway, it is my misfortune, and the Americans, that at this moment Kep's likely to refuse any invitation that would involve even a day's absence from Hong Kong. You know as well as I why she agreed to this little outing.'

'Do I?'

'Marcel, she is blinded in every eye she possesses!'

'I have three daughters in Europe,' Jacot-Descombes said. 'Two are older than Kep.'

'Which arithmetic I have done myself,' Wantana said. 'Many times.'

'You amaze me.'

'That I'm not happy about it?!'

'Young Kep! You really think I…'

'I am sorry,' Wantana said. 'I apologise. I would trust you with my life, and my sister's.'

This was something the Frenchman had learnt. That freely Wantana produced statements like this.

'These things pass,' Jacot-Descombes said, his sudden tone of detachment cruel against the heat-dammed air.

'Let us hope so,' Wantana replied.

'Then why did you ask her to join us?' Jacot-Descombes said.

'Because I am thinking of her. She is going to suffer, she is suffering now, and possibly there's a way to treat the pain. Which is precisely to open her eyes. I decided she should have the opportunity to perceive you more clearly. Hong Kong is kind to men like you. It lets you appear like gods. For someone like my sister anyway. The lives that you build here in the East, I mean you and your counterparts, middle-aged Europeans, Americans, they are gained under false pretences. These young women are deceived. And in your case, there are more than enough of them.'

'You exaggerate. It is your way.'

'I see you in Hong Kong. I see you in your cubicle at the YMCA. And I see you sitting there surrounded by letters from your daughters. And then you leave your room somewhat late in the evening. To go where? An Eastern city's daughters wait.'

'It is not like that.'

'Every week these letters come. That's what you tell me.'

'Yes, but it's not like you describe,' Jacot-Descombes said.

'No, I do not expect that it is.'

'Nevertheless you decided that Kep should have the chance to recognize this ancient European for what he was.'

'I wanted to close the physical distance between you. How else does a person get to use his eyes?'

'So by including your sister in our group, you would leave this place with something, even if in the end you are persuaded that America is one step too far, even for you.'

'Will I be persuaded of that?'

'This is beyond my level. Pass me a crayon, I will show you a thing or two. Beyond that I'm not about to delude myself.'

'Show me everything. Enlightenment! Where the world isn't mine.'

'You really think I can help?'

'You think Hong Kong can help...?'

'Try a room at the YMCA.'

'No, everywhere isn't the same.'

'Of course, you are right.'

'The places I intend to go to – I need guidance! Who am I? An entrepreneur out of Hong Kong! And Chinese! God that makes me an innocent in your cities. You help me. When you speak about things you do. I have to confess, it's not many I will listen to. I wouldn't even ask.'

'America! I've never set foot there. I've never set foot...To build like you! Every day to thrust off into the unknown on a prodigious scale. It's your covenant with life. With yourself.'

'See, there are things you have to say.'

'But what is any of that?' Jacot-Descombes said. 'I'm relating something everyone knows about you. Start with the one word: business. There is an opportunity and where there is an opportunity you are the man who will act on it.'

'Exactly,' Wantana said.

'You have told me that the American company is in serious difficulty. That is why the oil and gas group are so keen to offload their shareholding.'

'Camondo, or rather his father, committed to spending vast sums on developing a technology to power watches that has no future. The tuning fork mechanism. I have the company blurb off by heart: "October 25, 1960 - Recutron, the first watch to keep time through electronics, is introduced. It is the most spectacular breakthrough in timekeeping since the invention of the wristwatch. This revolutionary timekeeping concept of a watch without springs or escapement is operated by an electronically activated tuning fork. Why does Recutron record time so faultlessly? In place of the usual wheels and springs, time is measured by a tiny, electronically-driven tuning fork that vibrates 360 times per second. This principle makes it possible to give with each Recutron timepiece a written guarantee of accuracy to within a minute a month."'-

Back in the fifties, Marcel, the best mechanical watches relied on a prime moving element with a frequency of around 2Hz., that is, about two 'beats' per second. By the novel idea of applying an electric current to a tuning fork, a frequency of 360Hz. was realised. But the sad fact is that by applying current to a quartz crystal, a far higher frequency is achieved. This is a watch company out on a limb, compelled for reasons of the investment they have made, and no less for reasons of pride, to pursue a science that already is dead in the water. They boasted of themselves as pioneers and they never were. The whole organization was turned over to a massive delusion. With this watch science they make such a noise about, what in fact have we got? Sadly, we're not even talking the pickings from the palace. Quartz is the future for watches. One thing I know about Andrew Camondo: he is alone now. It doesn't matter how many he employs, when a crisis of this scale strikes, there isn't anyone else. The responsibility rests with him. I might be the first and last opportunity he has to save his organization, Chinese or not, you might say.'

'To fix this company you will have to remake it.'

'Yes, but will they take it? Will they take it from one such as me? I am asking you.'

'Are you asking me?'

'Yes, you my friend. Not anyone else.'

'What can I say?'

'You will give me your answer. And before we leave this place.'

'All that you have done till now is dead for you, isn't it? Everything is dead for you but the idea of America.'

'If you become satisfied with something, everything stops,' Wantana said. 'In any case…'

'What?'

'This is my bid for freedom.'

'Your father?'

Pracha Wantana looked at the French architect, but said nothing.

Then he averted his head, his gaze sliding off to the orphan row of unworldly beach quarters. Amazingly, they had indeed continued to exist, the restaurant no less, and came over as substantially unchanged. He laughed, but not out loud. It was for himself. Taking the exterior look of them, it was like the pieces of a large sailing craft come to grief on rocks had been gathered and put to use. On the outside each chalet was the embodiment of the rough and ready, abrupt uneven wood planks finding a niche against others entirely arbitrarily. Two segments to the beach and concentrating on the part enclosing the line of brusque holiday homes, it was as though they had come upon a scene that had stood undisturbed for a hundred years or more. Once, a long time before, an unknown man had happened on the spot by accident. Succumbing to vast weariness he hadn't been able to continue with his journey. Pressed for his sanity's sake to some activity, any activity, with the five simplistic beach dwellings that in the evening light were like the nameless manifestations accompanying some primitive tribal rite had proceeded to leave his mark. No being had set foot here in the time since. In Wantana's eyes that man had been Jacot-Descombes.

Too true he had broken with this place from his childhood. The Bidayas had kept on with it. Their interest was differently formed since they owned the land. And visiting they left things alone. What feudal lord would tamper with an ageless fishing community? In amongst the trees existed a sort of tinderbox of the untouchable. Another of his sisters lived in Switzerland. She had married a farmer, though the man had been persuaded off the land and into one of his watch component factories in La Chaux-de-Fonds; someone who had proved effective inside a factory. A fishing village, a farm, the signal didn't arise with the summons of a bell or the glare of a clock-face, it was a tempo, a tempo bound with leaving a table and returning to the table, which gave the lead. The yesterdays, the tomorrows, they stroked the back of each other in a pact of lovers. At length the faces rotated, children came about and grew, yet still it was a tomorrow of yesterdays, the slant of a man's back in the fields a verse like the passing clouds. Spreading the nets, leading the ploughs, it was endeavour following with the wildflowers the rain the wind, endeavour eternally pitched, that eternity so much the one picked up in the sound of a man whistling. The boats making their imperishable way out from the shore, the boats themselves, it was a knot that went for time. And watching from the bay, eyes half-closed, the dumb hunch-back which was the island, the lonely enigmatic rock outcropping, older than everything in its clasp with the bay, its clasp with the shore, and in its constant gazing at the shore some of that pitiful trusting expectancy the grievously lame gave off while waiting upon their warden, he or she their sole voice in the world.

Yes, he, Wantana, he did stray. The odd moment it happened. A sort of trance set in, his stillness of mind, his concentration, feeling to him akin to the bonfires Indian tribes in America were in the habit of lighting outside their tents. The vigil taking him over was man in his setting, everything forgotten but the cruel phenomena. It was debate he was drawn towards, to know where it was he inhabited. He didn't want the discourse especially and the people he spent his time with in his business universe couldn't have suspected. He was conscious of hidden eloquence, this lost lamb on his inside. It had found its way out in the spur to realise a rare industrial building. He saw it like that. Possessed of no special aptitude, eloquence was left to meditate in the abstract. It wandered the street. Personally, he nursed a fortune. A part was available, of course. Thailand, Bangkok, the needy existed, and they bore young faces, very young. The experience of poverty in a city was the jungle. Were he on the side, without fanfare, to launch some small charitable trust, it wouldn't be necessary to live in the country. But he took it no further. Folklore had him as the all-out hard-bitten business operator. To an extent he was convinced; enough that he forgot a mind's freakish tilts. Besides, they didn't interrupt anything, not for long. A business thought started, he was back.

The island: what did it know? The sea wedged it, the sea owned it. From the beach he had made this movement with his head all those years ago, if it was once it was a hundred times every hour. Always the island was there. And now he was doing it again.

Jacot-Descombes appeared tranquil. But that was deceptive. He had Wantana next to him at the table. To begin to approach this Chinese man sent you into a black contest with yourself. Getting close in bodily the personal magnetisms came at you like an axe. In the first days the sensation had compelled his trust, his obedience. But already, allowing for some of the things he had witnessed in their relatively short relationship, his generosity, his eagerness, was now meeting severe obstruction.

His mounting disturbance at Wantana was like dice he kept flipping from his hand. He wanted to say things, he wanted to speak out; what was necessary was expiation of the deluge on his heart; what was necessary was to find a name for things. But if he did speak there had to be a beginning, and the beginning shouldn't be unkind for, after all, Wantana had been crucial to turning him around. So he would make a start in some simple statement, no meanness to it, not at the outset:

that here was someone that though to the finish bore an overriding impulse for action, not meditation or anything like it; that, his consideration slightly less benign now, this was a man for whom the magic of the world lay in its potential to be broken down on a monetary scale; the magic of the world was that man facing man its constituent parts could be bartered; the magic of the world was in the conception of vast production lines. He wanted to say, definitely on the attack now and not frightened of the nastiness appearing in his heart, that really the talent was for rabid egomania, rabid self-promotion. He wanted to say that the political consciousness went no further than the creed which apportions rights according to a man's status in society. He wanted to say that on an especially bad day, significant westerners present in his office, pressures built in him leading him to behave like a performing bear, the bluster overtaking him just crude, and likely accompanied by imbecilic statements; and he wanted to ask why he was never like that with him. He wanted to say that there were shadowy interludes when spite was never far from his lips, when malice took him over incurably as it can a child, the worst of the spite invariably following a spasm of intense jealously at one of his brothers. He wanted to say that in the moments when he turned to puppet performer the rampant self-confidence on display stank, the stench getting to your nostrils advising of some lonely character inhabited by a wake of insecurity. He wanted to say that this was a man building a business empire as his devout protection from the world.

But in trying to say these things, he was interrupted: as incontrovertible as all of it struck him, it nevertheless missed its target. No, not a barbarian, better to say a maverick, one who with a careless wave of his hand, facing the devastation of a long-serving member of his staff whose wife had been diagnosed with cancer, in a second's decision took on himself the load of every last one of the medical bills. No, not a barbarian, just a maverick, and once without a clue, naïve enough in the early stages of his career to protest, to be wounded, at being asked for a contract: his word was his contract and if he established proof of one thing in his life it would be this. That naïve maverick who as a schoolboy excelled at Greek studies and who as a grown man never tired of boasting of it; and moreover belonged to the aristocracy which is the fluently multi-lingual, never having to strain for this, as if pirating complete languages wherever he found himself and as if in a day's business. No, not a barbarian, rather a maverick, one pulled to hand out alms not merely to the needy but to anyone who showed him a day's decent respect, to any who wandered across his path and stayed out of respect. No, not barbarian, but pure individualist, one who went to the head of the table not simply out of vanity but because he was volunteering for the load of leadership; he couldn't have done a thing in life without this burden; remove one of his limbs but never, never, dislodge him from his answerability for sums of money in the way of the economy of a small nation, for his answerability to the thousands upon thousands who endured out of his drive to be. No, not a barbarian, confine the judgement to maverick, one who rumour had it, colonial Hong Kong being one of the world's keener rumour mills, had paid a ransom of one hundred thousand American dollars to get a brother off a manslaughter charge following a traffic incident; still in any case, someone who through to his bones dwelt and dwelt again on the issue of family.

An idea in relation to Wantana was gaining strength with the architect. He wanted to say, and with immense sympathy, that the industrialist was a man in whom there were no quiet roads. And that made it hard for a man because unquiet roads hadn't to be easily appeased.

Jacot-Descombes kept on marvelling. If the whole enterprise of this four day break felt somewhat bizarre to the Frenchman, still it was recognizably the hand of Pracha Wantana that was at work; a hand that arose from a lavish turn of mind. He would never be without it. And wasn't the proof of it to be found where he and Wantana looked? With three guests to accommodate, he had produced an entire 'house' for each of them. But it wasn't enough to decide that where there was one guest, there should be a property exclusive to them, and where there was another so would another sole residence be found. It wasn't enough to place an ocean at all their front doors. No, none of that was sufficient. He had decided, for reasons his own, to include a young woman amongst them. Nor was it just any young woman (of course, neither could it ever be; a girl as girl was utterly forbidden; he would take you to a hostess club in Hong Kong, but carry a young female along with them on an outing like this: do not dare to go near the thought). Jacot-Descombes understood the depth of honour accorded to both himself and Richard Marshall. That a man such as Wantana had instigated the presence of a sister of his was unprecedented. Yet really it could never have been other than a sister.

From the doorway of the third chalet along the twenty-two year old person Kep appeared. Straightaway the two men at the restaurant table fixed on her. One of course was her brother, but not the other. Arriving in the East, Jacot-Descombes had been forced into a solitary vigil, a vigil whose object wasn't permitted to him, a vigil which came with depths of silence because not only did it threaten condemnation, it risked personal betrayal the more fervently he was to seek a product from it; a vigil of impossibility, but what was also impossible was to forgo it.

From his cell in the YMCA he went out to dine in Hong Kong with a stream of limber upbeat office girls, their tight frames trained to a Chinese girl's studious frocks; at their place next to him crossing the vestibules of the cinemas and restaurants, each in turn these pintsized girls melded with his tallness as if it was their destiny. East and West did meet. Jacot-Descombes had discovered it.

Wantana's sister set off for the restaurant tables in the company of Richard Marshall, who had descended from his own door, the chalet furthest along, soon after Kep had come out. The crop top was white and sleeveless. Where it stopped a circling band of deft flesh was deposited into deft circulation. The sailor shorts were without precedent in this family. Making her way to the tables that bare midriff of hers led a life of its own. Her brother looked, meditated; America went further than his particular obsession with it.

A Frenchman was attentive, no less. Taking her awkward steps, this young person rose at him as if from a ladle. The skin was brown, its count of young womanliness impossible to ignore. Evening and its developing shadow parted to let her through, it parted to let you see her. The stamp of her waist flirted with the idea of a true rare slenderness. That patently it would never quite achieve this was not in any way to its cost. The waist broke to a regatta of force and passion. The hips just radiated, burnt through with substance, but in a manner that was controlled and even sinuous. Where her contours were memorably, solidly rounded, paradoxically this obeyed a sequence that was yet nimble and lissom. Your eyes advanced and as they did this dishy line she had with its enigmatic tightness crept out of its nest. She possessed a body that persisted in alluding to things it wasn't. This ignited the body she had. Something in her overall form resisted description. These curves of hers were at once festive and disciplined, a mysterious ingredient policing all of this shapeliness, kneading it to a stubborn taut grace.

It was the ambiguous robustness at her waist and hips that seemed to give this young woman her stride. She walked heavily, but not with the heaviness of any man. Though it must be said a certain heaviness of form lurked throughout this Thai-Chinese family. Across their physical bounds the physical expression of it varied from one to the other. In the case of the youngest of the daughters, her walk was a lope that spilled her youth. In height only degrees saved her from the hinterlands of a marked tallness. Watching her Jacot-Descombes again caught this strange reluctance of hers to give rein to the moons of her legginess. Before her movement became a walk, it was invariably a kind of abashed shuffle, and not because she went in fear of the slight ungainliness that characterised her regular movement, but as if out of an innate understanding of the bloom of sensuality that her full-bloodied motions unlocked everywhere across her body. This sensuality belonged to her, and yet it didn't; a devilish radiance behind which there appeared the separate image of a person who conformed to a calmer, more resolute scale. There was an air about her that said she was perpetually caught between these two poles. Sliding towards one, she immediately veered to the other. It seemed to leave her constantly looking over her shoulder, in search not of another person but of herself.

Whenever Jacot-Descombes set eyes on Kep he was stirred into recalling some words he had read once. The writer was describing an encounter with a stranger whom he had met with when travelling in distant regions: 'He spoke about bright young faces, eager students of poetry and literature, scholars who lived in conditions of medieval clerks.' Jacot-Descombes could not explain it, but in his mind Kep shone with these words, notwithstanding that in the main the places she dwelt in resounded with natural advantage; he did understand that it was related to things he was observing on his visits to the country which was Vietnam; he had seen people there and in them he had seen Wantana's youngest sister, and in her now he could see all of them.

Returning to Hong Kong from one of his excursions to Vietnam, his dreams were beset. He saw etched figures journeying alone along the crests of verdant ridges, cut off, lost, fleeing in hopelessness, seeking in hopelessness, out to its borders their country gone to war's quicksand, their lives quicksand. Vietnam was broken, families asunder; motion helped if you had been made an orphan, or wore the stigma of deserter, two, three persons together, or braving it unaccompanied, friendless. The young were in Khaki denims. If it was the one person and no one else, and the face was beautiful, the khaki stamped them with the cut of young revolutionaries. In fact the revolution was bitter, bitter, in mass the khaki just bleak. His dreams confirmed it: thousand-fold on thousand-fold the young were being thrown to their end, the numbers easy the commander's nod sending the phalanxes forward, his nod to throw lives away easy, all of it easy, easy like sprinkling tulips in the air.

Perhaps he was seeing as only someone of his kind could, but a man like him, this visitor to the East, this trespasser, he found that he had to narrow it down. The impressions he was receiving became a morass unless he looked for a few simple images he could pin up before his eyes as if they were pictures framed on a wall. Everywhere the grace of form that he confronted in the East was a thing stretched to breaking point, and nowhere more so than in the line of some of the young women. Such edge to the terrible fineness, the fairness of aspect, and wonder in your mind that all of it could hold and not shatter. And everywhere in the East were doorways that out of some quality you couldn't define transcended their function as mere gateway to some run-of-the-mill building. Bound up in any one entrance was the shadow of the drama of all the others.

He was French, and having accepted a working position in Hong Kong, it happened that by the time he reached the landing strip of Hong Kong's Kai Tak he was in the grip of a plan where to head for with his time-off. Somewhere amongst the many passages of a long flight a word tumbled forward, opening out of the ether. It opened to an intelligence hardly indifferent to the word. A jet aircraft on a path eastwards he was spurred to the word like the nation France came about in him. The reason was in the word: Vietnam.

Jacot Descombes turned to Pracha Wantana:

'It is strange,' the architect said. 'You are the oldest son. Kep is the youngest daughter. Between you and her there are five daughters and another two sons. Nor does it end with Kep. After her come three additional male heirs. Yet your father sent only you and Kep to the West for your schooling. He has not granted this to one other of his offspring.'

'Nor will he, I think,' Wantana said. 'But in any case, she is the most intelligent amongst us.'

'I would expect that from you.'

'That I am ready to admit it?'

'A degree in social anthropology,' Jacot-Descombes said. 'I for one am impressed. But more than that, looking at her, it's exactly what you'd expect.'

'Need I tell you,' Wantana said. 'You have seen. There are moments when she will not let up. She comes to her voice like someone on a mission. A mission she discovered that morning. She is fortunate she is young and a young woman. But I am glad of her powers. She reaches me from the family, after all. But who can talk like she does. Not anyone I speak to. What it is to have a young sister who graduated in the last year. We ignore her at our peril.'

As she neared the tables Wantana's gaze remained settled on Kep, the long novice legs just so game for the world. Don't fail me now, sister, he pronounced to himself, show this man Marshall every courtesy. Really that is why you are here. You are family. If I can say it, the best of the family and for the next days this man will eat at the table next to you. I am inclined to make this available to him.

Yes? Did he have this right? He felt bound to honour Marshall even as he was preparing to pull the ground from under his feet?

He hadn't just employed Marshall, he had gathered him up, had called on him to follow, had pointed to the place at his side, had promised him riches and all because he was one of those he had sympathy for. And how many were there, in truth. Best not to get into that.

He had never admitted it but the experience of the western academies had left him with feelings of deep inferiority before westerners. It was Richard Marshall, he and his father, who had come to his aid, who had helped him discover the belief with which to see off the curse on him. How he had been disarmed by the instance of a man of the West seemingly desperate to ingratiate himself with him, Wantana, of a man of the West placing eyes on him of open reverence. It was to occur again, but never as with Richard Marshall. Fifteen years? An odyssey lay between them, inestimable on both sides. Yet no one shakes hands without their body makes an entrance. The largeness they had had for each other reverberated in the first reckoning as a physical matter. A division of skins, yet not so; on the day of their meeting was certainly that encounter of two people where the width of seas lap at your legs. And yet amazingly, with the gulf of race dividing them, they had stared across the space to see their very own images.

What had reached their eyes had dazzled them, found them mesmerised to their shoes. He and Marshall, the starting point had been endless fascination: equal in height, equal in figure, that figure short and stocky; complementary as to their hair, which is to say, cleanly parted, glossy black in firmament; then also within six months of each other in age; then also the identical background of a family in business. It didn't allow for escape, the magnification each had for the other brought to bear by the wonder of these mirror likenesses being founded, critically, on otherness, that indeed of race.

It had been that ardour which is sameness found where sameness is ruled out. He wasn't inhibited to apply the word. Ardour it had been. Marshall understood this, enough that his evident calculations about defying his employer against all odds began from it. No one was going to dismiss him, least of all the man who had effectively demanded his allegiance, who had begged for it, who had, yes, been free with the insinuation he was assuming responsibility for him, who had with resolution granted him the title of honorary brother. Marshall's tactic was to grasp hold of the past and remind Wantana. Wantana couldn't be who he was without Richard Marshal. So Richard Marshall intended to bring it home to Wantana.

But he, Wantana, knew it in any case: Richard Marshall just wasn't any man. No? Well, in any case he was bored by it, this one connection. He had liked Marshall, he had treasured a man in his employment unmistakeably of the West and moved on any day to do honour to him, Pracha Wantana, who kept on undeterred in his solicitude, who never wavered in his devotion. But he just couldn't find Marshall's face anymore, someone who arrived in his office every three or four months. The vast weariness men came to with each other – it seemed to exist in direct proportion to the eagerness with which they had begun.

These men in his pay: it was tantalising how he could play with all of it, moving the pieces on the board without compunction. Forward, sideways, back; forward, sideways, back. It was his game, his refreshment. Goodbye, done cold, done in ignominy, done in exhilaration.

Every excuse had been used up. This time the filthy work was his to take on; certainly if he aspired to maintain cordial relations with himself in the future. A man to be given the elbow, always he delegated the task. Which is to say he ran and hid; he, Wantana.

But not this time. This time he would stand directly in front of the man. This time the man would get it from his, Wantana's, lips, get it plain, hard, at a distance of inches. Dead of night or not, a beach in Thailand or not, this time he would stare into the man's eyes, deliver the news, give a last look, then turn his back, clean as you like.

The beauty of it, that spin away, that switch off.

Yes, the relationship had had a beginning, and yes, he, Wantana, was the one who had to own up. And had much changed? Contemptuous of many, at moments rude as a man can be, still his was a figure ever overeager to impress, and to the extent it saw a man famously loose with his offers, which soon left him confronting the impossibility of living up to them. And besides, he wasn't interested to for a minute. People were always looking to him for some special dispensation. He was out on his own not solely because he sought it but because he was eastern man who western man had elevated of his own free will, and western man never put eastern man on a pedestal like this without he didn't expect favours, a long story of them. So he, Wantana, had learnt.

Surely they knew: he threw his offers around like confetti because he was so uncertain of himself next to his fellow man.

Little more than a year had gone by since he had witnessed his sister's re-emergence in Hong Kong, her own time inside the western colleges gone through to its finish. He had welcomed someone whose outward image had rather discouraged him, a student's apathy in the matter of personal appearance cruelly discourteous to the definite female charms that existed. She carried the disregard as if the immovable filter through which she met the world. On the day of her re-entry she had been a girl hidden inside a welter of unkempt hair that grew as it came to it and in gusts went off where it liked. In this black mane of hers and its dread absence of lustre he had divined the memorable tinge that characterises tool steel after it has been oil-hardened inside an open flame. Visiting the engineering shops in his earliest factory Wantana had relished standing and regarding the process, a block of steel first quenched in thick oil then held in fire, specifically the open blaze of an acetylene torch, the flame dancing, going around the block like a mouth, gorging like a mouth, the oil burning away beneath the fire-god's attack to leave the square of steel etched to a count of black colour as purely dead in tone as will ever be witnessed on a material surface. That black, its flatness, its lifelessness, was an image rooted in his mind like the island.

The length and breadth of the production floors under his authority he saw other tomboyish girls, ranks of them, their many thousand skulls sheeted with coarse sunless hair. Hair like this was wire, and arid like metal. Young heads, but ancient warrior-like thickets growing from a good number of them. His sister arrived back in Hong Kong in a storm of broken jeans and coltish levitation. She had returned to find that her brother had erected a marble palace as industrial headquarters. In flashes she could spy the edifice as yard by yard, a sleek airliner turning belly-heavy in the way of an albatross, her plane lowered itself in the gullies between the skyscrapers, the city tentacles reaching up, the city tentacles hooking about the glinting silver shape, ensnaring it, so that gates fastened around the jet well before it ever made contact with the ground, an embrace rendering the heavens non-existent, forgotten.

Pracha Wantana was ready to reward his youngest sister for her degree in social anthropology. He would have forgiven himself if he had seen mystical powers in her newly won accreditation. He was in difficulty. In his arresting immensely collected Hong Kong factory plant – technocracy-smooth walls that at the four corners were hung off building-high single-piece rectangular granite stanchions as broad as the pillars of a mighty bridge, the whole outside finished to a solid bronze coloration, bronze the bass amongst colours, and this deep-baked Martian brown so empowering the edifice spiritually it just oozed pity for the neighbouring structures with their regulation stucco walls, the regulation white the walls had – ten manufacturing levels were at full-bore. The breadth of the activity had caused the administration floor at the summit of the building to drop the baton. The required professionalism didn't exist. With the numbers at the manufacturing face spiralling, the understanding of how to tether the beast to a system, of how to monitor it according to a science of rigid practise, hadn't kept pace. The imported production technicians were doing their job, but he had ignored the need for abler administrators. At the spot where an organization organised, where the purpose was to watch and worry like mother, the mothers were short of talent. In no time a growing industrial unit had outgrown their level of competence.

For one thing, there wasn't such a thing as a functioning personnel department.

Aware that his sister was back in Hong Kong, he had invited her to the factory. A day had been arranged. Thus had she come to his magnificent new plant. As it turned out a day he would always know, always go back to. The invitation had directed her to come at lunchtime. She needed to present herself at the reception on the ground floor, nothing more. There she would receive directions.

With the creation of his futuristic watch component factory one entire floor, the fifth, had been set aside to serve as the company canteen. Soon it was that two sittings were asked for. It was when the workers broke off from their labours that the beast was revealed. The thirteen floors encompassed battalions. Ready for nourishment, out of the lifts, so much like the trucks of a building-site, the operatives surged deluge upon deluge.

The factory canteen was a vice on the eyes for the very reason that it was here that the eyes were let into the secret of the apparent limitlessness of the area making a single floor in the building, on this floor the idea always to leave the greater part of the thirty-six thousand square feet perfectly open. The advance of uncorrupted space, and precisely because it was an interior space, dazzled as simple phenomenon. The perimeter walls were in sight, but the better description was that they were off somewhere, all the pull on the eyes the free-running yardage of the floor. On and on the yards travelled.

The factory canteen down its length saw lines of tables set out rank upon rank. The factory canteen at the appointed hour fixed bodies to these tables in the manner of the canteen in a penitentiary, each one of the rows of tables like an estuary with its phalanx of human forms. The factory canteen made explicit not so much the echelons of commonly-attired figures but the heads of these thousand upon thousand persons in eerie isolation, skulls more alive to the eye than will be experienced in a lifetime of individual encounters. The factory canteen in minutes turned electric with what two or three thousand heads will do on two or three thousand pairs of shoulders when these people are aglow with camaraderie and the business of food.

On the inward side of the rectangle where the lifts were located the factory canteen was watched over by the massive steel counter from which the dishes were served, a troupe of chefs lined up behind it, all sporting the outfit proper to the occasion, hats included. The factory canteen invited the workers to present themselves at the counter. The factory canteen saw them keen to do it.

The factory canteen at the one end designated a complete row of tables, the first in the sequence, or the last, for the use of the family who owned the organization together with their most senior executives. The factory canteen had something like a year ago witnessed his youngest sister enter the area through the door at the farthest point from where the family congregated at their exclusive station.

He had seen her straightaway and straightaway had understood the nightmare engulfing a young woman. His eyes never left her as she undertook the hike down the entire length of the floor to get to him. It just shouldn't have been asked of her. Every eye in the place had gone to her, and a place like this had never existed, or been imaginable, when she had travelled off to the western colleges, a place like this and the measureless hordes it was host to; and not one of these people who in the second she appeared didn't shift in their seats, shift to stare at this young woman standing alone and cut-off. It was a daughter of the family, but more than that the youngest of the daughters, someone the workers had never seen, but someone the workers could divine immediately in all her status. If the individual was of the family, that individual was guessed at immediately.

In a flash she had sensed the scope of the gaze that rested on her. He had seen her baulk at the impossibility. She couldn't do it. Then he had seen her gather herself, and known that in this second, with the outrageousness of the test, she had needed to learn how to do this. He had seen her come to the ability as if in the space of a few strides. And he had seen how eventually she relaxed, those legs of hers whose slight sturdiness she shrank from in herself finding a gaiety, a feminine gaiety, inside the arch of the knee-length frock. Blue it was, a blue to say grace over, the sparse overprinted flower design like shoots from the quick of a girl every which way a girl, if only she but knew it. The darts of the frock had echoed with one young woman's resin legs. Twelve children his father had had, and mysteriously he and his youngest sister possessed darker skin than the rest. The two of them, they were the peasant stock in the family. That was his verdict on the mystery, and announcing it to himself always cheered him.

With that heroic trek down the long, long channel dividing the tables from the serving counter she had been transported between worlds. Observing her on that day, he had known, intimately so, what it was to return from a western college that door having closed behind you forever. But going from one world to another, even he had not stepped out of a classroom to be flung into a single vast reservoir where really an Eastern city was crashed; and the unbelievable noise that could pour from those tables; an hour in the day chimed, the workers flung to their break, and that was to give free expression to their human enthusiasm for each other. Let off the leash it was the voices that came to life, whatever was the day, whatever was the week. The canteen? The sound was a birdhouse, nation-size. Better than anywhere in the world China was in his factory canteen during the two hours in the day. He was making China even as his heart was set on becoming something, somebody, where the corral, the personage, spelled out royal western soul.

He had sent out an invitation to his sister. He wished her to come to his spanking new industrial castle. But he had not anticipated he would have another guest on the day. Beside him at the family's special spot in the canteen had been Jacot-Descombes.

As location for a fully-fledged personnel department she had told her brother it was her preference to go deep into the factory. The administration floor up at the pinnacle of the factory she distrusted. With her work she should be near the heat of the action, yoked with the beating heart of a plant, the flesh in the corridors that which ended the day not a little unclean, smelly.

But was it her wish also to put distance between her and her brother?

He had requisitioned a part of the floor home to the creation of the company's line of watch dials, in fact a floor where no one broke sweat at all. It was the science-trite machines that everything was asked of. And ask the limit because that was what a machine was, their sweat never sweat. Science was too dumb for that.

The room which was her office lay on two levels, the desk itself located at the centre of the raised up portion extending out from the wall furthest from the door. He set his little sister down on this dais and soon she seemed born to it, because in weeks a change had been worked. Awed slightly, he had speculated and continued to speculate. An eight hour day and at varying times didn't her duties send her out across the factory spaces to mingle and take note? Each floor had its nucleus of western technicians, overseers in coats of green and blue that never quite seemed to fit; in the circumstances in which they found themselves, watchful men, despite their maturity, or because of it. Returned to the decks of an eastern universe was it the gaze of these European males, with their harmed, dented faces, that pierced the consciousness of a Chinese girl fresh from university in the West. Hadn't her experience in America kept her at a distance from men just drier in their seed? A day's business taking her in under the eaves of a man, older, authoritative, professional, should he think that social anthropologist was no more, Personnel Director even less so. It was a case only of a young woman, Chinese, wanting to understand she was attractive. The seal for that lay nowhere but with them, the formidable unsmiling men he had placed in his plant to let him win through to success.

One morning Wantana had gone to visit, striding from his office towards the row of lifts. He had discovered that the person he had escorted to her newly-built quarters a matter of weeks before was no longer in residence. In sculpting a kind of throne for her, it seemed he had acted with prescience. The exquisite mortal seated behind the desk gleamed. Where they played on the surface of the desk, the fingers flexed to a new music. Letting your eyes rest on them for a second the fingers appeared worldly-wise and somehow drawn out to new-found length and slenderness. Beyond it was as though one head of hair had been exchanged for another. There grew locks, fanned to artful definition. The tresses were piled, they curled, they swanned. The transformation in her dress completed the magnetism of the rebirth, fabric and line bearing the heraldry and blossom of a Milanese catwalk. The family was rich and now she was the overt symbol of the money where really none had existed.

Reaching the beach restaurant Kep felt compelled to tug out a chair for Richard Marshall. A quality in the energized face suggested relief that she had safely delivered this 'parcel' she had found herself entrusted with. Of course, she understood that as for Richard Marshall the moment had arrived. How was her brother going to accomplish it? Every senior person in his organization was waiting for him to do the deed. One of the constant pressures on him was to hold onto the respect of his senior people. Richard Marshall hadn't a friend left in the company. The organization had turned against him. Her brother was expected to show himself a leader. But the proof of that now lay in just the one matter: the sending away forever of Richard Marshall.

'Is this a bare canvass, Mr. Architect?' Kep said, some froth risen in her just at being with these men. 'Or are you people slave to the city to the exclusion of all else?

'If the commission is a beach front, I'm ready,' Jacot-Descombes said.

'My brother won't give it to you,' Kep said excessively sombrely. 'If you want to know why ask him about his pedigree chickens.'

She saw the Englishman's blank bewilderment. His face just glazed over. It delighted her because she knew it was for her to release him from his confusion. She also realised that for her brother and Marshall to sit facing each other over the next three days depended largely on her. She had received some instructions from her brother. She was the diversion. Be her young self. Be forthcoming. However it took her. She would try to comply, though she had serious misgivings about her brother's approach in the matter. To do what he was building himself up to carry out she considered her brother had made it just so much worse for himself by bringing Marshall to the beach. And was there honour in stretching something out? Rather honour the man by not wasting time. Honour the man by giving it to him straight, without a minute's delay. But she also sensed that this thing that was Richard Marshall and her brother was outside anything else in her brother's existence. In these ties you stumbled into blind with your fellow man, you couldn't keep pace with honour. Honour your guide your feet were in mud. The places you reached in your relations with another weren't to be prophesied. Honour couldn't be brought in to it. Whose honour anyway?! It was always murder, a small sort, or something larger, on the day making the here and now, on the day to be ten years hence. Get the least accommodation you could. It was at the back of every conversation that broke out. And in fact was her brother planning to say the word? What was his plan? Cutting himself off with Marshall was to find an answer. Yet did the answer exist. The two of them had journeyed to the beach; they had extricated themselves from the cars; they had inspected their surroundings; they had walked over to the beach chalets; they had put away their things. A contest was taking place. No less than that a human bond was in flow, still, this noose about their necks.

'If you don't already know – but of course you do know – this family has two fixations,' Kep said, transferring her attention to Richard Marshall, 'watches and property construction. But, yes, watches – with us they overwhelm everything else. Still, as a side-line my brother started dabbling in property construction. In Hong Kong it is almost a duty if you pretend to be a man of affairs. Whatever else you are doing, you must involve yourself in putting up some kind of building or other. The men of the Hong Kong business community cannot take their eyes off each other. And who follows the herd like a man? But my brother has gone beyond dabbling. Something else: my brother has a liking for audiences. He is famous for it. Entertaining an audience he has his routines. It's at these moments he turns into the showman that essentially, deep down, is the thing he is anyway. Let me tell you about my brother. The pleasures of an audience will likely enslave him. What goes to work on him more than the naked evidence of the impact he can have on poor gullible foot-soldier. But that wasn't what I was saying, was it? I was trying to explain about the chickens. Well, in this one particular routine he begins in a tone of interrogation. A group assembled in front of him, he will direct a question at these people: "Ladies and Gentleman, have you ever seen a naked chicken?'' At this, everyone will begin to stare at each other in complete bemusement. The more so since my brother's question will for certain appear utterly unrelated to the very prosaic matters they have been discussing till then. Pracha, yes, so much the showman, will savour this for a second before continuing: "I mean chickens plucked clean of the last one of their feathers." By now my brother will be full of himself, like only he can be. ''Come, good people, there must have been times when you were confronted by such a sight,'' he will proclaim in all innocence. "This is Hong Kong. In the street markets outside these offices fowl are hung up in rows exactly as I describe." Oh yes, the master he is at coaxing consternation to a fever point. The greed he has for this!

Eventually those making up his audience of the day will start to nod, even though they remain as flummoxed as when Pracha began. But with these heads wagging in front of him, as it only comes to the Chinese perhaps, my brother sees his opportunity. And it is as though he launches himself: ''Well, there you have it. Naked chickens! That is what I build. These great modern towers of glass and steel that I am erecting in Hong Kong, this is what they are. Naked chickens!" It always seems that my brother is as proud of this statement as he is of the constructions he is making allusion to. See the bay of Hong Kong. See its array of naked chickens. '

It felt to Richard Marshall as if he had to go in search of the levity he knew was expected of him. A show of amusement did break out across his face. The struggle he was engaged in to connect with his surroundings he experienced as a kind of echoing separation from himself.

'I recall a time...,' Marshall said,

'Tell us, 'Kep said.

'Pracha was a frequent visitor to England in those days,' Marshall said.'

'It's right, Wantana said, 'I liked to go there.'

'He had these ideas about how to broaden his investments in my country,' Marshall went on. 'A move into property development was one of the possibilities he actively contemplated. Then another year he investigated whether to go after a listing on the London Stock Exchange.'

'It's still an objective of mine,' Wantana said. 'I mean...a listing in London!'

'But a building in London, why not?' Kep said. 'Why shouldn't we do this? We have just the man for it.'

Her eyes swivelled. Jacot-Descombes met her gaze.

'For that you will have to find someone else,' Jacot-Descombes said. 'Europe? No, I'm not inclined to retrace my steps. My life is in Hong Kong now.'

'A room at the YMCA?' Kep said. 'What kind of life is that?

'She never relents mocking me for this,' Jacot-Descombes said, looking directly at Richard Marshall. 'As does her brother. But I am alone now. What else do I require?'

'In any case, it is America now that fills Pracha's head,' Kep said, dismissing the Frenchman.

She did not quite know who she was addressing, but if she was there to provide the 'space' in which her brother could look hard and long at Richard Marshall, she had to keep busy. The addition of Jacot-Descombes was in part also predicated on the identical reasoning. But further than that her brother had wanted another westerner present, but not just any westerner. In this he was displaying some sensitivity towards Richard Marshall. As to why alone amongst the family Wantana had decided to take her into his confidence on the deafening matter of his American aims, she was not at this juncture ready to speculate. It dazzled her, of course, to be confided in, and to the degree that she feared for her brother in what he had decided to attempt in the business realm. With regard to Jacot-Descombes, her brother wanted the Frenchman's impartiality and the strength of his manhood, being respectful of both. As to Richard Marshall, it seemed bizarre to be seeking the advice of a man you were girding yourself to expel from the organization. But really, if you thought about, such twists went with occupying a seat of power. To succeed with your responsibilities while seeking honesty in your relations with the hands – in your dreams!

And then the States! Was he really interested in anything the three of them had to say on his ideas to reinvent his organization through taking control of the historic American watch company? Hadn't he taken his decision? The beach from his early life was mere prelude before the fury of action.

It was on the issue of Richard Marshall that her brother was thrashing about in his mind. She sensed the awful strain it was for him to bring a man's brain round unambiguously to a subject that minute to minute it closed its eyes to. Coming to the beach was so as to apply force. An issue to be focused upon, a man to be found, he was after applying pressure to himself, like a whip.

The cross of passion took thought with it. Thought was the worst wilfulness until there was an object of love. Left to himself now, her brother swooned to the incredible plan for his organization. His every pulse was with America, with Andrew Camondo, with the great business enterprise Camondo was at the tip of. Once he was in pursuit of a specific dream, her brother's attention to the needs of those the endeavour hinged on was wondrous in its scope. In her short time inside his organization she had learnt that her brother was blessed with powers of insight denied to the majority. But it was as if in the main he just couldn't be bothered. He ignored his capacities. He only turned to them when he was captive to the vision of some new business conquest. Then she had a brother so solicitous the memory refused to fade. Let this mindfulness, this responsiveness, float forward on the kind of charm that was able to infuse his impulses as a man and you could be moved to pity for the victim. At times he could see right into a person. That one so self-enamoured was armed with such intuitiveness seemed a contradiction. Did he convince himself of his good intentions towards these people? Or didn't he care one way or the other? The thing was at all costs to get the thing you wanted from the person. Once upon a time, Richard Marshall had been the 'victim' in her brother's sight, the object of his excessive advances. He had had to withstand the inundation of those advances, except, of course, he hadn't. Pracha had asked Richard Marshall and his father to sell their company to him and there hadn't been any answer but yes. Now Marshall, in the sense of her brother's former obsession with him, had metamorphosed into Andrew Camondo. Never mind the years that this had involved, it constituted a different level of things altogether.

Camondo and her brother: she had this image of men locked together in a fearful embrace, but wholly unlike the very mortal snare he had come to with Richard Marshall. Between Camondo and her brother was the cold-steel contest which is rulers vying over a world. Two men, two mammoth organizations, the men, their organizations, divided by continents, by differing ways of life; every moment was a single moment in time but some much more so than others. This one had its hand on her. The fate of two very considerable commercial enterprises waited on the thoughts and decisions of the one pair of individuals. She was enthralled. Only with the obsessions of powerful men did the great bird of being go out to all its glory. Possessed by this vision of his, this goal, dream, ambition, however you were minded to term it, her brother would explore as only a few minds did explore.

And he had grandly informed the three of them they were ones he chose to explore with at this stage. And out of consideration of the risks that three men could pose to each other in circumstances where they were thrown on each other's company to the exclusion of everything else, he had been persuaded of the benefits of a larger group, one that ran to the presence of a woman.

He in his office, she in hers, the hard deluge of nine weighty industrial floors inserted between them, she didn't doubt he was preparing to offer himself as a kind of mentor, that is, if she was willing to commit herself to his organization. He couldn't hide his reservations in respect of his other brothers and sisters, not if the prospects for his company were the measure of things. He knew of the 'crush' she had for Jacot-Descombes. But she had to suppose that he trusted the Frenchman. He probably estimated that Jacot-Descombes, possibly without a word even, would in phases set her right. For the first time there was an opportunity for a genuine physical proximity with the architect. That her brother and Richard Marshall hovered nearby didn't cut across that. Her good brother carried an impressive engineering diploma from a school in Switzerland. With this visit to the beach he was engineering to his heart's relish. With his own quest notionally in the foreground, he would permit her this crazy pursuit. He would allow it being confident of the outcome. She needed to be enlightened, and only Jacot-Descombes in person could accomplish that. Her brother was forcing her to confront the question that she had avoided asking herself: in truth, did the Frenchman even notice her, beyond extending her the due appropriate to her status as Pracha Wantana's sister. She would have her answer in the next days.

But was she in fact even thinking of this? It was her brother she was suddenly concerned about. Suddenly she could read his mind. In himself he was terrified. He was terrified to think how insignificant he might appear in the eyes of the American, Andrew Camondo. America and this slightly overweight Chinese businessman from Hong Kong: what fantasy was this!? Her brother was seated at the table in such apparent calmness. But with these desires that he had for his life, it was surely a dam that kept bursting over him, unleashing his anguish that none of these things could ever be.

'Look at this place!' Kep said. 'We might be the survivors of a shipwreck. Cast up on an unknown shore.' A triumphant note radiated through her laughter, a rush of sound purely that of youthful credulity.

'It doesn't matter that there are people working in the restaurant,' Richard Marshall said. 'I have the sense that the four of us are completely cut off. I feel if I wandered away for a leisurely walk I would not meet another human for miles.'

He had little idea what to say to these people. It did not help that he remained ignorant as to whether Wantana's sister and Jacot-Descombes were aware of the precariousness of his position in Wantana's organization. How much of this issue had Wantana disclosed to the other two? That out of the blue Wantana had invited him to join an informal but intimate group created exclusively, as it had been explained, for the purpose of casting a critical eye at Wantana's American calculations had at the first suddenly made him feel welcome again in the house of Wantana; the thought that he had won a reprieve seemed to confirm him in his strategy of obtuseness whereby he shamelessly placed himself at the mercy of Wantana, head down like a penitent, no less the closed lips of the mortally weak. Not with another living person would he adopt an attitude of such despicable passivity, whatever the circumstances. Soon, though, he had realised how deceived he was in his newfound optimism. Wantana's idea of entering into a searching review of his American ambitions had been as spontaneous as his decision regarding the venue for this so-called reassessment. The fact was nothing and no one was going to keep Wantana back from America. It left one asking why they had come to this bleak lonely spot.

In Wantana's obvious enthusiasm for Jacot-Descombes, Marshall discerned something of the brightness and sympathy which the 'great man' had once displayed towards him. But even in those earlier times he had understood that many in Hong Kong, and many in Wantana's wider family, were fiercely opposed to the person who Wantana had appointed to represent their interests in England. Pracha had always set himself against these voices, to the extent almost of a willed deafness, not unlike the stance he himself had now adopted before Wantana as a response to the desperate shakiness of his place inside the organization. No, for years Wantana wouldn't hear a word from anyone. Richard Marshall was his man and let no one be in any doubt about it. Time had gone on and Wantana had remained a fortress in the face of the disfavour that one day the name Marshall had started to elicit in many parts of the organization, and also within the wider Wantana family itself. But now, finally, the last of these walls was down. Pracha Wantana was listening, and listening with intentness. As a result the voices were reborn in their fury, baying at Wantana to dismiss the unexceptional, as gravely mistaken as was the view, individual at the head of his United Kingdom operation.

'I wouldn't advise straying far,' Wantana said, his fathomless yet somehow fatherly stare picking out the Englishman with particular concentration. 'The beach is where everyone should stay.'

Effectively, it had been the death of Richard Marshall's father that had reminded him, as it were, of the very existence of his subsidiary in the United Kingdom. Had he so tired of Richard Marshall personally that a mental block had resulted on the subject of his interests in Britain? Was he redoubled in his attention to all the other dimensions of the organization demanding of his mediation because he was someone in flight; that which he was incapable of resolving his mind by some adept process became skilled at putting aside almost so as to expunge it from his mental world. And this even though there was an unfavourable economic dimension to the impasse. The offshoot in England was handicapping the progress of the larger organization. To many of the senior people working in his Hong Kong headquarters his neglect in this matter was not merely unreasonable but bordering on the criminal. It was a publically quoted company. The obligations on the leader, those to the wider unit under his authority, demanded allegiance to professional codes set in stone.

He watched his staff watching him. He saw the reprimand. As answer some days he wanted to shout that a man sat behind his desk with blood in his veins. And that dreadful red deluge had standards too!

The Marshall business had indeed been the very first commercial enterprise he had acquired outside Hong Kong. The first was beautiful but the first was doomed. Wasn't this the refrain? It had been the first because of what he had discovered in London on the occasion when he had met Walter Marshall to confirm their original distribution agreement, knowing nothing of that man previously beyond what he had discerned from their correspondence. When eastern businessmen set out to link up with western concerns, it had to be seen that they were put off by those western individuals who were dominating personalities, no matter to what degree they themselves might be overbearing characters. Walter Marshall's innate reserve had been at odds with the brash forwardness universally synonymous with man the commercial animal. Yet now, some fifteen years later, he, Pracha Wantana, he saw that many buyers must have been won over by the senior Marshall's essential quietness of manner. Without question, this was the factor that had swayed him before anything else. In London it had not been a test to sit with the older Marshall. In fact, it had been quite the reverse.

So much had he been influenced by Walter Marshall's easy tranquil courtliness that on returning to Hong Kong from London he had found himself eager not for any mere distribution arrangement but for complete domination of

H.R.Marshall and Co. This old-established English organization would be his. He had invited Walter Marshall to Hong Kong in order that the esteemed gentleman could make his way around the proposition that he, the young upstart Hong Kong businessman, had decided to put to him: for all time to align his family's destiny with that of Wantana's own. Of course, neither of them had thought of it in exactly those terms. The proposal had been for a simple commercial take-over. Thus had Walter Marshall arrived in colony. As for himself, this Hong Kong-based entrepreneur of Thai-Chinese background, the confrontation had roundly been a first. In due course such confrontations would become familiar to him. There it would come time and time again, as though a form of contraband, the inexorable exotic that was a significant meeting of East and West.

How naive he and Marshall had been. And what had the senior Marshall in fact represented to him then? As the two of them had explored the possibility of actual union, where in truth had they been positioned in relation to each other? The representatives of two families, or simply two men privately encased with their private calculations: their families as backdrop, but nevertheless men alone as men and having arrived at a seminal moment in this ineffable dynamic of separateness and individual isolation? Whatever the field of activity they were engaged in, men were continually proposing unions amongst themselves. But what did any of this say? As they planted images of the glories waiting from joining together, as they acted in time-honoured fashion to upgrade the organizations they stood for, as they outlined arguments of advancement and increasing stability for a commercial concern only achievable through linking up, as mortal beings at the personal level they stood off from each other with such finality, it might be equivalent to occupying different dimensions of time, and this even as they faced each other across a conference table.

He had been eager to show Walter Marshall the city. Keen to escort him out onto the streets, this aging man who had known so little of the wider world for all the maturity of his years. It was a case of the younger man taking in hand the older, someone who perhaps arrived at a place on those streets that taxed him with regret for not coming to the East sooner in his life, for rarely making the effort to travel more often to any destination outside his country. Or had Marshall's reaction been the reverse, Hong Kong just repulsive to him? He would not have said, of course; a matter of civility.

The sea at their shoulders this exorbitant pacing, deliberate, arrogant, like the pad of a lone lion in the bush, out of the sky stillness of heart, wistfulness, engulfed his nerve ends, sending him to remembering a man, dead now. With Richard Marshall sitting directly in front of him, he just absented himself from the image. His thought surged to the father. Not least, in a way, it had been Walter Marshall who had clinched a young Chinese person's entry to manhood. His first expedition outside Hong Kong as an adult businessman had been undertaken in order to appoint Marshall as the United Kingdom distributor for the watch bracelets that comprised his earliest output as a manufacturer.

Initially it had not gone well. He had bought his ticket, set off for London by himself, Walter Marshall's promise loud in his ears to collect him at Heathrow. In his mind now he referred to it as the time of the mix-up over his name. Walter Marshall had kept his word in so far as he had gone out to Heathrow. But once there had been confounded. Of Wantana there wasn't a sign, this young Chinese gentleman it was his responsibility to take in hand. Somehow in the throngs they missed each other. And then everything had got worse, the girl on the desk informing him that no one answering to the name Daniel. T.K. Bai was on the flight. Wantana's great omission had been his failure to inform the Englishman that he travelled under his Thai name, Pracha Wantana. Marshall was oblivious of any identity but his Hong Kong one.

In one thing Wantana and Walter Marshall were alike. They shared a rampant streak of impetuosity. Walter Marshall had abruptly abandoned the airport. He had been helped in this by his foresight in choosing to advise Wantana beforehand of the London hotel where he had reserved rooms for the two of them. Thrown on his own resources Wantana had duly set out. True to form, the face in the back of the taxi young and Chinese, the good English cabbie hadn't passed up the opportunity. Someone to rip off, he had done just that. What a tribe, temptation their high-priest.

Arriving at the hotel he had been as disconcerted as a man from the East could be. Which is to say that Walter Marshal had surrendered his right to be considered a member of the human race. But coming on each other they had quickly made up. He, Wantana, had taken responsibility for the misfortune.

The next day they had walked together along Oxford Street. Oxford Street, of the name, of the genius and climate that there were to some names, tensions and reverberations that if they carried anywhere it was to places far-off, places less anointed. Places that he, Pracha Wantana, came from. Oxford Street, with its inordinate compression of people and peoples, the crush on some days registering as the progression of a single unflagging unbroken chain, on others as the oncoming of innumerable bands, each in turn these squads shuffling along like so many prison work details. Oxford Street, with its long tunnel of morose, disdainful, city-sly shop windows dying their death, met with in a week or after a long decade of trading, the hard sell down the pavements of that remorselessness which later would be the word on him, Wantana. He had felt he had known the road even for the fact he was standing on it for the first time. Cities deviated, but not so far in truth.

The offices, the meetings, left behind, in their place the light breathing of a beach at sundown, suddenly he was rediscovering Walter Marshall, someone largely his mental universe had shed through to the finish. He conceived of this figure high up on a castle wall, vigorously patrolling the ramparts of an undue civility and human graciousness. Yet Walter Marshall had never upheld such worthy standards of conduct through rigid personal doctrine, through a conscious effort to be proper. In hindsight his civility had gone hand in hand with an eye-catching nonchalance of manner. You could not separate the courteousness that flowed off him from the way he carried himself. This affecting looseness of limb of his was kindness. His graciousness at the human level was as if a felt grown out of his definite cool physical style. The smooth ease with which he carried himself sweetened the air, leant repose to a room. If you were the one he had responsibility for on the day, the one he was acting the host to, it was a sort of blessing that came your way, and without Marshall barely uttering a single sentence in your direction.

Much was evident in the way a man moved, and wide was the embrace it sent out, for good or ill.

Hearing of the death of Walter Marshall in the past months he had done nothing. The senior Marshall had died and from the East there had come absolute gory silence. Not the beginnings of a message voiced or scrawled. Of course, he had his excuse ready, ready for himself, that is. It represented the most impeccable pardon. Since he had been on the point of ridding himself of the Marshalls, father and son, wouldn't any word have been a travesty in the circumstances? Whenever he deemed it necessary his secretary became an impassable wall for whoever it was trying to get in touch with him. For days or even weeks he could sit atop his organization and be beyond contact by any who worked for him. This was the void that he had deliberately left Richard Marshall to face. The poor man had had this news of his father, the message that it comes but once to relay, but the person his every instinct informed him should be the first outside the family to know hadn't been reachable.

He, Wantana, was the person the two Marshalls had decided to follow. Though commercial life provided the setting, wasn't he talking about something that for a period had developed a value demonstrably in excess of a mundane business liaison? Yet it was always business that told in the end. That was who was. That was the responsibility he had. Finally, both Walter Marshall and Richard Marshall had to be judged in the context of what value they had at the business level as servants of the organization. Yet still, though eventually he had tired of them both, what had grown between himself and this father and son combination had for a time defied simple explanation. Now he found himself plagued by the image of this empty seat on the day Walter Marshall was laid to rest. What would it have cost him to attend the funeral; the pain of one more journey of tedious duration inside an aircraft? It sounded pitiable. Yet the lapse, if that was what it was, stood. By no power on earth was it to be undone.

His mind seeking for a man he was suddenly overtaken by the sense of an outstanding duty towards Walter Marshall never to be set right. Let him accept he hadn't been equal to the moment when it had arrived. But let him think also that it was indeed fortunate that in the face of this obligation he had found the resolve with which to spurn it, cold as anything. That he had been man enough to stare the duty down was an outright blessing. Then again, to have attended the funeral and immediately thereafter to have given notice to the son would also have demanded a good share of resounding maleness. Since a man was always caught between competing claims of what it was to be authoritative in a masculine sense, you couldn't escape being a criminal in someone's eyes, while to another a weak-willed fool.

He was more than aware that as to the question of Richard Marshall, the consensus in Hong Kong was that he was being inexcusably feeble. But having got to this isolated spot he could no more concentrate on the issue than in all the preceding months. He hadn't the least appetite to go in search of an answer. He was even sorry he had asked Richard Marshall along. Long ago he had flagrantly abandoned the father, Walter Marshall, in favour of the son. In Hong Kong on the occasion of their fateful negotiations for the sale of the Marshall family concern, Walter Marshall's reserved way had put him in mind of his own father. Even as the two of them finalised the details of the take-over, he had had a vision of the inevitable tone of his future contact with Walter Marshall. Whether or not he was in the dominant position as the company owner, it would have been unfailing deference that would have been asked of him in his continuing dealings with the older man. The deference would have been the senior Marshall's due. Honour made it so. The consideration and high regard involved would have been of an altogether different order to that implicit to the repartee he enjoyed with Jacot-Descombes. It would have been possible for him, not least because he had liked Walter Marshall. But the thought of another father had sent him into retreat.

Being as young as he was, as unformed as he was, he had wanted to experiment with himself. He had known exactly who he would be beside the elder of the Marshalls. The silence necessary would have been his silence, the respect rightful to the occasion his willing respect, but won at the cost of suppressing other things about himself just as valid. At one of his cores, a burning selfhood had been on the march, and was still. In a sense it was to be appeased only by asking of his compatriots that they turn themselves into a kind of blood sacrifice. With some he felt the widest licence, and so swiftly this had become absolutely necessary to him. In order to do justice to the naked ambition that overtook a man, you were diverted away from your nobler features. Effectively, he had decided on men to whom he could freely extend the worst in himself whilst being certain it would be accepted without complaint. The lack of restriction he was looking for he had met in Richard Marshall, the son of Walter Marshall.

But the appeal of Richard Marshall had had other dimensions. Each of these fascinations had struck hard. In terms of the licence it would permit him, Richard Marshall had, whether through calculation or not, presented him with a demeanour as fertile as he could have wished for. The fact that only six months separated them in age had also been significant. From that alone comforts had abounded that are gained nowhere else. Divided in face, the equivalence in age, height and build had proved compelling. He might say that for a time there had been that oneness that is precisely and exclusively the product of a racial chasm, a oneness whose consuming interest is always itself. Looking at each other, they had been transfixed. To a degree they had proceeded not only as brothers but as something more than brothers.

But was it beholden on him to excavate with a crueller eye? Had the junior Marshall all along been as artful as a man could be, divining exactly the pose asked of him if he was to cement his relationship with the man from Hong Kong? In this small party he had formed, a new Richard Marshall was making his appearance, and he, Wantana, wasn't sure of this person in the least. Whereas the former Richard Marshall he had been confident of to the last detail, every one of those details in service to his own enhancement. Still the enigmatic figure before him surely was Richard Marshall, and whatever outward semblance of normality was to be read into the conversation going between them, it was yet a deadly contest they were engaged in, a thing just not to be made speech however near to each other they got. No more so than the sum of the human mysteries that had seen them joined. The struggle to break an embrace like this assailed a man if he allowed it. Know that carelessness might be a better way. Truth be told, with most he had a ready way with carelessness; so why the wrenching nervous to and fro in this case?

There were things he could enlighten Richard Marshall about, except that it was impossible at so late a date. It was impossible anyway. At the time Walter Marshall and his company had been a catch to stir his heart. But this man, the senior Marshall, his history, his country, and most of all his organization, it had all begun to pale for him even as the ink hadn't yet dried on the document transferring ownership of H.R. Marshall and Co. to his own enterprise. The onset of boredom had been swift and lethal. The status and prestige that Walter Marshall and his company had for a time enjoyed in his eyes had perished out of sight as if in a matter of days. In fact, he had awoken one morning to find the scale laughable. This wasn't his proper level, or anything remotely like it.

For a number of years, though, this essential indifference towards the company H.R. Marshall and Co. hadn't interceded in his relationship with Richard Marshall. As he stared out across the bay, stirred by the image into a sense of his own beginnings, he contemplated the savagery with which he had dismissed and forgotten so many in his drive to advance. In the time it took for one moment to pass into the next a man could swivel his face away from a colleague with deafening infinite finality. Just this slick, darting, venomous twirl of the head and the arctic erasure was done. A man need never look back. He thought of someone throwing down the stub of a cigarette and grinding it underfoot. How many had he disposed of as peremptorily as that? What should he say? That finally it could never be overlooked that the business sphere was amongst the operations of man, the people assembled therein possessed of a human foundation like all other mortal persons, a foundation that being so human would often prove to be viciously lacking in the human.

Yes, why shouldn't he respond to his detractors with the perfectly cynical barb? Then there was cynicism as an argument of office. It might be kinder than knowing the facts about oneself. The actions of a primitive! This was the slur that kept being levelled at him following some of his dealings. Had Walter Marshall died mouthing curses? Had there been a number aimed at him? What had been the older Marshall's memory of the day of his entry into his life, this invader from another world? It hadn't been battalions or legions gathering outside the city gates. Absolutely not, just a solitary man stepping from his carriage, his weaponry confined to the beguiling way with which he had slid the gloves from his hands. Here was that uncontainable charm born of the spires of the far-off dominions.

But even though the first handshake had been fashioned just for him, soon Marshall had had to watch as the invader and his son had become lost to an epic coming together wherein perhaps it is two coinciding human souls that are converging. A conspiracy of rejection had descended around Walter Marshall. North, south, east and west, it did not matter where the senior Marshall faced, the message scythed forward. See who you are! Aging (and what an eyesore that is to the Eastern neophyte with inordinate entrepreneurial ambitions); incurably invested with a business ethos as quaint as a three-penny cycle, accepting it has a certain charm; nostalgic in that the organization the invader wants for his own carries to your heart like blood; and worst of all possessed of the physical face that all who work in the firm accept as the indisputable seal of the enterprise they serve. Once you appeared in a room there was realised the organization root and branch. Was there ever a greater crime? To undermine by your mere presence the man who was supposed to be the business' new owner.

So in silence the onslaught began. You, Walter Marshall, your indoctrination started; your re-education. You were allowed an office, but uniquely designed to advance but the one outlook: there in cinemascope this view of the young, the two young, the two thunderstruck young, like lovers even when the one was off in his base in Hong Kong. It had been an office to perpetuate but the one eternal lesson: a man's time ended. There you had had sat until the day your son Richard Marshall had returned from a visit to Hong Kong and handed you his father a letter, signed by the company's new lord and master, instructing you to vacate the premises altogether. You should not think to return. You were not wanted. The letter that your son delivered to you in person set it out plain. The 'brothers' had reached a pact, their first. The older man was for the scrap yard.

He and Richard Marshall: East opposed by West, but in something matched. He and Richard Marshall: across the miles, across the years, the one asked, the other consented. He and Richard Marshall: the entanglement set in deeper with each and every phone call; each and every phone call the knot went another two rungs. He and Richard Marshall: A Judas knot.

Admit it though, you Mr Walter Marshall, father to your son. Wasn't the devil impressive, the sloe-eyed raider from the other side of the world; a true serpent of destiny. It was stated in the way the tunic stretched across his back. Fiefdoms were pledged to him. The land itself must make way and offer itself up. No one gleaned better than he did that to observe his figure told everything. Ask how it is? Ask how it will be? Why bother? All would be known soon enough. Simply it would be in the one man's pronouncement. And the time was when that man had been no one so much as you yourself.

In the year of his initial engagement with the Marshalls his career had been in its first infancy. For Walter Marshall himself the commercial relationship that had developed from a straightforward distribution agreement had surely to be taken as the most significant business link-up he was ever to enter into in his life. He saw now that Walter Marshall had wanted this communion with him. But he had turned away. Once the sale of the Marshall organization had been completed, he had gone away to barely ever speak to the man again. One day even that rare word had ceased. He had communicated through his subalterns, which in this case meant he had communicated through Marshall's own son. He had gone off to a march of kings, one business acquired than another, mostly in Switzerland and Japan. A Hong Kong bank had passed through his hands. He had stuffed shares in the bank into the pocket of Richard Marshall. 'Take them, take them. You are amongst my most trusted.' Yes, the first was beautiful, but the first was doomed. Absolutely, it was as the shamans said. Like anyone in the East, shop assistant or industrial baron, he used them.

It was true: for a period what had grown between him and the Marshalls did defy simple analysis. But the issue was no longer Walter Marshall, it was his son. Everything had its time and for him the compulsion of Richard Marshall had expired in all its dimensions. Yet, having brought the director of his United Kingdom operations to this stark outpost, a human specimen was about that he couldn't situate in the years of his contact with the man. For all that Marshall, as it seemed to him, was, so ingloriously, asking for pity, a rare aloofness and determination was yet in evidence in the bearing of the Englishman, that given the unsparing spiritual fatigue he, Wantana, was now experiencing at the mention of Marshall's name, visited him almost as revelation. And suddenly it was Richard Marshall who was talking, the intonation immensely careful and formal, cold almost.

'You came to this place when you were young,' Marshall asked. 'It was here that your family took its vacations?'

He had passed years in conversation with this man who was his employer, but as to the personal background of the Eastern industrialist he had little more insight than when it had all begun. Nor really had he ever been possessed of the interest to learn. Richard Marshall was a man who to function was dependent on a voice of authority somewhere at his back; a voice that spelled out the day's itinerary, that laid down the day's itinerary. And this even as from early on he had gone after a role for himself significant for the command over others it enshrined. Meeting Wantana had been the critical introduction of his life. With the appearance of Wantana his deepest need had been answered.

'We have always shared this beach with another family,' Wantana said. 'A Thai family. In fact the beach, the fishing village, everything you see is land that the family I speak about owns outright. '

'It's hardly believable but it's my first time here,' Kep said, 'and no one has ever told me about the Bidaya family. Not really.'

Wantana shot a look at her. But his sister stood her ground unrepentant. She appeared challenged at her brother's glance.

'What have I said?' Kep protested. 'Can't we ever talk about this? It's my brother who has chosen to lead us to this spot. How can we remain in this place for three more days and not refer to these things. Look at this beach. There's nothing here. But in fact there is. There's a story here. And it can be told now because now the Wantana family is successful in its own right. And I would like to know. Because… Doing well are we, not beholden to anyone, yes? Let's be frank, the Wantana family is obsessed still. It goes on. To this day we're thieves on the run, scared to send one glance back. Because there they remain, the Bidayas.'

In the company of these men, the invidiousness of her extreme youth and insignificance she experienced like death chains. To be the most junior amongst them left her gripped by a fearful intensity. Assailed by the idea of her lowliness, it sent her to the one reserve she had with which to fight back in the circumstances: her power of speech. She would be reckoned with. The three men would remember. They wouldn't leave this place and not remember. They would remember her.

Quickly, Wantana conquered his initial surprise at Kep's rash talk. He decided to give his sister her head. Hadn't he included her in the party so that she could provide an unpredictable factor? Didn't such things sometimes produce effects that could not have been anticipated? Often deadly, yes. But on occasion the wild ingredient turned out to be the catalyst that struck down what had seemed an impassable obstruction. He had no idea how his sister was supposed to help him resolve the question of Richard Marshall. Was he to look to her for the strength and fortitude that he lacked? Of course, this so-called resort represented the wildest factor of all. But he and Richard Marshall needed to be diverted. Steering the conversations towards his American calculations would be the first of the diversions. If the distractions were many it might be that cumulatively they realized a kind of sleight of hand that might see him clearer in mind as to what he owed the Englishman, if anything. But in any case, hadn't he effectively adopted his sister in a way he might a lost creature he came upon on the street? He had taken her up with an attention that exceeded the trails of their blood connection. It had happened the day she returned from the western colleges. If the truth be known, he had little enthusiasm to see any of his other sisters working inside his developing organization. Only this one.

'My sister exaggerates,' Wantana said, a slow, meditative note in his voice, the subject filling him with caution. 'But this family we are talking about does have a significant place in our lives. That is undeniable. Many years ago my father met a man. His name: Suthin Bidaya. It has been a remarkable friendship.'

But what he did not say was that this friendship of his father's had left the older Wantana cursed by a feeling of obligation. It was a web or net that his father was entangled in, one that he flailed against to no avail, one whose ropes were relentless in their diabolism. The stream of gifts going from his father to the man he had encountered one day in a Bangkok gymnasium never ceased. It achieved little. If anything the sense of being in a man's debt gripped harder, the liability burned onto his father's soul imperishable. The burden of a present for the giver was the honour involved. Since the obligation his father felt had a weight that engulfed him it produced shackles of honour such that the offering of some shiny object felt an act of mockery. It mocked Suthin Bidaya, it mocked the defendant in the matter, the one making the gift. And the fact that the two men had inserted a sea between them hadn't provided solace for his father. On the contrary, it had increased the vigil of being in man's debt. It was a lonely business, and endless. For his father was as he was.

With the name Suthin Bidaya on his lips, Pracha Wantana paused. The name would mean nothing to Richard Marshall. But at this moment his thoughts weren't with Marshall. He was wrong to go on pronouncing to himself that for the Wantanas in their eastern universe everything had begun with his own father. It had not. It had begun with another man; a native of Bangkok; he the one of the gym; Bidaya, Suthin Bidaya. But his sister was right, to the degree anyway that the Wantana family did have its pride now. It had been worked for, and yes, there was a freedom in that.

He swept his arm around, the motion characteristically expansive. When he spoke it was not without awareness of the net that Richard Marshall had him entangled in.

'Yes, Suthin Bidaya,' Wantana said. 'Look about you, know the name.'

The words sprang from his tongue. That there was an undue energy and expressiveness in the sound signalled even to him that for too long he had denied himself the free use of the two words and that the obstruction had been burdensome to him. But that he was amused at himself for experiencing this relief also gave rise to the strength in his voice.

'Do not forget Joti,' Kep said. 'Do not forget Joti Bidaya.'

'I never forget him,' Wantana said, his head turned to his sister.

'Like you, Joti is the eldest,' Kep said, 'the first son of Suthin Bidaya.'

'That's one fact. What else should we say to our two friends?'

'You mean we shouldn't say anything,' Kep said.

'Suthin Bidaya,' Wantana said. 'I have just pronounced the name, as firmly as I could.'

'And he has two sons. But like you, Joti has pride of place.'

'And what else can you inform us about the Bidayas?'

'Haven't I just said? The story of the Bidayas has been kept from me. The information I have I've had to scrape for. But it amounts to little.'

'You use the name Joti Bidaya with confidence.'

'Not knowing a story, properly, you form your own ideas, right or wrong.'

'And the figure that interests you is Joti?'

'The figure that interests me is my own brother. And if there's a key to my brother it is Joti Bidaya.'

'It sounds as if the scholar amongst us is preparing to enlighten us with one of her theories. And you have many theories, my young sister.'

'It isn't a theory I have. Just a question for my brother.'

Richard Marshall and Jacot-Descombes were watching now. They were watching the Chinese man and his sister. And Pracha Wantana, otherwise Daniel T.K. Bai, knew that they were watching.

'Didn't I employ you to ask questions?'

'Haven't you been satisfied?'

'I never imagined the...rigorousness.'

'My brother felt confident enough to ask me to join his party.'

'And which of us here would ask that I had not done? Wantana said.

'Then am I not to speak,' Kep said.

'You imply that I have some authority in the matter.'

'Please never doubt it.'

'I commend you to silence and there it will rest?'

'It is your good name you fear for if I proceed.'

'No sister. That's futility itself.'

'It's the first thing you say.'

'What?'

'You buy some company somewhere in the world, you announce to the staff, "I care because it's my name I'm putting to your firm."'

'I've never heard anything so hollow,' Wantana said. 'The man who speaks these words is a fool.'

'I pray you don't repeat them in America.'

'That's your advice to me?'

'It's the reason you invited me, no?'

'Think of it how you choose.'

'I can't do that.'

'Why?'

'This is serious. What you are planning.'

'I don't live a moment that isn't serious.'

'Am I to be condemned so quickly? The sister with a tongue.'

'I prefer to say a sister brave of tongue.' Wantana said. 'But we will listen to your question.'

'What?'

'You had a question.'

'Of your contemporaries, Joti is the one man you look up to.' Kep said. 'He has a hold on your imagination like no other.'

'And what does that mean?' Wantana said. 'Do I need to tell you that it was as though we grew up together? He might be my brother.'

'So you admit it.

'But what is it that I admit to?' Wantana said, his laughter slightly uncertain.

'That as with most, there is one you submit to in your heart. The man you just want to be like.'

'Never underestimate what is accomplished simply out of the need to emulate someone,' Pracha Wantana said, glancing at Richard Marshall.

'Nor out of the need to vanquish that person,' Kep said.

'And that is what I have to do?'

'You can never be comfortable in Thailand,' his sister said. 'Because it is Joti's domain. In Thailand you live under a shadow. His!'

'Joti puts down a shadow,' Wantana said. 'I will accept that. But a nation? You're the one over impressed.'

'You think so?'

'Look about you.'

'What's that mean?'

'Joti is here,' Wantana said. 'The beach!'

'I don't…'

'You are after a man's shadow? Look where he fell, or where he proved himself different.'

'What did he do?'

'The last time the Bidayas and Wantanas vacationed here together,' Wantana said, 'Joti decided to swim out to the island. He walked down to the edge of the water and did it.'

He pointed to the little Gibralter that lay some two and a half thousand metres out from the beach, this isolated stack of grey black rock, mounted on the flat proud sea, its form broad and swollen low down, but this the precursor to shapes and faces that steering upwards tapered by degrees until finally a definite lonely pinnacle of sorts projected, its skywards aim in the image of a solitary mountain peak. If you visited the beach from year to year, the distance to the island became a goad because whilst it was a challenging distance, it wasn't at all an impossible one, not if you were twenty-one years old. A man got into the sea, he swam. Something took over. Should it be a time of war he had it in him to tow another, someone wounded. A few could persist, turning the corner of the shoreline until it was a count of miles they'd put away. Be that as it may. The distance that held him taut was the gap dividing the beach from the island. At your place on the beach, it was where you looked, where you studied, where you imagined.

No longer pointing, Wantana went on staring out towards the island. What was conveyed to him in any thought about Joti Bidaya, was a tranquillity and prepossession that he believed was lost to him. Fervently, he knew his own unrest. The urging on his inside disqualified him from the innate dignity of a Joti Bidaya. To him it felt like so. The elegant slowness in some flesh, the spikiness and inconsolability in other flesh; or should it be seen like this: that what was on the inside of a man had way of fitting itself around the man? The map of a man was in his aura.

If in some sense he had been nursing his sister along deliberately, at once terrified and entranced by the risk, then why retreat now? He was aware of the heedlessness and blindness that might fly into her mouth. An unruly element existed. The belief that her terrible lack of years somehow gave her knowledge previously unknown to man was a visitation she seemed prey to. Needless to say, it was a description appropriate to the young everywhere. She had so much to say, so much to prove. But he was willing to use it at this moment. She escaped what she said for the simple reason so many were moved to spare her any cruelty. That there was a person seated with them who affected them like that should make them feel thankful. If over these few days they were to advance anywhere, they had to discover some conversation together. And he was determined that they would. He had devised the expedition for many reasons. That was how he interpreted it anyway.

'I could not stop Joti doing this,' Wantana said. 'No one could. He was around twenty then. Five years older than me. '

'Are these waters safe?' Marshall said. 'But safe or not, you don't take on a swim like that lightly. This has to be an unusually brave man we are talking about.'

'Or a very foolhardy one,' Jacot-Descombes interceded.

'Joti knew what he was doing,' Wantana said. 'He was more than just an accomplished swimmer. He was a swimmer to international standard. It was in the evening. He swam back the next morning. He said that he had had the idea in his head for some years. That was how we parted that last year.'

'Joti Bidaya went on to train as an architect,' Kep said. 'For some reason my brother is fascinated by architects. No, in fact he is in awe of them.'

'And why not,' Richard Marshall said. 'It's our privilege to be in the company of such a man.'

'Mr Marshall, we are in your debt,' Kep said. 'How could we have forgotten?'

The two western men smiled, and they understood that Pracha Wantana was also amused, but they had to ask themselves how they were aware of this because the face of the Thai-Chinese industrialist wasn't enlivened by the smallest movement. Nor was it ever, if you stopped to think about it.

'And there's something else,' Kep said. 'We are talking about a bold fearless man in his own right. This too needs acknowledging?'

A tide in her was up and burning. As it had been ever since her brother had asked her to accompany them.

'Here is someone who by choice spends many of his weekends in Vietnam,' Kep went on. 'It doesn't matter to him that this is a land at war.'

'Perhaps there is a war,' Jacot-Descombes said. 'Nevertheless, it remains entirely accessible as a country, even for someone like me.'

'As you have discovered,' Kep said.

'Yes,' Jacot-Descombes said.

'It seems that you need this, you and your kind,' Kep said.

'Is that right?' Jacot-Descombes said.

'While you are there, do you find the time to get together with these… brothers of yours?' Kep said. 'I mean, do you come across any of them?'

'Who are you referring to?' Jacot-Descombes asked.

'A land out at the edge: what a pull it is for a certain kind of man from America, from Europe. You are all searching for one of these places. And it doesn't require anyone to explain that it has to be one of the eastern territories. At this point of your lives nothing else is going to suffice. Not for any of you.'

'I live in Hong Kong.' Jacot-Descombes said. 'I work there, as you know.'

'So what is Vietnam?' Kep said.

'France once,' Jacot-Descombes said. 'I was curious. One weekend I took a trip out of Hong Kong. I chose Saigon and it turned out I met someone. A lady I am keen to go back and see sometimes.'

'Not sometimes,' Kep said. 'Saigon: as soon as you have time to yourself, this is your complete itinerary now. You do your duty in Hong Kong, but you are just waiting.'

She had her chance now. He couldn't not hear her.

But unexpectedly Marshall got in the way.

'I imagine that the presence of the Americans, those in uniform, should we say, is of benefit to the wider region,' Richard Marshall said. 'To those in business hereabouts anyway.'

It was a remark that Wantana might have made himself, and he recognized it immediately; in its way, a comment of shameless sterility; a hollow condescending platitude. Lead a man to a new day, the platitudes were feed. So many of the ideas he had of his fellow beings were born out of his experience of the men in his employment. The involvement didn't leave him with feelings of generosity. Not where it was the male constituent of the company's payroll. Never mind that it was his obsessions endowing a man with the sense of purpose anyone needed to stay eager in his speech, for simple interest to take hold, he was contemptuous of the product this realised on the an average day. Whether at their posts under his roof, or freed to their own resources, the train was loudness, vulgarity, simplicity, submission to the crowd, dependence upon the crowd, dullness of imagination, vapidity, coarseness, lachrymose sentimentality; and as if bearing the suspicion that every bit of was designed purposely to show the talker in the worst possible light; as if the exaggeration of his crudity was irresistible, a straight out compulsion; as if in the exaggeration was empowerment; as if in the exaggeration was a sort of pact, a pact he made with himself for survival. Perhaps men were born with a passing thought of rebellion, they were not, however, born with the capacity for it. Finally society never left off correcting men in their purer delusions. Unseen by themselves perhaps, men lived lives of spiritual fracturing, accretions of deaths. Where else to locate their docility, that quota of apathy essential to human existence?

Nevertheless, just as Marshall had done with his comment, he too, he used these lifeless observations, these spontaneous but empty verbalisms, these stock phrases. He consciously entered into an identical artifice that on the surface aligned him with what was expected of him in his role in life, in his case, business tycoon. It was as though he chose the moments when to lay claim to an overwhelming mental prejudice and consequent insensibility. He saw his own obsessiveness. He saw only too clearly a consciousness that on some days was closed to anything but the one perspective. He had his mind, but at certain times what could you conclude was assembled inside his head but this deadly treacle of commercial calculation? Life pinned to the one ensign. Men telephoned him from everywhere across the globe. His first words to them hardly ever varied. 'How's business?' Any day he would ask the question and with enormous heartiness. As stale as the phrase was, it had his undying enthusiasm. He didn't tire of it. And whilst the weakness of it as a greeting could be seen as reflecting the strength of the divide existing between him and the caller, it was also his manner of taking on that gulf and mitigating it. However confident you might be, to go where men had a foreign look out of an aim to involve yourself in those seas at a dominating level, you needed simple verbal constructions to parry the divides. Men could sound like buffoons, but the seeming idiocy they grasped at with such spontaneity and relish often worked for them. More, it allowed them to advance.

The statement of Marshall's observed what it observed and travelled to where it travelled. The remark knew very well what it was. To Wantana's mind, it had sought a deliberate derision, to be derision. Surveying Marshall, he again had the sense of a transfigured individual. Of a person he had not met with before. Yes, this pitiable stance of mute submission to whatever his chief decreed in the final reckoning could be taken as of a piece with the Marshall of old. That was someone wise to the value of a silent appeal to the emotions. That was someone calculating of the gains to be had through turning oneself into an object of commiseration. That was someone determined to believe he had the measure of the man; which man, of course, was he, Wantana. In the end a man with a heart, who ultimately would be moved to pity for the director of his British operations. A man who finally would recognize an unspoken pledge was involved here. Yes, all of this was evidence of the Marshall he knew. Nevertheless, somehow the passivity wasn't as previously. Another Marshall was at the table no less. Someone redoubled; someone of a rare, disturbing quietude hinting at a rare manhood even. A quietude that spoke of absolute separation, of fateful resignation, of enormous detachment, of an impregnable self-belief, of the knowledge that finally everyone stood alone, of the strength this knowledge brought, a strength that said a man remained a man, and considerable with it, however he was victimized and humiliated.

Of course, in the last months Marshall had lost his father. That had to be a consideration. His father gone, his very position in life mortally at risk, did a man grow in the face of such a deluge? To anyone observing it couldn't have appeared a more normal scene at the table. Two of those at the table strived to believe in the show of ordinariness, endeavoured not to lift their eyes to find the other, pitted themselves like dogs to achieve forgetfulness, gave their all to go in ignorance of the maelstrom they carried, fought to be rid of every bit of the vortex, the murderous thoughts, the outright contempt, the pity, the disgust at another, the despair at another, the recrimination, the tearing consternation, the blank seizures at a situation, the disbelief at oneself, the self-hatred, the curses at man, at existence, the curses at a man, the endless pleas for deliverance, and in the case of one of them, the base cry: Let go!

The clinch was terrible; the clinch was amity, passionate amity, passed to the grave.

Richard Marshall's observation about the material advantage that can amass for a territory when the American military machine arrived to erect its tents disturbed Wantana immensely. There had been a tone not of spontaneity, but of calculated amusement. But the contempt was not for the American soldiers or for their nation. The contempt was aimed back at his own person it was directed at the man he was with, Pracha Wantana.

He couldn't say why but sitting in his chair Wantana had the devout sense that he was being ridiculed, that the man on the other side of the table was quietly laughing at him.

'Without doubt,' Wantana said, staring hard at the ambivalence in Marshall's voice. 'It seems the American soldiers have a passion for watches. My father could tell you about that. As businessman and commercial distributor this whole region is his region. He is more than willing to explain the impact that the American soldiers have had on the fortunes of his watch agency. At this moment they are one of the foundations of the business. He doesn't hide it. The American soldiers - he will not hear a word against them.'

Well, did the new man have a new face? With immense effort, a powerful sense of resignation dragging at him, Wantana brought his full attention around to Richard Marshall. Might it be that the remade individual, the reconstituted man, came with an altered countenance? If he looked again, would he rediscover some of his past enthusiasm for Marshall? If his father had formed a rare alliance with Suthin Bidaya, hadn't he and Richard Marshall in turn also known one of these indefinable human bonds that the two persons involved were less capable of understanding than anyone? So let him take in the face before him, no matter the years it had figured in his life. No matter these years?! It was for the very reason of the years that he should do it.

The physical hallmark of the man was his tall brow, the bevels at the outer peripheries of an emphasis of line like brick gives. The nose too, it blazed a path, the length handsome, the structure proud, the planes cleanly symmetrical. An arrow pointed, drawn back in the bow. Of the crazy energy of the area which was Marshall's forehead Wantana had great experience. The wonder was that there weren't even more lines inscribed into the tome. Yet here there did seem the suggestion of an actual physical change in a man's visage. Strangely the brow had stilled, just as had all of him. But as ever had been the case, it was the fate of these upper elements of the face to act as a sop for those aspects that were lost to any such handsomeness. Above all, it was the mouth that was the family embarrassment, the sickly amputee in the family. Feeble and compressed and luckless, it was a huddled thing. Yet as finicky as was its air, as oddly stunted its proportion, it was the mouth more than any other feature that seethed with allusion. To Wantana it betrayed the deep gratification that this strangely reborn man had begun to gain from his own person. That segment of the face that was weak and miserly was somehow critically in touch with the weird stealth of the wider person, this person he barely recognized as the man who had worked for him for so long. It was a stealth that knew how to dress and move. A careful, uncluttered elegance came from the very grain of the man, an aspect of him that had never been apparent before to Wantana.

Richard Marshall? Think of a man changing in his culture, nearly.

Doors opened in a culture, and then closed behind you in the interim as you passed inside, and once through to the inside vague scurrying sounds reached you that said numerous feet were busy in the shadows off at the sides. But for all the sense you had of this commotion, it never gave anything away, it never showed itself properly. A door held open you went in, yet whatever the effusiveness of the greeting, there arrived gusts impervious, impregnable, utterly self-betrothed. A self-congratulation like treason it was so wanton.

Wantana inched towards his own assessments of the apparently re-girded figure that was Richard Marshall. Finally, these assessments wouldn't matter that much. Once he discovered the strength with which to take the decision that was weighing so heavily on him, Marshall would withdraw from his sight never to be encountered again. Still a relatively young industrialist he, Wantana, had met with countless men. It was how a wide-ranging industrial concern was built. Without his naiveté he wouldn't have approached many of these people. And in the end had he a care for the faces; whether in the old days or now? Generally he didn't give them a second look. In all honesty the past entire he just dismissed.

It was 1971 and what mattered was a word, creation's newest word, newest offering, and the fierceness of it could never abate: America. What did the soothsayers say? They said that there is the planet Earth and there is the planet China. And for the planet Earth the coming will be the planet China. But that just wasn't true. He was about to make his entry, he was about to set out, but not for what he was, nor as the vanguard of anything, but in pain to possess the word. In fact, two words: America, Camondo.

But again the one haunting issue bit hard, searing his brain with the ridicule it tipped at him. A Chinese businessman from Hong Kong and this legendary American corporation – how could these ideas be intelligently entertained by anyone? But even as Wantana appealed to himself to come to his senses, so the idea of something burst at his face all over again. Something held him and having hold of him was larger than a man's intelligence. And in any case, a chance had appeared. He couldn't let it go. As for Richard Marshall, he just didn't know.

Silent now, and wanting to maintain his silence, again Pracha Wantana gave thanks to whatever had impelled him to invite his sister along, because at that moment she stepped in as if he had whispered to her. He was thirty-five years old, but with Kep before him he couldn't ignore what it was to be at the beginning of your journey. Your misfortune to be decidedly tender in years, then the more was the voice you owned a thing to be put on display, this age of yours a number so sore to the touch, and never as acutely as when it was your own kin occupying the other chairs and the family an especially sizeable one. For the youngest in a tribe the audience that was your original family was persecution and goad. In this isolated resort he was her audience. But however incalculable he was in this respect he was aware that another audience pressed down on her at that small table. It carried the name Jacot-Descombes.

'You have your war to go to, Mr Architect,' Kep said, 'as a tourist at least. But what is your view of that war. As Mr Marshall comprehends, my father and brother aren't so indifferent to the numbers it adds to the company balance sheet.'

Jacot-Descombes couldn't answer. The face of the young war widow he was involved with broke at him. With this brooding word, Vietnam, was now for him a massing of emotional response impossible to decipher. Say what he believed? He hadn't an idea what he believed. He got into the country, then left to go back to his desk in Hong Kong. And doing his work his mind would likely stray, the winds of an indescribable body of reportage drawing around him. The wind that was a signal people; the wind that was a stern land fed through with the lush veldts of rice paddies; with spates of enamelled flora; the wind that was a sapid land endlessly stalked; the wind that was a land seemingly under sentence for its collection of light-legged damsels, girls old in their grace, fresh as kites in their grace; the wind that was war succeeding to war; the wind that was the spectre of the re-education camp; the wind that was the spectre of cold ideology and its cattle prods; the wind that no matter the sounds of the current war was a land so dampened by aftermath a sense was in the street of this moth amongst nations; the wind that was a people possessed of a step like the motion you have negotiating a trail of stones placed across a brook. Lands cried river, and rivers cried the weight of the land's tortured past, not least because the torrents around their surface were a magnet for a warrior's gore. In time the water cleaned itself up, yet it could not. The devil in the colour red was the echo it fixed.

Comprehension of some infringement, some trespass, hers, bore in at Wantana's young sister.

'Thailand has a part in the war,' she said, excessively brightly. 'Curious I can tell you.'

It was as though she was at once summoning these men to listen to her and willing them to. One by one they brought their eyes slowly round, something to the action like a man searching grudgingly inside his pocket before taking out an odd coin and placing it on the table in front of him. Whilst this didn't satisfy her, she accepted it for what it was. These men didn't realise what opportunity the smallest opening gave her.

They knew so little, in fact. She thought that the three of them were carrying their heads heavily.

Indeed they were, presenting the image of men facing untold hardships. They weren't in a hurry. She had all the time she wanted.

Suddenly though her brother started, a force of reaction showing.

'This war is not Thailand's business,' Wantana protested.

'I didn't say that,' his sister said.

'What then? Wantana said.

'Well, France for one thing,' she said, pinning down Jacot-Descombes with her quick look at him. 'Weren't they, the French, in Vietnam before the Americans? So now what we have are two wars in an embrace. Taken as one not the war of the century but to someone like me it feels like it. And all of that asked for a man. You want his story there's a place in Thailand that has to be considered. It's there to visit. For many the journey is essential. They go as pilgrims. I'm talking about the Ban Na Jok region in Thailand. What occurred there…Well, it was the start of everything…no? Of course, Marcel might already be informed about this.'

'I am in complete ignorance,' Jacot-Descombes said.

'Tell us,' Wantana said.

'In the forests of Ba Na Jok the courses of nations were taken in hand, surely,' Kep said with insistence. 'I don't see how else you can think of it…'

Her voice died.

'Go on,' Jacot-Descombes said. 'I ask you.'

'Probably this isn't of interest to anyone,' she said.

'It is to me,' the architect said.

'It's not necessary to be polite,' she said.

'I am more than keen to hear about this,' Jacot-Descombes said.

'If you wish,' she said.

'Absolutely,' the architect said

'Another day I think,' she said.

Inert and distant in manner, nevertheless it couldn't veil the mix of stubbornness, contrariness, self-pity ensnaring one young woman in the moment.

'You can't stop now,' Wantana said.

'You men have things to discuss,' she said.

'Please,' Jacot-Descombes urged.

'What is wrong,' Pracha Wantana said.

'I'm in the way,' she said.

'That is priceless,' Wantana said.

'Don't make fun of me,' she said.

'I could speak for our two colleagues here,' Wantana exclaimed.

'How?' she said.

'That I am the one in the way.'

'Oh, what a charmer my brother is.' she said

'Ask them then!' Wantana said.

'About what?' she said.

'In the way..?' Wantana said. 'If you weren't here, there wouldn't be anything.'

Kep looked at her brother's face.

'You really want to hear?' she said.

'You have something to say about the French in Vietnam,' Jacot-Descombes said.

'It's not about them,' she said.

'Not about them?' Jacot-Descombes said.

'No,' she said.

'But I thought...'

'Sister!' Wantana said.

'Yes?' she said.

'I beg you,' Jacot-Descombes said.

'I was saying…' she said.

They all watched her.

'Ban Na Jok: the quilt laid across the region is forest, thick, daunting. It is relentless. Seen from above the land is drowned out. It was so once. It is so now. No one can expect a thing will alter. Not giving way the forest basin reaches to the Mekong River, at a place where it stands as the boundary between Thailand and Laos. Amongst the trees there is a site that carries to all Vietnamese people. It's to be found four or five miles in from the river. Ban Na Jok: know it for the assembled trees. Know that these woods won over a certain Ho Chi Minh. At the time he was on the lookout for the ideal retreat in which to hide away before engaging openly in the struggle against the French. He needed a place to prepare. First he sent a trusted colleague to the region in 1921. On reaching the Ban Na Jok area this man immediately married a Vietnamese woman he found living in the vicinity. Ho Chi Minh himself followed in 1923. He arrived in the company of four or five other friends. There in a forest in Thailand, just inside the border, they followed an existence as mundane as can be imagined. What the lowliest homesteaders though the ages have gone about, so ensued the patterns they kept to. Coconut and carambola trees adorned the spot. Out of these trees and the rest they fashioned the lumber that formed the basis of the house that forthwith would be known as Ho Chi Minh's house. Ho Chi Minh took to the days as just one more smallholder. He grew rice and vegetables. He had to earn a living. With the passing of time his hands became as fertile as the rain. This became his life for the next seven years. Throughout the period his colleagues travelled back and forth to Vietnam, emissaries of a very special kind in that it was their mission to relay the strategies that Ho was developing for the liberation of his country. Ultimately, of course, Ho Chi Minh went back to his native country and never returned to this home he had made in Thailand. The house is now a ruin. But whatever its state, it is Ho Chi Minh's house and always will be. He was here, in Thailand, and then it started…'

Her sound built a chapel, for hush there came as she spoke. Inside the peace and quiet was born the soundless music of her hands so fantastically did they take to the air. Words could not arrive on her lips without this launching of her hands. She needed no attendants for her hands were her constant attendants. But it wasn't them alone. Her attendances were many and powerful. It was a style and more than a style that was hatching from her body.

Willing himself to it Richard Marshall's eyes stayed fastened upon Wantana's sister as she described these events, but the strength to actually listen to her eluded him. Increasingly, the speech of others asked of him an interest and attention that he found impossible. That he should be addressed directly forced him into one pose after another. Whatever the discourse, and sometimes it was his own talk, enthusiastic even, reaching his ears, little in it persuaded him. The silence inside him and his mounting silence amongst his fellows he knew as a sort of slum of being; but yet a slum with resources, determinations. Giving himself up to it, he had discovered the resolve with which to confront Wantana's decreasing interest in him. He was helpless not to make it clear to Wantana that he wished to remain in the organization for he could not conceive of another existence. But strangely, inside his slum, it was the beginnings of a man's strength he was feeling his way towards; a strength that, as hollow as the prospect left him, saw him at least ready to conceive of a life without Wantana. He could entertain the possibility of it now. The cesspit of removal lurking at his core left him so possessed an individual, bravery flowed from his heart that had never been his. Of course, he would continue to resist his fate right to the end, caring not how shameful others thought his tactics. They didn't understand anyway. What lay between him and Wantana was without measure or reference. Not a single other living soul could enter, could contrive the first idea. The combatants themselves hadn't a way in. And anyway, was it so despicable the manner he put himself on Wantana? He would make it as demanding and embarrassing for Wantana as he could because that was where he had reached with the man. The parting, if that it should be, had always promised to be excruciating. He saw that now. And what was also preordained was his, Marshall's, pure compulsion to increase the burden for Wantana. He wanted something from Wantana. He was owed it. He refused to make it easy for the celebrated industrialist. He would simply wait, and Wantana would see him waiting. The great man would not see anything else. So he, Richard Marshall, was to be despatched. Well, let Wantana take him off to the side and utter the words. These were words he was prepared to hear now. But where were they? Because still Wantana could not bring himself to speak them.

What Wantana didn't owe him! It was endless in the ramifications. He was being asked to take responsibility for Wantana's own incompetence. Many of the business plans he had had to adhere to, the sales targets he was under orders to achieve on pain of death, had been so much madness. Wantana was incapable of keeping to an even path. So glaringly, his shift to the idea of America was the newest evidence of the fact. Immense upheaval was augured. The guiding hand behind one of the world's legendary watch brands – Wantana was stepping outside his range, prodigious empire-builder or not. The entire group he had succeeded in constructing to this date would be put at risk. The man found the long view impossible. To set a forward-looking company policy that would ground the company in a definite reality for years to come, and which all its workers could relate to from week to week was the antithesis of Wantana. He was interested only in today. To work for such a man led to chaos. If the organization was about to make a sacrifice of him, Richard Marshall, it should impose the same penalty on its ultimate leader. Joined to Wantana he was. The only justice was that he should not fall alone. Wantana too should pay and precisely with his job. On the rebound the man was assembling a business colossus, but as a leader he was a travesty.

Bitter? You could say so, yes. Wantana had had the best of him. Willingly he had handed it over. Five days a week they cleaned his guts off his desk. To work for Wantana called for it. It did if your desk lay seven thousand miles from his. The miles were free rein to him, bond between men notwithstanding. What he, Marshall, would say!

Wantana's great flaw was an addiction to the chase bearing the promise to climax in the hour; that must absolutely reach a resolution before the next dawn interceded. But meet Wantana at the level of family and he was someone else entirely. As just one more member of a major Eastern industrial family he would wait and go on waiting. Indeed, so extremely he could bequeath the vigil to his children. And no one should protest that this was nothing but exaggeration because if he, Richard Marshall, had learnt one thing in his contact with Wantana, with China, it was that in certain contexts a facility for exaggeration went so far as to provide a channel to the truth that was revelatory. He fully accepted he had never been particularly interested in Wantana's background, but he hadn't been closed to everything.

For all the searing hostilities evident inside the Wantana family, the truth was that at the heart of the life of the family the year advanced not according to the rotation of months but in measure to a series of rigid family rites paying tribute to the very chain of birth and disintegration out of which came the fall of generations, one succeeding to another. In fact, essentially the year was to be seen as divided in two. There was the time before the father's birthday, there was the time after. Always, it was a mammoth affair, a good part of one of Hong Kong's five star hotels taken over for the night. The esteemed gentleman would stand side by side with his wife at the entrance of the section of the hotel sequestered off so as to greet the guests, queuing in an endless line, and somewhere in the background the high clatter of the mah-jong tables.

But Wantana the individual, the driven industrialist, was devoid of any such certainty. Fundamentally, he, Richard Marshall, had always needed Wantana's orders, but on too many days the orders had been grievously wayward. It had cost them both dreadfully. Yet if the years with Wantana had educated him in something else it was that you could not ever tell a man from China that he did not know what he was doing.

Making the decision to travel to Hong Kong unannounced, the determination gripping him suddenly to place himself directly in front of Wantana whatever the consequences, had at least forced him to his feet. He was losing his job, but by the pouring fever of his melancholy, the mountings of a life on earth were going begging.

He barely knew who he was anymore. Fearing for his sanity, the contest with Wantana brought him his one direction.

The slum had begun with his father's illness. He understood that. And he did fully comprehend that he had his own illness now. But the dreadfulness of it was that it was simultaneously an illness of withdrawal and an illness of desire. Strangely, in defiance of the accepted wisdoms of his condition, his interest in his appearance hadn't flagged. Rather, his sensitivity towards how he presented himself was now like a gigolo's. It had a bearing on what he sought. If he could not speak, he was possessed of an immense greed for the beauty of woman. He had begun a desperate inconsolable dialogue with the image which was fair woman undressed. He would know these bodies. He was filled with gratitude that the girl was with them, sister of Wantana's or not. This was the physical incarnate. Yet what was he doing in this place? Thailand: How had it happened? What had he and his father been thinking when they had agreed to this alliance, relation, association, with a major Far-Eastern industrial family? They had willingly leveraged their lives to the whims of a Thai-Chinese businessman they barely knew. Ever since the sell-out he had had to undertake the journey to Hong Kong every two or three months. His new masters needed and expected reports. His new masters might even like your face, such as it was. Basically, the journey had become a principle of his existence. But he had forced himself to make the latest journey to Hong Kong not out of fear for his position in the organization – in that he discerned the better strategy was to keep to the margins – but out of shock at his accelerating physical immobility.

In the face of the crisis in his relationship with Wantana, it was the difficulty of his own condition that terrorized him, that absorbed him. The slum on his inside was the deepest drowning. In England the one bridge left to him was the way to his office. The buckles he snapped at dawn dressing, the buckles he snapped taking to his car, allowed him a whisper of normality. The grind of a city's rush hour traffic was bigger salvation. But once he closed his office door behind him he realized the target wasn't to involve himself in anything, but to shut himself away within the only set of walls other than those of his home he trusted. Once inside the room he became marooned there, detached from the organization that spread outwards from those four walls. So far did the organization stretch in its reach; it was a kind of statehood. That was what his family had built up over the generations. What they had made a gift of to the young Chinese gentleman. Yet, with his father gone it just passed him by. His office served him purely as a hole of sanctuary. But soon, immovable in his chair, he had started to crave raw unthinking physical activity, physical release of any description. He had wanted to experiment, the need to appease the physical aspect of his being overwhelming.

His growing carnal embrace of all the creaturely drives in a man was bloodcurdling even to him. This dreadful consuming indolence, yet it was his consciousness of his body and what was open to it that formed the lone horizon reasonable to him. The rest was worthless. He had expanded his powers in the sense that he could devour one physical experience after another with tireless fury. He was spitting them out in disgust at the pitifulness of the experience. Always he needed something more. But what did this say? Was it some terrible risk and mortal danger he was thirsting for? He did not know. But though his mind lunged everywhere in the hope of discovering new physical tests, new ratcheted-up spreads in the sensual realm, though he desired to grasp hold of something with all the power and relish of the flesh that a man could call on, out on the street he could not swing his arms without the cold hand of apathy locking hard against his chest. The nerve ends of his physicality raw with desire, his ardour for the physical world like a flood, still all of this was a torrent that laughed at him. He seemed to be driven to expend himself precisely out of a sense of futility that he could ever be satisfied. He would try anything. Though this was born of arching passion, it was also born of yawning disinterest. He was resigned in advance to what would be the outcome for him. But this just drove him on with new endeavour to discover the physical breadth of a man.

The memorable restriction of the vestibule area of his father's house was a sort of swindle in that it gave the wrong idea about the main living areas beyond. Those spaces marched on freely. As a pointer to the bedrooms though the entrance was blameless. In the cell containing his father for those long final months a number of dated photographs had looked down on the figure propped against the leather bedhead, the very platonic gaze the images maintained from their place on the walls simultaneously wanting of meaning and hollow with meaning. During the hours of his frequent lone vigils beside his father near to the end, it wasn't his father's silence that ate into his skin but the vast detached silence of a room a step away from overarching constriction. He was the one who grew invisible there, not his terribly weakened father. Illness was the thing that could not be invisible. The constant battle was to recover from it the very vitality that was the power of perception, because so easily illness took down everything, for victim and onlooker alike. But it couldn't take down the room. The stunted room was always there, the man resting in it, a younger man watching from the side. In fact, what was a man on his inside but a collection of boxes in the style of the rectangles a house packaged so adeptly, there on his inside a set of enabling chambers and caves? How else to describe the inner physical construction? A man's powers advanced off the scope of the various core inward compartments that chance design had blessed him with. It might be severe restriction giving him his breath, it might be floor areas broader in range, laying the potential for an enhanced existence. But essentially, a man had to be an incurably blind small thing. What his inward motive caves amounted to determined what he was. Further, place and compulsion enclosed a man. Strapped to such restricted frontiers, and to so small a quantity, it came about that each morning that a man awoke therein was the scheme that gave rise to the individual. A man couldn't appear in the world larger than his vital caves, what they were. A man was led by the hand. Being was the prison on his interior.

At his station in the bedroom, his entrails bruised and ripped from the long evenings with his father, on some days his heart had narrowed, generosity towards others, towards himself, towards existence, not an inclination at all. Like the dead hand that was a vulture's gaze, faithfully his eyes would go to their chilling patrols in that claustrophobic room. The mounded fingers spread out over the bed-sheets by themselves pointed to the toll of years. But in any case there were the photographs, that black and white of theirs leaving a man's life as a series of iron casts. Taken together the photographs on the walls represented a vault of sepia to be sifted through for the various milestones. One by one his father had approached those milestones in actuality. He had married like a man does, he had had children, he had served his country in uniform. Staring at the photographs, no matter the absurdity, he had wished that some essence, condensed and brilliant like a gemstone, so much in advance of the mere homilies of a photograph, might be kneaded from the pictures, that when brought close to his father's eyes this the shining evidence of where he had been during his days and what he had done might go to work to suck out the poison of infirmity, might go to work to conjure some mystery of solace or resurrection.

A time had been, and not very long previously, when Richard Marshall had had this ailing man in front of him. But it hadn't just been a man prostrate in the room but a passage, the article that was a man's passage, an article as purely its own thing as anything could ever be, as unrepeatable as anything could ever be, as separate as anything could ever be, suddenly in one small forgettable room come to completion, and in the completion suddenly was the article, and the weight of it was terrible. His vigil beside his father had been combat. The sin of your own eyes: onward they devoured, onward they went with their cold testimony. They never let up. And his hadn't. They had ground the room to shreds. They had crossed the room back and forth. They had crossed in consuming anger, in consuming disinterest. And finally they had crossed in fervent prayer: that somewhere there be a presence to acknowledge and receive this unknown scale that was a man's life, and to receive it from his two arms, because it was there that these ashes were lain out.

None of this, regardless of the time he had known Wantana, he saw as communicable to his employer. Was it to anyone? As to themselves, theirs had been a bond, but to attempt to look into each other just didn't occur to them; except, of course, a moment had arrived when he was filled with one vast question: could Wantana carry it through? Could he fire him, clean, cold? He had power over Wantana, he knew that, he had always known it, and no doubt at this minute he was exploiting all of it in the saddest of fashions. But he couldn't help it. He couldn't help it. And then, the great red orb ghosting down to start its slow internment in the horizon, propelled to a singular ornateness by the drawn-out descent, in its carbon glow the unimaginable celestial plateau which was the ocean surface warped and wrinkled like sheet metal, at last proper understanding of something shot forward into Richard Marshall's eyes, his eyes as if widening at the revelation. In the flush of recognition he lowered his head: the years were just too many now. Not long hence a day of days would dawn. He might not know this day on the actual day, but he would in the period following after. Then the day would be shown stark to him, the day that brought his last sight of Pracha Wantana, otherwise Daniel T.K. Bai.

Three girls appeared amongst the tables. The minutes, hours advancing on the rough and ready pavilion constituting the focal point of the restaurant area, belonging at once to the sand and to the trees immediately at its back, appeared as if deserted, the tables outside left to their own resources. Then suddenly, like the sun slipping out from behind cloud, these working girls were all about, live and active.

The pregnant young woman was missing from the three.

Behind the shack the heat holding in the spaces between the trees, a stirring intensely physical, seemed to close in upon itself, as though curtains had been drawn about it. The dark of evening setting in lady nature got busy with untold mysteries in and around the beach. Those in charge of the unsophisticated eating premises might have taken a cue from it. In the window to the right of the cabin's entrance a robust fish tank had been placed on a table. Its iron frame was crusted like the bottom of rowing boats. The glass sides of the fish-tank were spy-holes as if offering a glimpse of the actual ocean floor. From behind the glass was conveyed a sense of the eeriness and unholy depth. Nameless blotches of iridescent colour, as concentrated as glue, could suddenly stir into life and slide along the insides of the glass. The orbits of other foetus-like shapes were to be discovered. Spindly trails of green marine growth flickered and swelled up in the swirling murk of the water.

The three girls too, they were a sort of plantain, unfurling to their meanderings; going round the tables they fashioned a straight-backed saunter that somehow elongated their figures. The poise in this movement was the absolute diffidence of their limbs. Devoid of any conviction their arms swung back and forth, slow like the girls were passing out, the strokes wider and wider each yard they advanced. Inside their long tapering skirts their legs appeared in their own dimension of time no less, this stride they had so much a coasting motion, the languor and vacuity in the action the sleep of angels. Bending, they set about dragging up two of the remaining tables towards the one occupied by Wantana and his guests. This task completed they returned to the cabin. But it was only to reappear in cycles as they carried out the bowls of food.

The question of the dishes had been passed into the care of Pracha Wantana. He knew how to do this and was always fulfilled by it. Should he be presented with a starving multitude, he was ready to adopt these people in a second, and ready to pay, so long as the power to choose the plates was given over to him. It didn't matter where he was or who his guests were, nor in fact whether guests existed on the day or not, the host in him was never far adrift. He might put everything aside to pass into this role. With these instincts at the fore, a feast it was that was all too likely to arrive on the tables.

And so proved the case on this occasion; the tables that the three girls had brought together were soon overwhelmed. That this drab anonymous 'way-station' had produced such things was inexplicable, not least to Richard Marshall. The shiitake mushrooms could be picked up with chopsticks and eaten as an appetiser with wine and beer. The dish called for garlic and the large cloves had been peeled and sautéed in butter. An oyster and soy sauce completed the starter. Pracha Wantana was fond of pasta with salted fish and given the treacherous divisions in palate existing at the table, he was possibly seduced by the security that pasta seemed to offer. Probably he had played safe too in his decisions in respect of some of the main dishes. The German pork leg could be served with gravy and mashed potato. But for himself and his sister he had specified steamed rice to accompany the pork. It needed a dipping sauce to be spooned over the meat, the more so if the pork was greasy. He dared to settle for a spice-laden sauce, one involving chilli peppers and lime juice. With the steak that he had ordered so as to extend the possibilities for his guests, the appropriate sauce was the example known all over Thailand as 'Jaew'. It was associated with the North Eastern province of Isan, and consisted of fish sauce, tamarind juice, dried chilli peppers, toasted rice kernels, sliced shallots and chopped green onions. The steak had been sliced into thin sections after cooking. Wantana knew that the sweetness of the meat went well with the saltiness and spiciness of the sauce, the hot rice absorbing all the harsh flavours with its starch.

Ready to push his plate away as soon as it was polite, Richard Marshall could look past the shoulders of the two people opposite him, Wantana and his sister, to see what they could not. Perhaps he faced the ocean as a man faces his quarry. Amidst nothingness a man discovered inside him this betrothal to the sea. In a vague form it was there at the beginning, surely, and without question it was there at the end, as had been made obvious to him during his father's decline. Hearing his father reminisce, on the days the voice held, the tone changed when it got to the matter of the oceans. His face took on a different aspect, the eyes in the face taking their leave of you, a little. An individual's everlasting communion was revealed; a life's absorption denoting the simplest pulses of a person; a correspondence of the heart where the rolling wagon of career and family didn't set foot. Learning of his father's secret, he had instinctively known it to be true of men in their tens of thousands and tens of thousands more besides. The sea was this term bringing together all the seas. There lived a man the word had never penetrated? There lived a man deaf in his soul to the image of the waves and their path of solitude only the clouds watched? Standing next to his son, there lived a man who not once had cradled these waters as a kind of invaluable offering that it was to him alone to bequeath to his own?

But the reverence wasn't confined to the unchallengeable ponds which were the oceans. In conversation with his offspring, rivers came into it. Didn't they speak to the raw sense of seniority and survival a man could be overcome with in the presence of his child? Faced by his son a man risked an air of preaching telling of the stretch of river that at a point in his life he had fished faithfully, the torrent where his float stood up vertical, lithe, curling, at once so energized and apathetic?

Water in its open territorial state as a colossus of the natural order was like that. For a man come to the end, the image of the sea could appear in the nature of a dark messenger bidding for his life as he called it back to himself.

In all of this he was certain. In all of it was the weight of his last vigil next to a man. In all of it was an account conceived through witness to but the one man: the father he had had.

'You look out there and the island just stares back at you,' Richard Marshall said.

'Once you have known this place, the island stares at you wherever you are,' Wantana said.

'So let us do it, Pracha,' Marshall said.

'Do what?' Wantana asked.

'You have brought us here,' Marshall said. 'We should swim to the island.'

'I think not,' Wantana said, smiling, seeing it as a moment's jest between colleagues.

'We are young still,' Marshall said.

'Some would say so,' Wantana said.

'Only six months separates us,' Marshall said.

'But which is the older?' Jacot-Descombes said.

'It is the one with the authority,' Marshall said.

Wantana's head moved back, its angle more telling of the cold silence in his heart than the eyes bearing in at Marshall.

'And what would you have me do with it, Richard? My authority.'

'It is our privilege to wait on that,' Marshall said. 'All of us who work for you.'

'Yes…?' Wantana said.

'What do I say?' Marshall said. 'You're at the top. You call the shots. It's the same everywhere.'

'This is dangerous talk, Richard,' Wantana said.

'That sounds like a threat, Pracha,' Marshall said.

'You think so,' Wantana said, laughing. 'My dear man, I'm at the top, remember.'

'Are we in fact?' Marshall said.

'You will have to explain…' Wantana said.

'Are we…men?'

'I think the question is to be addressed to you.'

'You were bound to say that,' Marshall said.

'I could say more,' Wantana said.

'What?' Marshall said.

'Prove it,' Wantana said. 'Prove you're a man.'

'Nice, Pracha,' Marshall said.

'Then will you?' Wantana said.

'I might,' Marshall said.

'You might? Wantana said.

'At this minute I'm more interested in the island.' Marshall said.

'You're avoiding the issue,' Wantana said.

'No, you are,' Marshall said.

Wantana sat rigid.

'Are you frightened, Pracha?' Richard Marshall said.

Jacot-Descombes looked between Wantana and Marshall, the deadly seriousness of the moment invading him.

'We put our trunks on and walk to the water,' Marshall said. 'That's all. Why be scared?'

‘No, Pracha,’ Kep said.

Wantana flicked his eyes over at his sister, realizing that but for her presence he could just ignore the oafish Richard Marshall.

‘Is this the reason we’re here,’ Jacot-Descombes said. ‘In fact, neither of you is that young.’

‘It seems that Richard is the one deciding the reason we’re here,’ Wantana said. ‘He thinks I’m shaking in my shoes.’

‘You are,’ Marshall said.

Now their eyes were locked. Time passed.

‘You two are just play-acting,’ Jacot-Descombes said abruptly, desperately, seeking for anything. ‘It’s all to impress this beautiful young woman.’

Which young woman sat looking at Richard Marshall. Which young woman asked herself one more time just what lay between this man and her brother?

‘Do you know the best image I have of Pracha,’ Marshall asked.

‘Tell us,’ Wantana said.

‘It was a man’s head bobbing above the waves. I was standing on a beach in Hong Kong. Pracha was some fifty yards out from the sand, an afternoon’s swim.’

‘What did you like about the image?’ Wantana said.

‘I thought you looked human,’ Marshall said.

No one spoke.

‘I have listened to you talk about Joti Bidaya,’ Marshall said.

‘So the good man from England presumes to place himself on a level with Joti?’ Wantana said.

‘I have never met him, but I know I can swim to that island,’ Marshall said.

‘I am not going to allow it,’ Jacot-Descombes said.

‘Then I will do it alone,’ Marshall said. ‘It’s not for you to intervene. Nor anyone else.’

‘If you determined to, I will not stop you,’ Jacot-Descombes said. ‘It’s Pracha I’m concerned about.’

‘But surely Pracha will decide for himself,’ Marshall said.

'You will have your wish, Richard,' Wantana said. 'You want to see me swim to the island? So be it.'

'No,' Marshall said. 'I want you to do it with me.'

'Why won't you listen?' Kep said. 'Marcel is right.'

'Listen, sister!?' Wantana said. 'When do I not? They line up outside my door with their petitions, their pleas. Where is the one who will allow me a second's rest? Thousands rely on me. What children they are! I say this: if Richard enters the water, then it's the two of us. I don't want another word from anyone.'

'Then at least we can have a boat standing off,' Jacot-Descombes said.

'You mean one of the trawlers?' Wantana said.

'Or one of their smaller vessels,' Jacot-Descombes said. 'It would be madness not to have a boat in attendance. They are here, these people. These are their waters. And how do you intend to get back? Do you propose to swim back?'

'We will go to the village in the morning,' Wantana said. 'We will ask them.'

3

The village lay in a hollow and the path to it descended through trees. It wasn't a distance they had to cover from the beach. Never mind, the trail was rugged in parts, the trees impressively solid, massed, and with this world of theirs seeming not in the present. Hardly to be confused with a military troupe of course, nevertheless the single file the four people abided by had come about of itself, silently, quickly, a ranging Frenchman getting the vote for the advance position in equal fashion. One other westerner amongst them, he had been determined to bring up the rear.

Making their way into the trees a strong smell of cinnamon became evident. Soon it felt like an animal's stiffened carcass pressing against their faces. This was the heat. The edge of the narrow track was garlanded by mushrooms. Keeping to the trail the party edged past a small number of cedars that obtruded like cathedrals. The unknown invention was their girth. Wantana remembered that partridges collected in the branches braced over their heads.

Observing the back of the austere, long-limbed Frenchman, he marvelled at the instinct with which the foreigner took to the landscape. Weren't there certain Europeans who seemed born to these trails in a way that not even the hardiest amongst the region's own people could match? Indochina was a resonant word and Indochina lived. During earlier periods it wasn't the terrain that caused the lone European voyageurs to founder so much as the customs that held sway in the sphere of taxation as it was applied across the region. A distinction was drawn between territorial jurisdiction and personal jurisdiction. Thus it was that if an individual shifted between territories, he paid tax to the governor of the region he was officially settled in because he was a man of that territory, and territorial tax to the chief of the domain where he chose to stop off for a time on his travels. In general the latter exceeded the former twice over.

With his sister directly in front of him, Wantana was aware of the marked deadness of her step. She advanced only feet from the heels of Jacot-Decombes. The defiant, almost insolent tone she could adopt when speaking to the Frenchman concealed little. He had his friendship with the architect. That made it difficult for his sister. He asked himself whether he should intentionally strike down his relationship with Jacot-Descombes. Friend it was he would lose, the man who was this exception, this 'grace' he could seek out when he was driven to retreat from his regular retinue.

Of course, he needed his clique of minders, this private staff of flatterers he maintained. Having an entourage was how he lived a great part of his life. Executives on his payroll, yes, but these retainers, an inner circle and more, amounted to wheels, to camouflage, to a ring of defence, they added up to one leader's insurance. With his cadre of 'bad guys' he was let into understanding of himself and of what he needed at a fundamental level; pulling these men around him to some extent allowed him to tame the elusiveness of existence; their presence brought about a way of being he was comfortable with; his confidence in their existence was the signal permitting his parts to slide into place at the start of a day. To think of himself as any common soul alone and naked on the streets was an unbelievable conception. At daybreak let these people descend on him for their instructions. Let him see them hovering around him, sworn to him, the symbol of all he held sway over.

On his outings from his office in Hong Kong, looking out from the back seat of the limousine, faithfully it was that his gaze encountered construction sites. One after the other they came into view, complete with their towers of scaffolding. The spectacle was a constituent of Hong Kong. Passing by in his car he gained a vague sense of something. The business empire he was intent on forging, wasn't it itself really the thing he was beholding, purely a kind of scaffolding. Finally what this scaffolding realised and serviced was one man, amongst humankind's powerful, amongst humankind's movers and doers. The channel to his full function as a human being lay in this scaffolding. Every industrial building under his control, in whatever part of the globe, the work going on inside these buildings, all of the men and women who scurried to his orders, could be viewed as components fashioning the unwieldy vehicle he lived through, a vehicle as critical to him as his limbs. He could not live in any other way. Be it known that an empire builder was occupied like no one else. Be it known also that the thing under construction held him, together. To live a simple existence would undermine him leave him, Wantana, wretched and vulnerable. He would be terrorized by existence.

He became conscious of the comparative tallness of his sister's figure. Marching behind her he sometimes lifted his eyes all the way. It was like counting off all the routes of emerging selfhood of the phantom. Phantom she was in this sudden, mighty redrawing of herself. A fuse was lit in her. It showered feminine glad rags, feminine ceremonies, the gamut of the female graces. From the first he had been intrigued by the change in her, being completely in favour of the development. He accepted that for him considerable difficulty was augured by the fact of six sisters. It was in some way a life's connection never to find an answer to. They would surely figure, but how? If he were to look about the family for a suggestion of the dynastic, here it was. The brothers of his sisters, he one of them, worked and bustled, the husbands of his sisters worked and bustled, all these men in turn challenged to achieve something definite, all understanding they were watched, and that the watchers were addressed by signposts that surfaced not to any man's eye but to the eyes of the earth's female element alone.

Already he had needed to ask his sisters' forgiveness. By marrying so late he had tested everyone's patience. A Thai-Chinese family, yes, but if China is there nothing sets it aside for a moment. The stamp on a family is diamond clear, diamond hard. Say the word China, a lined empire of cultural tariff passes to the eyes, reckonings for the native born like a last reveille. For this family of many offspring, amongst the commands coming out of the valleys was the one directing that since the eldest son was the eldest overall none of his siblings could marry until he had done the business. It was only Kep, far away in the American university, purely young, no thought of nuptials in her head, who had not experienced the desperate annoyance at him. All the rest in the family had had to look on helplessly as the handsome, recklessly decisive oldest in the tribe had delayed, had appeared torn, unfulfilled, desirous of something he was unable to quantify, and ultimately it seemed, reduced to accepting the dishonour of an enduring bachelor status, an outcome that would overturn everything that was expected of him as the most senior. Then, worse still, the news had spread that he had begun an impossible relationship with a woman in Switzerland who was establishing a significant reputation for herself as a sculptor.

Of course, eventually he had married. And where had he met his future wife but in a gymnasium, this time one of Hong Kong's. The woman destined to be his bride had been working as a physiotherapist and fitness trainer.

At his place behind his sister, suddenly he went off to a moment's flight of the imagination. Suppose it had been Andrew Camondo in his office in Hong Kong and not Richard Marshall. Suppose with his impetuosity he had decided to risk everything and invite the American to this place so as to allow Camondo to gain a better appreciation of his Chinese suitor, though he would not have known that that was Wantana's ambition. And suppose that at dawn on one of the days the American had simply wandered off. Trudging along in the tracks of Jacot-Descombes and his sister he was captured by the fantasy. A man far from his own land, a man he was acting host to gone missing; yes, but hardly any man. The event would quickly become a nightmare. The sense of it took hold of him. He saw the fingers pointing at him from New York, every hand that of a race of superior beings. Andrew Camondo lost! It would be horror. It would be America converging, as only it did, about one of its sons. It would be a man amongst a nation's elite, stepping out from the security of his national habitat and into the jaws of an opposing universe, placing himself into the care of the man whose universe it was, whose invitation it had been.

It would be the radiant sector of the globe coming down on its poorer cousin, the misdeed the greater for the divergence. Going in search of the American, he would be this person flailing around in body and spirit, the wealth of his elaborate identity coming away in his hands like so much dead skin. Deep amongst the trees he would be ready to let out an insane noise in the urge to call out Camondo's name. Only the presence of his sister might hold him back. Andrew Camondo not to be found – he wouldn't be able to grasp the event. His mind would spin into blankness. He would act out of obedience to a vague conception of what a man might do in the circumstances, his legs moving but without any reality to himself. He would just be this dazed creature with thoughts about his sister's hair. A vision of the unremitting savagery he would draw down on himself swept over him. They would not spare him, nor would he spare himself. His very life would be tainted, and for evermore. New York: the image grew brighter than ever in his mind because now it had been taken from him for ever, all of it ended in the circumstances of one man on a moment's impulse and curiosity going off on his own where, yes, it was not safe.

His moment of make-believe died on him. The problem of Richard Marshall broke through in force. Finally it did. The actual plod of a man's two feet reached him from over his shoulder. It was fitting. He knew himself to be stalked. He was being stalked when Marshall was in his office in England and he was in his in Hong Kong. Oh, were the issue to be solely just a question of whether one individual was deemed suitable to continue in his position or not. A man judged purely against his effectiveness in the post he occupied. In order to resolve the matter would that it was no more than this. But for Richard Marshall and him…No, he could not deceive himself. His cadre of senior Chinese executives in Hong Kong, his father, other family members, they just were not able to comprehend the difficulties he was in over this one figure. What did he owe

Marshall? His father should be able to understand the insolubility of a question like that because hadn't he had to ask himself countless times what he owed Suthin Bidaya.

In his mind now Marshall dangled as outright specimen. He, Wantana, had questions, hard questions. It could be that with his interrogation he was seeking to absolve himself in the decision he was about to take. But never mind, he was suddenly filled with doubts with regard to Marshall's sincerity towards him. It just hadn't entered his head before to put Marshall, to put their relationship, to the test of sincerity, sincerity on Marshall's part. But, yes, a vision of something was reaching at him. That all along Marshall had been manipulating him to his own ends as coldly as a man ever did. Of course, at one level this existed in every human relationship. But just what lengths had it gone to with Marshall in his links to the man from the East. Hadn't it been a case of a man, Richard Marshall, being so in touch with this critical need of his to have something like a father figure at his back, someone who he could rely on as authority, as bulwark, that once this man appeared – and amazingly revealing himself to be more than eager to take him, Richard Marshall, on board – he had been led to a calculation and guile with which to control, to stage-manage, the very figure of dominance he craved. Dependent emotionally on another's confidence, decisiveness, he knowingly went about constructing a persona that he sensed his employer would be unable to resist.

Indeed, the question did have to be put: Between himself and Marshall, which in truth had served which? Ask the question once, ask it again, go on asking.

But what was sincerity in a case like this? Could one even presume to apply the term? Whatever were the convolutions of Marshall's mind and heart, he, Wantana, had to acknowledge that today Marshall was there for him as much as he had ever been, no matter what lay behind such willingness. It was he himself who was overcome with fatigue for the connection. He should remember that something had existed once. He should recognize too that something had preceded it. He could hear it now: the keening of a man frantic to receive the voice of command, frantic to be taken up by a leader, and somewhere in a distant region the one who was born to lead carrying a hidden wish for a follower whose heart would bleed to defend his name. And if that individual turned out to possess a foreign face, a western face, then he, Pracha Wantana, he would be attracted, overcome, disarmed by the wonder of such a man deferring without hesitation to his person. If he had believed in the thing that was Marshall's apparent veneration of him, it was because he had needed to believe. Yes, the leader was not without his grievous insecurities. In order to be satisfied, doubt-free, the leader had, always, to be confirmed in his natural might. And for this it wasn't a vote he sought but an unashamed and helpless display of homage in the ranks of those he commanded directly; as Marshall, unconsciously no doubt, had searched hard for him, so he, Wantana, had been searching for Marshall all those years ago.

Jacot-Descombes pulled up without warning. Some fifty yards ahead of them an old woman with a load strapped to her back was toiling across a clearing. In this spot the charred trunks of trees lay about everywhere. The woman was not alone. Two children, two urchins, were hunting around at her side. But as soon as their eyes alighted on the Frenchman, they abandoned the woman and scampered away. Hopping like monkeys from trunk to trunk, they kept turning to deride the village dowager for her dreadful slowness. That she was bent over beneath her burden seemed only to strengthen the enthusiasm with which they goaded her. Still, there appeared no spite to their wilfulness.

'We need to get on,' Pracha Wantana said.

The party of four arrived at the edge of a much larger clearing; a crudely fashioned bamboo frame, tall, rectangular in form, and spare as some children's hoop, had been erected at the exact centre of the patch. It stood alone, completely, serenely.

'It is ceremonial,' Wantana said, 'a formal gateway announcing the start of the village territories.'

He had no recollection of it. Yet years ago he had surely come this way.

At the sight of the somewhat surreal archway, an object cut-off in space, they drew up in simple instinctive respect. In silence the party separated, taking to either side of the construction in an exaggerated show of avoidance. In the massively still air the damp, grey vaporous light wasn't even in its texture. It had congealed into a pillared effect, these shards seeming to hang before them like icicles from the roof of a cave.

Numerous children came to meet them; as they went towards the youngsters an unaccountable murmur of voices, the sound low, voluminous, droning, started up, quickly gaining strength, pressing at them from the immediate distance. Even the toddlers paused in their capers, somehow responding not so much with their ears as with their nostrils. Wantana's group looked where the heads of the children were turned, the four of them pestered to understand the path to follow to get to the heart of the settlement. But nothing seemed to be centred anywhere. The few dwellings they could see lay about in random isolation. Their distribution had no pattern. It was like confronting the remnants of a community, a community that had suffered a terrible decline. An odd dwelling spotted in amongst the trees, it seemed to represent just another blind turning that led nowhere. The only signpost they had was the swelling undertone of voices trespassing through the trees. The sound indicated a small multitude.

Pracha Wantana was alerted to the anxiety in the faces of his colleagues. The hum of voices filling the air had made them uneasy.

'It is the way of the people,' Wantana said to assure them. 'They are excited, even fearful, when strangers make an appearance.'

'But no one has seen us,' Jacot-Descombes said. 'It's only the children who realise we are here.'

'Our presence is known,' Wantana replied with conviction.

They were startled by a new single voice that broke out very close to them. A man, perhaps forty years old, appeared to their right, whistling and singing as he went. He was driving a solitary steer before him, its side caved-in, one beast's tracks of bones set out like goal-posts. The dungarees the man wore were turned up at the bottoms. He walked on bare feet. His singlet was like a boxer's training vest, dirt-spotted, perfunctory, and cut-away at the shoulders. In the light of day the long wiry arms told of years of straight-out manual effort. A sort of sheet was circled about the man's head. A trailing piece flapped at his back. Miners have their faces. Is it any different with a quintessential village face from one of the developing countries? The accumulated weight of an unremitting exposure to the sky can lie on the human face like a skin-graft.

For a moment Wantana was back in his daydream. It was as if he could hear himself addressing the drover. They were searching for someone, a foreigner. Had the man seen anyone? No, the nightmare couldn't continue. It would surely end in the next second. An American would stride forth from the shadows amongst the trees and everything would be resolved. How they would stamp around on their feet to assuage the derision they experienced at themselves. Hadn't they been resigned, almost, to the idea of the worst possible outcome? Laughter would grip them as they made their way back to the beach, the foolishness they felt at themselves flooding into their faces.

The herdsman stood before them stubbornly silent, his eyes going from one to the other as he peered hard at the strangers.

'These voices that we can hear,' Wantana asked the man, 'what is this about?'

So shy was the poor fellow it left him staring without discretion. Behind his air of disconsolateness appeared a mind obstinate with but the one hope: that he had only to look away and the strangers and all memory of them would be expunged forever. Abruptly, though, he gestured in a jocular fashion that they should follow him.

'I do not know,' the man said. 'We will have to go along and find out.'

He prodded the bovine with his stick. They saw the beast's neck with its hanging folds snatch up slightly.

It was once told that in every man of Siam there lurked an excellent farmer. Though this was in the first instance a village of fishermen, Wantana was incited to repeat this adage to himself as his eyes went about; notwithstanding that his Chinese identity, his city identity, Pracha Wantana was sensitive to this compact with the land that illuminated so many of the people of Thailand. Nor was the partnership confined to the poor of the nation. In times of old the cultivation of fruit trees had been a favourite pastime of wealthy men. Discovering the riches of the soil was a delight that brought a certain comfort to these men's lives. Would these have been the inclinations of his father if the man had reached Thailand in a previous era? In different ways, all of them in the family had an ambiguous relationship with the Thailand. But wasn't that true even of the natives of the land. Pracha Wantana knew this about the country that was Thailand: that everywhere you went, north, south, east or west, you proceeded forward in harness to a vague feeling of dissatisfaction that you could not account for to yourself. Whether you faced mouse-coloured slopes, the short grass that grew so luxuriantly in places, the green of sheltered glens, the morning fogs with their hazy dews, whether you listened to the wind sighing as it fed through the long-leaved pines, you always expected that in the next moment you would see something else, something more, something scaled up, something even of a feeling close to magic. But how did he know these things because the place that he knew was Bangkok? But was Bangkok any different. It kept insinuating discoveries, potentials that never quite unfolded for you. You couldn't name these things. But the sense that revelation awaited you wouldn't stop hounding you. The next day the promise would be made good. Yes, the next day.

The village seemed a mishmash of disconnected clearings. Following behind the scrawny drover they came into one containing a large haystack, as gloriously isolated in its space as the symbolic entrance arch that they had encountered. Another of the tykes, a little girl of about five years old, emerged around one side of the haystack. Jacot-Descombes beckoned to her to come nearer, but the man with the bullock shook his head violently. He began to jabber without pause, his face contorted into a high state of excitement. The Frenchman was forced to look towards Pracha Wantana.

'What is he saying?' Jacot-Descombes asked.

Wantana ignored the architect for a moment as he concentrated on the rant of the village man. Then he swung back to his colleague.

'You mustn't trust me on any of this,' Wantana said. 'I believe he is saying that the girl is not right in her head. He speaks of her as an idiot. It seems that one day not long ago a man brought her into the village, giving her into the care of the village elders. The stranger explained to everyone that he had found the infant wandering around alone. That she hadn't eaten was obvious. Before preparing a meal for her they carried the child to a stream to bathe her. Her condition demanded it. But the little thing fought them with a strength no one could credit in a five year old. It's a jumble. But that's what I could make out.'

'She appears hungry this minute,' Jacot-Descombes said.

'Well, the story is not unknown in Thailand,' Wantana said, 'a young mother whose husband has left her falls ill. She decides she can no longer care for her child. She looks for a busy road, convincing herself that some passer-by is bound to pick the child up if she leaves it.'

'Did we see any busy roads on our way in?' Jacot-Descombes said.

Pracha Wantana looked away.

'Where is our friend taking us?' the Frenchman asked.

'I told him that we wished to speak with the headman of the village,' Wantana said with a resigned voice.

'Two days ago we were in Bangkok,' the architect said. 'The day before that, Hong Kong.'

'Yes,' Wantana said, 'how many times have I repeated that to myself?'

The architect was conscious of how Wantana and Marshall resolutely stood off from each other by some ten yards or so. It was obvious they were not disposed to narrow the distance.

Moreover, they hadn't so much as a word for one another. Now the group had broken to a free formation, walking along side by side, with every step the two were at pains to avoid their eyes meeting. It had been like this since their group had broken up after the dinner the previous evening. Jacot-Descombes felt that he and Kep had become mere bystanders to something.

He saw that Marshall had increased the pressure on Wantana. He saw that Wantana had done it for himself. The two of them brought together at the remote beach, it was Marshall who was presented with opportunity. Was it too far-fetched to suggest that for Wantana to reach a position of resolve with regard to Marshall required something superhuman of him? He himself, he didn't know Marshall, but it had quickly been his notion that the Englishman was possessed of an unerring instinct for the intricacies of his relationship with Wantana and it led him to an unerring sense of which devices of the heart he might employ to maintain his place with Wantana. The lonely beach left Wantana at the mercy of Richard Marshall. Had that been Wantana's awful miscalculation? This alliance had been forged and maintained across incalculable distances and at the very moment he could have employed these divides for precisely his own ends, some wretched sympathy of Wantana's had had him hesitating. Where he might have kept the Englishman at arm's length, merely informing him by letter or emissary that his service with the organization was at an end, he had decided Marshall was owed more. But of course he hadn't decided that for he hadn't decided anything. He couldn't decide. Standing out stark on Wantana at this moment was the most grievous mortal trap there was: not just the inability to decide, but the terrible labour to know what it be that you yourself wished for in the affair. It seemed like that to Jacot-Descombes.

Should he say poor Marshall, or should he say poor Wantana? As to the Englishman this was someone facing the prospect of losing a whole way of life. He would have to bring this news to his family. As much a European as Marshall, he dared not speculate as to what it would be like were Wantana to turn against you out of sudden deadly hostility. As yet, as yet, this did not describe the situation existing between the Englishman and the Thai-Chinese industrialist. But if Richard Marshall was desperate, so was Pracha Wantana. The mortal struggle of two men had the potential to go to any barbarism. You thought so looking at this pair, having gained a vague sense of the devastating human mix going between them. Caught in something past reason, a man was in charge of himself only so far. Or rather a point came where he threatened to pass out of the recognizable person.

Yet men maintained level minds conscious the shells weren't for the sky but for the ground their troop had orders to cross. Be it Vietnam or elsewhere, the battlefield was learnt, it was born, enough even to want to extract the experience.

Where he, this innocent French observer, was standing today, was exactly the place Richard Marshall had once stood. If Wantana was of a mind to take you up, you faced a charm offensive like a geyser. Unremitting power of personality just not in your experience descended laser-like. You had the feeling suddenly of being ten men and for the reason you had caught the eye of but a single individual, someone who just wasn't like others, or anyone.

Accepting a position with a firm of architects in Hong Kong, he had begun to encounter a handful of individuals he could not dismiss. One amongst them had stood out especially. Some distinctness was involved rarely come upon. In fact, he soon realised he had stumbled on an emperor. But one yet to be properly crowned. The man he had happened on had a Chinese name and a Thai name. Also, he was in possession of a stride surging with impatience. Witnessing Wantana in motion was to intercept the ceaseless collision of a man with his ambition. This stride of his bayed at you like some fierce dog.

Pracha Wantana had almost yelled at him: 'The Y.M.C.A! What sane man can live there? You work for me, you will have an address! You can take one of these apartments.' With that he had tossed across a list of enviable properties. But though on any given morning he had fully expected the arrival of a band of Wantana's 'heavies' under orders to eject him from his little cell, he had resisted his new friend. He had resisted with a return to laughter rightfully owed, as he had realised, to the impassioned Thai-Chinese man he had discovered. Standing next to this man the streets and roads took on a different list. The world was a platitude placed at the disposal of Pracha Wantana. And if he liked you, this man appeared eager to offer you the entire city as his personal gift. Received from his hand, the most banal of the city's streets metamorphosed into mystery, enchantment. Soon he had known himself to be one of the few that the industrialist was willing to treat as an equal.

Pracha Wantana could undoubtedly be cruel, not least when he was overcome by jealousy of one of his brothers, but this cruelty wasn't the man. For some reason you had to insist on this with yourself. Occupying this privileged vantage point he had discerned that as a rule Wantana was most comfortable in his dealings with his fellow beings when he could convince himself that he enjoyed a definite prestige that they did not, however artificial might be the basis of this elevation. With or without a significant position in life, some presumed their essential distinction in relation to their colleagues and were never undone in their certainty. Of Pracha Wantana it could be said that this was the one presumption he was never quite able to carry off in himself, though he willed it of himself with a passion. And he, Jacot-Descombes, hadn't needed Kep to point out that her brother was compelled to treat architects with a respect bordering on reverence. He had felt it at his first meeting with the Chinese magnate.

As powerful as Wantana had been in his insistence, he had not allowed himself to be turned out of his frugal quarters. There were things he would not have attempted to explain to anyone. His room at the Y.M.C.A spoke of what he wanted from Hong Kong. With his tallness opening to him as a kind of unaccountable comfort, he had slotted into the multitudes on Hong Hong's streets, letting himself be swept along. It had been aimless, but he had relished the movement. He had relished the ruggedness of being surrounded by an alien horde. Lost in the midst of these people, he had discovered the sacrament of his separation from them. For this it was necessary to drink of the people in their swarms. It had been a faceless communion, but one which had straightened his back. He had understood that by embracing this tempest, like a dam-burst across a few of the streets, he had consented to a process that was slowly siphoning off some of the congestion around his heart. The union with his wife had been long, the penurious route to the day of ruin a progression no less protracted. Where was the beginning of the breakdown, where was its point of no return? From a certain moment in time a purely dying marriage and going down so dreadfully peaceably; this had been the house this had been its mountain echoes. A marriage ultimately given over, a residence resigned from, the subjection had fed on as defiantly as a disease. In any case, an echo was what your heart was. An echo made of many echoes. And the East, that was another echo. You might be deep in the midst of it, echo was it nevertheless.

From the moment that they had arrived in the village the architect had been struggling to draw the settlement together in his mind. The sense of something marshalled, of something even vaguely persuasive of an underlying rationale, kept evading him. The thatched dwellings stood where they stood and pointed where they pointed. Their arrangement was spontaneity incarnate. With his disciplines he was urged to discover a standard governing their placement, but however his eyes worked they were doomed to a continuing frustration. The village mocked him, refusing to give back the sense he asked of it. A grandness of situation was common to the village properties he did pick out. Even where two dwellings did start to intrude on each other, still the proximity remained relative. Never was it overarching. Supported on its stilts, each primitive abode was a little manor in its setting. But travelling in the wake of the herdsman at last it was as if he had finally broken the code of the village. As he made his way between the utterly basic dwellings, as the clearings aligned to a stronger sense of partnership, an uneven but perceptible network of village routes, started to form to his eyes, displacing the memorable incoherence that had been transmitted to him until then.

Jacot-Descombes became alerted to the presence of an adolescent girl. She was watching the four of them from the balcony of one of the simple wood houses. His eyes going to her, she returned his look. It was a face generated of strong curvatures. The broadness of form had its counterpart in a girl's lips, fullness, ripeness there not a little incendiary. But what was more significant was the enormous placidness of her expression. Fixed of gaze, like the child she was, no less she observed these strangers that had arrived in the village with the calm of a holy sister. Jacot-Descombes fell a little behind the others. The deep anthracite gleam of the girl's hair reflected the signature black which a crow has, and the mass of it so wet through that in its look it appeared a true dead weight as it plunged downward. The girl started to comb out this mane of hers. Levelling an instrument that was too large for her hand, she was stirred sufficiently to throw her head down to one side. It was a mechanical action and the eternalness of it sprang at Jacot-Decombes.

His house in France had developed into a receptacle propping up the lives of his three daughters. In passing, it received their bodies, less randomly, it received their many objects. He had been a man surrounded. Not so much by four females as by their inimitable activities. Amongst this had been his daughter's interminable servicing of their hair. They had combed religiously, they had combed with apathy; an apathy that stretched away like their hair. Watching the dark languid figure of the village girl, he was in the grip of something. With such flatness and preternaturalness was the girl drawing out his eyes with her own, turning herself into a throne of detachment as all the time she went on with her task, her hand moving rhythmically. Each robust stroke of the crudely fashioned instrument pulled whole sections of her long hair around from her back. Their steadiness never veering, the impartialness of the eyes she placed on him was like the impartialness of the sky. What purpose took hold of a house when the daughters of the house advanced to the day of their nuptials each in turn. Each in turn his girls had become like gladiators, such had been the single-mindedness, physicality and self-laceration of their preparations as one after the other they had approached the day purely theirs and no one else's. Those had been rallying, garlanded years. And his wife? When a woman believed in something, how it acted on those she administered to. Four walls to the house like any other, but weren't these walls of new discovery while they retained the deities of four active women, three of them not just women but emergent women.

Hoisted up on their wood stilts, their balconies as if lashed together, and then lashed to the main structure, the rough-hewn village dwellings were like a form of raft. The tawny forest girl idling against the railings of her own balcony was a spirit that threatened to carry the Frenchman off. Seeing her young peasant skin, swamps pushed at him. In her shift-like clothes, it was a horde of crude jewellery she displayed. The silver hoops hanging down from her ears were flat expanses of dramatic crazy width, the spread three inches, four inches. Her neck and wrists trailed a girl's wares, the bands of metal and cane backed-up in number, the breadth of the pieces too not in the realm of sense. A melange of silver and cane sprouted everywhere on her. Sowed down one side of the full-length skirt she wore was a line of brash silver buttons to all intents won at a fair-ground.

Her combing drew to an end as if out of a collapse of will. Her arm had appeared increasingly sluggish in its movement, fervent shyness at one foreign man's concentration on her forcing up as if from a well. Finally the girl's arms dropped to her sides, hanging straight down in a gesture of hopelessness. The unwieldy comb fell from her hand. She didn't move to retrieve it from the planks at her feet. She made no movement of any kind. Yet even with the rush of bashfulness, her stillness carried inordinate patience for the two alien eyes angled up towards her. The bare-footed gazelle waited, all her shape mute, all her shape questioning, until finally, like a sphinx, she started to shrink backwards, the regret, the incomprehension, looking for the embrace of the doorway behind her. In a second the shadow at the inside claimed the last trace of her.

Trudging along next to him, Kep thought her brother wore a strained absorbed expression across his face that she couldn't associate with him. Marshall was walking at the other shoulder of her brother. From the time their party had entered the village it was perceptible how at first Marshall and her brother had kept away from each other. But now it was two men on a march, flanking one another, the image formidable for the sense of incurable partnership it was engraved with. But this didn't mean that either spoke. Both of the men had a look that said they were determined on silence. Not a general silence but one specifically aimed at the figure of the man alongside. The clamped mouths reverberated, a bond between humans, or the memory of a bond, visibly slung on the shoulders of two men, the actual men themselves. A party of four was making its way, but at the same time it was a party solidly of just two.

That she was there at all still astonished her. Though she had a resplendent office inside her brother's resplendent headquarters, and a significant mission to accomplish on behalf of the organization, she had returned from the American university to find her brother a rather remote figure. It was his liking to surround himself with a knot of confidantes and aides. Some worked directly for him, others did not. Having seen her brother once like this, it was how she always saw him now. To reach him even in her thoughts she had to penetrate this tangle of hard-eyed cohorts that cordoned off his robust frame throughout the daylight hours, and often through into the evening. Entering his office sometimes she had to take it on trust that he was there at all. To find him she needed to stay on the alert. The circle of suited bodies hiding her brother would open then close. In the gaps that appeared fleetingly was the one opportunity to glimpse her brother, this hunched form of a man seated at his big desk. Catching a sighting of her brother she could be overcome by the idea she had interrupted some gangster figure.

Jacot-Descombes was not amongst an organization's intense soldier subordinates. Nor could the courtier's role ever be his.

As they followed the path deeper into the village, she swung about in search of the dawdling Frenchman. In her beige cotton trousers, unconscious of the forthrightness of her stance, she planted herself in the middle of the track with legs braced wide apart. Jacot-Descombes turned his head in her direction. As their eyes met, she saw the start that went through him. He gave a little half-wave, springing up the track in a way that displayed disbelief at his conduct.

Wasn't he too old for this pair? Whether it was them or others, the question of his maturity was constantly at his back, harrying him on and off precisely because in this Asian setting the bare number you called out in your mind wasn't as translatable as previously. The friend he had in Vietnam didn't allow him his earlier reading of the matter. The gaze she sent at him never stopped painting the figure of a man, but he had no idea who this man was. In the wake of losing her husband to the war, she told him he had rescued her. But he couldn't believe her. Statements like that rang hollow to him. But she did things. There were small experiences that both in the moment of living them and then later visited him like unknown lands. That visited him as the thing called Indochina. During a dangerous two hour journey they had taken by taxi the one time she had lain across the rear seat with her head in his lap for almost the entire time. It was like the girl on the balcony; anything might be but he it was that had to decide. He was in Vietnam, this young woman's head was cushioned on his legs, the clock of life, of war, ticking out where the night was, and ticking too there on the inside of the car because desperately he didn't know the answer. It broke his heart, broke it in glory for he could drop his eyes to find her face, and whenever he did it was better than anything.

In her keeping he thought of his age as a sort of plasticine she was always toying with. Her fingers never left off, but she never let him see. The designs she fashioned were her secret, a secret she shared with herself when he had departed back to

Hong Kong. There was revelation to him that only she carried the knowledge of. That was how she made it seem. Going back to Hong Kong he left a man behind in Vietnam. The next weekend he would return to be that man. He wouldn't ever know him.

But whatever were his misgivings as he cantered up the path towards the Wantanas, he felt the eagerness in his legs. Brother and sister they were and somehow they persisted in making this place for him. Of course, these two were exploring the gulf in age that existed between themselves. It was one of the reasons Wantana had asked Kep to accompany them to Thailand. Offering her a serious position in his organization had forced him into a quest of rediscovery where his youngest sister was concerned. The Wantana family, large as it was, the gap to the youngest daughter from the eldest of the offspring a gap if ever there be.

'What's this then?' Kep said, keeping her eyes averted from Jacot-Descombes who had dropped into a position alongside her.

Ahead of them a considerable throng was gathered at the foot of one of the bare-boned village dwellings.

'This explains the voices we've been hearing,' Jacot-Descombes said.

At their approach, the low florid babble rising from the crowd began to fail until finally a pall of wary silence hung over the heads of the people. Faces swivelled towards them, but as they came round it was in effect a single face that stared up the track towards the party of strangers; a face that was sullen and fixed behind the tunnel of its glowering watchfulness; a face that as it stared bore the shame of centuries, understanding it itself to be the thing under examination when strangers appeared.

The tense stillness emitted by the crowd held a particular resonance for Pracha Wantana. A body of people watching as if with the whole of their bodies, he saw a state of confusion similar to that which sometimes gripped his own people when he was spurred to enter one of his factory departments unannounced. At his appearance in the doorway grown men could in an instant become like children caught in some dishonourable act, starting back as if dazed by a blow, the tools they held, dangling down from lifeless hands, just forgotten. Indulging in a spontaneous promenade through the world that he ruled, he was always conscious of the deftness that was required of him. Pausing for a moment of light interchange with one of his workers seemed such a small inconsequential matter. But in fact it wasn't, as he knew better than anyone. In each case it behoved him to adopt a certain attitude, a certain style, a certain cant of the head. That he should be successful in this was critical to his aims. At every stage of his journey, he had to take these men, all of them, with him if he was to triumph.

Once he had the mob of villagers in view the raunchy guide they had gathered up immediately lengthened his stride to some purpose, becoming divided from his ghastly cow. Even under pain of the hustling of its master the beast had showed itself struck dead in its will, the legs beneath it columns of crushing reluctance. But once it was spared the irritation of the stick in its ribs, matters got worse, profoundly so. The animal stopped to go not another step.

An ageing man with white hair stepped forward from the crowd to meet the herdsman. Cropped in a peremptory fashion, his hair sprouted vertically in dense tufts. The loose ends of his open white shirt were tied in a bow that dangled over the belt of his dungarees. At the bottoms the work pants flapped, brushing against rugged sandals. As he listened to what was being reported to him the village head never took his eyes off the group of visitors who stood some distance away.

'Are we to assume that this is the village chief?' Jacot-Descombes said.

'Without a doubt.' Wantana said.

Jacot-Descombes estimated the man to be some ten years older than himself.

Telling the others to wait for him, Wantana advanced to meet the village chief; getting closer the face of a person came into focus. A vast privacy in which was embedded too many of the years a man had lived flooded about the mouth of the village man.

The headman gesticulated at the drover, making it clear that he was not needed. Left alone together, Pracha Wantana and the village leader confronted each other in silence. The man was almost abrupt when he finally spoke.

'But we know you,' the headman said.

'No, you cannot,' Wantana answered.

A hue like teak to the skin, the village face he was looking at had condensed into a series of stark craters and grooves. The manliness of the face was tumultuous. In seconds it was a discomfiting face to concentrate on. For all of the handsomeness portrayed, the stern toll of years scored into the face stared back at Wantana with withering effect. Deep immemorial rivulets, almost a sort of heraldry, plunged downwards from beneath the eyes in striking curves, reaching as far as the jawbone. The ridges between the furrows sat up rope-like. The seared crustaceous eyes seemed burnt into the flesh. Behind the hard points of light glinting from them there might have been plates of metal.

'You are from the other family,' the village chief said.

'The other family?' Wantana said.

'There is the important family who own this land,' The man said, 'but once there was another family too. Sometimes they accompanied the important family on their visits here. But then one day it was just the important family who came.'

Wantana shuddered. The chief's words in his ears, too much of what he carried inside him broke from its leashes.

'You have a gift my friend,' Wantana said. 'You tell a story in a single sentence.'

'So I am right,' the village head said.

'How so?' Wantana said.

'You are the eldest in the other family,' the village leader said. 'It's Mr. Pracha, isn't it? A man now.'

Wantana laughed.

'No, it's not possible,' he said. 'I didn't even remember the road to take to reach here.'

'Does that mean your connection to the important family is at an end?'

What should he answer? The Bidayas? Well, old man, not so important now. He glanced up at the dwelling they were standing beneath. He had the strange sense that he would feel more secure talking to the village elder if they were enclosed inside the walls of a building. There was a forbidding authority to the figure before him that filled him with caution. The man had the strength of his surroundings. In the simplicity and lowliness of the surroundings was the harshest light of day; a light that redoubled the silhouettes of those born to this elemental existence. Curiously, in the outlines of the people you saw a sternness of fate so like that adhering to the figures of pioneer homesteaders of the new world as these figures were immortalized in old monochrome photographs. But this wasn't the new world. Fate didn't lie here. Pure being did. The leader of the village embodied this. A dour, intractable lineage was all of his countenance. By his own face and person he was lifted up. By his own face and person he was lionized. A true primary force if ever there was, Wantana thought. Standing in front of him, Wantana was no longer convinced of his own powers as a man.

'But it is years since we have seen anyone from your family,' the chief said.

'And you recognized me!?' Wantana said.

'I was certain of it,' the man said.

'Our own family went away from Thailand,' Wantana said. 'I had almost forgotten this place.'

'Are we so easy to forget?' the man said.

'I didn't mean it like that,' Wantana said. 'It was necessary for me to put it behind me.'

'The important family?' The village elder said.

Wantana kept his silence.

'Then why did you come back?' the man said.

Wantana swung his eyes towards the crowd. They were still watching him in their flat, expressionless way. This mute plaintive outpouring affected him. His gaze passing from one face to the next, it wasn't the features he saw so much as the prairies of a certain human innocence; prairies that the faces of certain tribal populations alone made manifest. The people filling the width of his gaze had pity for him, they had pity for themselves.

'Why are they here? Wantana asked. 'Why do they stand outside this house?'

'A woman of the village has been returned to us, temporarily,' the headman said. 'This is her son's home. She is not expected to live long. It is her wish to be with her family for a time.'

'I am sorry,' Wantana said.

'What do you know of our village?' the man said.

'Probably no more than I know of any village in this country.'

'But for years your family left the city to come to this place.'

'I was interested only in the beach.'

'And all the time, right beside you, there was an ancient village and its daily existence.'

'My life wasn't yours,' Wantana said. 'Even then I knew what my life would be.'

'We have our customs,' the chief said.

'I am sure,' Wantana said.

'There are people with you,' the headman said.

'They can wait,' Wantana said.

'Yes…?' The chief said.

'Is there anything I can do for this woman?' Wantana said. 'Or for her family?'

'A village from your childhood,' the chief said, 'and you confess you know little.'

'You want to scold me, you have the right.'

'In times gone by…' the village head started.

'Tell me,' Wantana said.

'A custom existed in some villages in this country. The dead were cast into a ravine. In days the heavy rains would carry the bodies down into the rivers.'

'And now?' Wantana asked.

'I will take you, Mr. Pracha,' the village chief said.

'What?' Wantana said.

He watched the headman bound away. But only as far as the stairs leading up to the balcony of the house they were beside. The chief climbed the five steps like a young man. Once past the railing at the top he turned to beckon to Wantana, throwing his arm up in an action like that of an outrider's. It was as if the throng of village people took this as a signal, starting to shift towards Wantana in a heaving swell, cutting him off. In the next second the region that separated him from the foot of the house was solid with villagers, the throng thickening before his eyes. In was then that the body of people began to part, dividing off into two huddled groups, the one backing off from the other. On each side the people began transferring about randomly on their feet in order to find a place for themselves in their own section. By that movement did the two sides secure a definite shape for themselves. Two lines started to emerge until soon Wantana found himself standing at the head of an actual passage, so much the condemned man.

Suddenly a terrible exhaustion overtook Pracha Wantana. He was aware of nothing but the eyes, scabrous and ever so mortal. They came slowly round in his direction, overpowering him, their concentration on him bringing a magnitude of human travail surpassing anything he found in the obsessive stares he received from two thousand or so of his workers when he entered the canteen area of his principal factory. There wasn't hostility, baying, showing in the faces of the villagers, nothing like that. He could trust them. They wouldn't hurt him. But he must go between them. He shouldn't refuse.

The alley facing him was resonant. Something in him started back, his gaze darkening to the deeply mistrustful eyes of the hunted. The tense passage filled his eyes, so unreasonably he could have believed of himself some accused of a previous time sentenced to run the gauntlet. The villagers seemingly determined on an impromptu honour guard, these people before him he suffered an onslaught of doubt in respect of his physical safety. In mass they were turning towards him. With such curiosity and obedience and expectancy did the many, many eyes finally settle on his face a tide of emotion was released in Wantana that for whatever reason impelled him to turn and beckon to Marshall to join him. His sister and Jacot-Descombes didn't need telling that it was only Richard Marshall that Wantana was addressing. Marshall hesitated, but then he moved to do what he was helpless not to do, going up to the side of Wantana.

'Do not ask where we are going,' Wantana said, 'because I do not know.'

These were the first words that had passed between them since dinner the evening before.

Moving into the channel separating the people, some dull instinct had them bending forward defensively, as if they half expected a fusillade of blows to rein down on them. But no sooner did they react like this than they straightened up, a shamefaced look about them. Then it was that they found their stride, forging ahead along the passage like they had swung side by side down countless corridors the world over, the buildings, offices, hotels, airport terminals, government premises; they followed the channel between the simple village folk like they had shoulder to shoulder and one year to the next crossed the vast spaces of innumerable trade shows in countless lands; like they had, just the two of them, sauntered city streets, the city just anywhere; like they had taken their places at innumerable boardroom tables, the two of them alone and flanking each other on one side of the colossal table, on the other a whole row of men, too often something like adversaries on the day; like they had, level with each other, climbed the broad concrete stairways to the great entrance arches of a thousand mighty business premises situated in any number of the great capitals.

But at the foot of the steps to the balcony of the village dwelling Marshall held back instinctively, letting Wantana go ahead, there not being the space on the short flight to allow them to ascend abreast of one another.

Arriving on the balcony the village chief looked at Wantana, blank, uncomprehending.

‘I must ask for your forbearance,’ Wantana said. ‘I realise the great imposition. I show disrespect. It is unforgiveable. But this man is from overseas. He is my guest. Our alliance has stood every test that human life will inflict. He has been like a brother to me. But he knows nothing of this place. He knows nothing of this country. He knows nothing of the people. It is time he saw. It is time he saw.’

‘Of course, Mr. Pracha,’ the village elder said. ‘You have only to say.’

Directly behind the old man was the door to the dwelling. Looking beyond it the swirling dimness on the inside was like a skin. As Richard Marshall’s eyes adjusted an amazing scene was brought to him. The immediate area the door led to was deep and broad. The people were packed in; wedges of humanity jammed together past sense; the press of bodies heaved.

The village headman swung around, stepping towards to the door opening assertively.

Marshall experienced this scream inside him. Enter! He refused to enter. He was beaten down with nervous divorce, staggering from a savage loss of bearings. The disorientation had struck the moment they freed themselves from the cars. What it was his whole system shrank from in revolt was the place he was, the land he was, in fact the full breadth of these the territories where he had arrived, the full breadth of the faces essential to the environment. His estrangement was the taking down of a man. The profound discomfort, the infernal feeling of terrible division from his surroundings, the vast discord gnashing at his cells at the confrontation with this landscape, at the confrontation with the decision he and his father had made all those years ago to join up with foreigners, at the confrontation with this image which was a jobless man, accelerated to the sensation of nightmarish dream. In his distress the murk on the inside of the door set its teeth into him, alien as death. He wanted no more of Wantana. He wanted no more of any of it.

But Wantana was speaking:

‘Your name?’ Wantana said. ‘Give me your name.’

'Opas,' the village chief said. 'My name is Opas.'

Resting on the planks at the side of the door was a beautifully ornate metal drum. Small shapes of frogs cast in brass formed the rim of the drum. As he edged across the threshold the village headman accidently nudged the drum with his foot.

Instinctively Wantana knew to stay right at the back of the indomitable Opas; but for the people on the inside to give way demanded of them a brute physicality commensurate to that which was asked of the person attempting to force his way into the area. It was a test of will on either side. To gain a yard the chief had to employ his shoulders with perceptible crudeness. Wantana began to appreciate that Opas was a character of iron. Whatever were the years he carried, somewhere there lurked potency apparently undiminished.

Dogged as anything Richard Marshall shoved up to Wantana's shoulder. He wouldn't be denied. He employed his strength like the village chief, not caring. The banging of bodies was toxic. Gaining ground in amongst the dark compression of people, Marshall closed his eyes, the hot breaths of men bringing the sense his face was blanketed by insects. Though he could make out little around him, he understood that the mighty Opas was intent on forcing a path to a side-room that lay directly off the dwelling's dominant section. Once they had won through to the door of this room the vortex of obstruction fell away in a single magical second.

But still there was the difficulty to actually see anything. Richard Marshall stood motionless, to all intents alone now, alone with himself, engaged in his senses at the level of reverie, at the level of tyranny. He hated the gloom ahead but was absorbed with it violently. As his eyes fought for a footing ideas flew at him. He thought he discerned a line of individual compartments, in the shadow like crevices set into rock, and large to accept a human being.

But searching hard with his eyes inside the cubicles he believed he saw, still he could not make out a single person. But he knew they were there. Someone was there. The shadow bore in on him, summoning him. It was something like intoxication he surrendered to. He was under siege in his parts in the effort to see, to understand.

Then he understood his gaze had found the far wall of the side room. Dangling there it seemed were the pelts of slaughtered animals hung out to cure. In stages the reality penetrated. A cord had been hung along the wall over which was draped an unholy miscellany of household items. He began to separate the items as best he could, in the process finding that people's whole lives stared back at him.

He was off the known tracks amongst those recognizably the bearers of the natural habitat, the earth's real, the earth's immovable, the earth's blameless, the first stock of the bare sea, of the bare land. Yet in fact he was somewhere he was more than acquainted with. The place he stood was the place he found himself when the plane landed at Hong Kong.

Be it the city, the village, it did reach him, this other opposing universe and he had never stopped making his personal record. He did it in the taxis going to his meetings with Wantana. Take Hong Kong, just so black in its stridency and invasiveness. It was a city whose lungs were diseased and it was shameless with the din of its constant retching. The people arrived on the pavements in herds and these herds were not tender of foot. In breaking over the streets, the crowds were never slow to give vent to their coarser foibles. In this city the energy, the phenomenon of driven man, was out in the open, and granite-hard in the spectre. An essence of the city was its refusal to be a shrinking violet, was the impossibility of it. The city hadn't propriety. The city brandished its intensities, its missions. Here was a population with lives and the lives were seen and heard. In some districts a sheer wall of brick lacking in a single window had a way of eavesdropping on the facts on the interior of the building that put to shame any amount of the glass of the imperious towers adorning the slickest areas of the city. In the lowlier neighbourhoods a single glance at a climbing surface of unbroken stone left you tossing hard against the naked knowledge of what lay on the inside. But if you required definite evidence then settle your eyes on the balconies. Life with its crowding, inebriation and sluice was hung across the exterior of many of the buildings with such candour it might have been a gallery of skulls lined up along the reams of balconies. Hong Kong had a way of making flags of its intestines, viscera rank, viscera the unwashed table in the basement.

The string running along the far wall of the side-room drooped from the weight of the accumulation of household objects thrown over it. He identified coarse clothing, rugs, blankets, matting. As he uncovered these things his eyes began to slice about with an increasing certainty. He was in a room drenched in the drugged atmospheres that developed when women did their homemaking off crude floors. Women could turn nature's floors into throne and hearth. Suddenly below him he deciphered earthenware strewn in all directions. He asked himself how he could have missed the groups of globular, thick-walled urns, pots, and bowls dispersed across the area.

Now the gangrenous shadow was helpless not to give up its secrets. The three women who were stretched out on the floor parallel to each other were simply the impressions of the human form in the first instant. But the realization that this was a female presence he didn't need to question. The ailing woman was the one in the centre. Extended flat on her back and very still in herself, her eyes were cast up to the roof. The two remaining women were reclined on their side as they concentrated on the sick person lying between them. All three lay on mats. Matting was to be detected everywhere across the floor. The chambers, compartments he had conceived of had never existed. It was an open space and the creature of the naked pine walls that formed and enclosed it. A potion filled the air, some incense made of the wood and heat.

Marshall did not see Opas gesture, but he recognized a signal had been given, the two women maintaining a vigil on each side of the desperate invalid moving to get to their feet. In front of his eyes a lethal indolence of woman, eastern in tenor, swelled out through the dimness, the shadow somehow piling on the spectacle. The robes draped about the two floated before him as if a quantity of scarves. Stirring the women went to their action, slowly lifting themselves, the movement a fantastic art seemingly spun out by intention, the planes of their essential languor following as if a step behind throughout.

Richard Marshall launched himself forward unheeding. No one held him back. Numbed, submissive, he was filled with the feeling that in any way that he could he had to fulfil every one of the tests that were being set before him, however inexplicable they appeared to him. He couldn't see beyond these trials. Nor even beyond this woman. Having reached her side it was a new effort that was asked of him. The prone figure beneath him drifted away from him, the harder he searched for her. Feeling himself to be no more than some dull tool of compliance, he fell to his knees beside the woman; and reeled at eyeballs that bulged out monstrously; at protruding spheres bearing that insensible slimy flesh-tissue white of organs cut from the body; at sickness-huge spheres glazed over like a blind person's; at sickness-huge spheres past a ray of sight. Rolled upwards, and expanded to a largeness that horrified him, the awful white orbs emitted terrible silent spasms, suggesting unceasing strangulation.

This wasn't breath. What breathed was an awful fracturing, body and entrails.

At the door to the room Wantana had been interested just to take a glance. He had gone into the room but only to linger at the door. He was disconsolate, wary, tired. But really none of it involved the village or its people, or even Richard Marshall. He was standing in the room but abruptly his mind started to work in isolation, as if of perverseness he had no power over. He was following what was occurring around him, recording the village house, taking note of the actions of Richard Marshall, filing every bit of it away, but equally a separate contemplation altogether had hold of him.

A tempest fell into his mind, scattering his mind down channels of dread, of despair. He thought of a man of his birth entering one of New York's heavyweight broad-on corporate strongholds, but not as any impoverished supplicant off the street, rather as wearer of the seal of office, the authority with power over the whole construction. Without America it was half a life. From Hong Kong he looked out at the planet and never did he struggle to grasp the boundaries in play. Contained inside the safety of a city he was at home in his heart thirsted at these boundaries. But looking out from an office in New York would he begin to flail? It would be necessary to confront a largeness whose aggregate somehow submerged all other lands in their totality, whose aggregate even outran the planet. In his new corporate quarters in New York would he find himself recoiling, the desire he believed he had withdrawing from him in an unstoppable rush? Setting his gaze at the world from the comfort of Hong Kong what in fact did he see? America? A landmass like this was untouchable until you approached it. But when you did approach, it accelerated to a weight and immensity that was like a plague.

If the nation were to be New York on its own, this he wouldn't have difficulty with. But in New York the genie in the streets would be the shadow cast by a vastness that he, Chinese or not, couldn't begin to engage with. The city would be instinctive to him, but to attempt to see into the infernal territorial mass which fed out from New York, would this prove his undoing?

But wasn't there a prospect daunting on another scale. Were they ready for him, all of the people working in the great office structure in New York, the headquarters of one of the nation's historic companies? Any time that on impulse he engaged in a walk amongst the desks of the staff would the faces lay bare the truth, not ever to be mentioned: that this wasn't the leader they wished for? As the head of the organization would he find himself marooned in a bastion of nativism looking to something that could never include him? Traditions and nuances and shapes so cemented it would leave him reeling from the revelation of what nativism was. It was only the outsider who was led to this understanding in all its dimensions. Would he be the spurned commander?

Frankly, would he be equal to any of it? Either where the confrontation was confined to the level of a single person – he would understand the language, but the tones of the daily interactions would surely be indicative of sensibilities simply indecipherable to him – or where it swept him into a reckoning with the wider imbroglio. Was this how it would end? America was to have been the brilliant monument to his name that he had always sought. A man like him, in order to establish his ascendancy amongst men, all men, he was driven to push out to the world's surpassing kingdom. He wanted a throne and there was only one.

Yes, America had been the single incomparable conquest that could suffice. Besides, he had known it in time: this was the one place that spoke to him. The one place that spoke to his heart, to the implacable ambition twinned with the blood his heart pumped. The one place fit for him, he might even say. And, yes, would it end before it began? Would he find himself in months back in Hong Kong, staring out from the deck of his yacht into the ether of what might have been, pleading for the strength to go on watching, to stay fixed as all of it spun away and away? He would stand rigid, unmoving, not wanting to remove his eyes ever. Over there in that far off country of countries he had for a passing moment been 'The Chinese Industrialist'. America named one, America knew one.

There it was, the vision, the recognition, the title, he had born in his imagination for years.

On his knees Richard Marshall looked and looked at the woman's face, wanting an account of a human being, of a stranger, wanting an account of the unknown. But his nearness to the woman brought him little feeling of connection to anything such as a person. The nearness he experienced was to this vast nameless sinking.

Turning his head to the hand placed on his shoulder he realised that it had been resting there for some moments. He surged with inexpressible relief, starting up with unashamed eagerness to follow the village elder to the door.

The main area in the dwelling was a different area now. The impossible crowd had evaporated. Not a single person stood anywhere. Crossing to the entrance to the house, Richard Marshall glanced at the television set that was standing on a small rectangle of shabby carpeting at the precise centre of the square space. It was the sole fixture. As the principal zone in a human abode the area felt little used. Shrouded in a half-light it did impress as a tribal space, but in that somehow was disinterest. Inside the area he was conscious not of the province which was a community people but of the province which was the naked forest.

Outside on the balcony, Wantana and Marshall gazed about themselves. Down below, immediately adjacent to the village dwelling was a blunt timber platform like a pallet. It was set directly on the ground and measured perhaps six feet square. The slender poles inserted at each corner supported a simple thatched awning. At the sides, the unit was open to the weather.

'Does someone live on that thing?' Richard Marshall asked.

Wantana threw a glance at Marshall. He put a question to the village chief and listened to his answer.

'It is the woman's home,' Wantana said. 'The woman we have just been to see.'

'Her home?!' Marshall said, not bothering to conceal his indignation.

'She is a widow,' Wantana said, his throat tensing.

'But her son has his house right alongside,' Marshall protested, the abuse he felt explicit in his face.

'Yes,' Wantana said

'Her husband passes on and she is condemned to live out her days in a kind of barrow!' Marshall said. 'And her son next door!'

The last sentence was almost a shout. His outrage, the level of his voice, broke every ordinance he had lived by in his relationship with Wantana. But far worse it showed him coldly indifferent to the code of behaviour he should honour as a guest in a foreign hamlet. Openly he trampled on the village.

'Her days are at an end,' Wantana said, rigid with the effort of keeping hold of himself.

'But before?' Marshall demanded, revealing something like contempt for the man he answered to.

Wantana was stunned. Where his life was bedded, he passed to ice. His fixed eyes terrorized the distance.

'Old age is a set of circumstances without circumstance,' he said emotionlessly.

'But she is not old like that,' Marshall said.

'No, perhaps not,' Wantana said. 'But this is how it is.'

'What has got into your friend,' the village leader said. 'Why is he speaking to you like this? What is this awful rage of his? I think you must take him away. It is not proper.'

Marshall did not know the speech but he didn't need to.

'Tell your man I apologise,' Marshall said. Tell him I am…overwhelmed. Tell him for a moment I wasn't in my right senses. I gave into raw emotion. The things I have met with these last days, it will never come again for me. I must go away never to return to this land for as long as I live. A part of my life has ended. It is my decision. Tell him that, yes, once you and I were like brothers. Once it was so. Tell him that after tomorrow we are to part for the last time. Tell him…Tell him any sweet thing you like…'

Marshall thrust off down the wood steps. Still a collection of villagers hovered about in the area at the base of the house. He pushed past two of them. When he got up to where Jacot-Descombes and Wantana's sister were waiting, he kept to his silence.

The man Opas gazed straight at the face of Wantana, waiting.

'Not long ago my friend lost his father,' Wantana said. 'What he found in the house disturbed him. He asks me to apologise for him. He is not himself today.'

Wantana said no more, setting his mouth.

Instantly the village leader graced to accept the explanation.

'I believe you are eager to speak to me, Mr. Pracha,' Opas said.

'I am,' Wantana said. 'Tomorrow I intend to swim to the island. I wish to ask if one of the boats could follow at a short distance.'

'Is this sensible?' Opas said.

'Of course not,' Wantana said. 'But it is what I will do regardless.'

'You mean with or without the boat you will do it.'

'Exactly.'

'And if I ask you to reconsider?'

'All I am requesting is a boat.'

'It would appear you are not to be put off.'

'It is something I have to do,' Wantana said.

'But why?' Opas said.

'It began a long time ago,' Wantana said.

'In the years when your family joined the important family here,' the chief said.

'Do I have to tell you?'

'You are confident you are up to this?'

'Without question.'

'In fact, this is not so extraordinary,' the village leader said. 'Men have always done it. The island is out there. It is never less than a temptation. To man to youth alike. Almost every year someone tries. And not just one.'

'I have seen this myself.'

'Of course you have.'

'Yes,' Wantana said.

'Who was it you saw?' Opas said.

'You know already. He belonged to the other family.'

'And the people you have brought with you today?'

'They are as keen as you to discourage me.'

'Did you return here for this alone?'

'Not at all,' Wantana said.

'But now you are here, you cannot escape it.'

'There are mountains of things I cannot escape. And it is never any different.'

'But this is different?'

'Yes.'

'And when you have accomplished it, what then?'

'Then, like my English friend, I do not think I will ever return to this shore.'

'And may I ask where you will be?'

'I have set my heart on America.'

'I take it that you are an important man yourself now, Mr. Pracha.'

‘Well, I do not go to America to dream away the days,’ Wantana laughed. ‘You see, old man, I have to build.’

‘You should not forget us, Mr. Pracha,’ the village chief said. ‘It’s a place you have here.’

Pracha Wantana looked at village head.

‘And tomorrow?’ Wantana said, after a moment.

‘I will give orders for a boat to be made ready,’ Opas said. ‘Tomorrow you are our responsibility.’

Wantana descended the stairs from the balcony. Walking off a short distance, he stopped. The three others came to meet him.

‘We can go back now,’ Wantana said. ‘Everything is arranged for the morning.’

4

As he walked down the beach at the side of Richard Marshall, Pracha Wantana raised his eyes to the ocean, his gaze striking out until it intercepted the unmistakeable outline of a rare individual. Jacot-Descombes was at his place. His rail-thin silhouette climbed up from the deck of the trawler designated to keep a close watch on the pair of swimmers. The one boat had broken away from the vessels grouped at their regular anchorage and moved to adopt a prominent station not far out from the shoreline. Concentrating on the Frenchman, Wantana experienced satisfaction at the sight. Would he have to call on the fishermen to haul him from the sea while Marshall swam on with languid assurance? Most probably this would be the inevitable outcome to the business, for all his efficiency as a swimmer. He had to think that but for the presence of Jacot-Descombes, he would not have embarked on this craziness, whatever the loss of face. The steely figure lodged in the bow of the trawler would indeed stand guard. At this moment it was clear who had effective charge of the fishing vessel. The man from France had only to speak.

Nevertheless, this wasn't someone he could take with him to America. Simply, it would not be appropriate. But he wasn't the person anyway. There was so much a kind for the occasion; a kind to arm himself with entering the critical talks. Which kind exactly was Richard Marshall. And Marshall he would have taken; for he never could have made the decision to dethrone him. He realised that. Simply, he would have delayed more. The sense of being torn, of it being an issue pulling him this way and that, had to be seen as a critical mass of his mind and heart acting out an intense rite of denial. Wasn't it so? In fact in this matter he had known his mind incontrovertibly. He just hadn't had the fortitude to act. Nor would it have come to him. He would have allowed Marshall to retain his position in the organization. For a time anyway.

In the final event, wasn't this the thing that distinguished him: the power to eject men from the posts that were everything to them? In this case, though, he would have gone on putting matters off. So, he could say a prayer of thanks to Marshall. He could say that he was forever in the man's debt. He could say whatever he liked. The essential point was that he was free now. Farewell Englishman. None of it interested him anymore.

Yes, Richard Marshall had figured in his life to a degree he couldn't explain. The beguilement was in the racial separation. Somewhere it was. Once he had needed Richard Marshall as much as Marshall had needed him. You carried someone because the wish to do it was implicit in the attraction. Yet didn't that mean that he carried you, no less. But then one day this thing in you, the compulsion, just started to lose air. A phase of your life was through. You learned that there couldn't be a brother who wasn't your brother. It was a matter written in blood, solely. He and Richard Marshall: all of it was there when they were both of youthful age, but a time come when neither was that young anymore, the thing no longer existed.

And yet: amazingly, he understood that despite everything, despite the overwhelming lack of sympathy risen up between them, still he would have gained a rare strength from having Marshall present at his shoulder when he arrived in New York to take on the incalculable challenge that he had set for himself in that far-off land that cut a man to the quick with the breadth of the triumph it promised. Young shores, but what they threw up was a determination and self-possession of such precocity a value arose matching all prior histories. In fact, this was a history you dared not equate. Therein were skies of no previous making. Their scale would be his scale. That was the promise, the promise he was gripped by. And yes, a part of him would have been glad to have Marshall included with the select few he directed to accompany him. He could not proceed anywhere without his retinue of the hour, a sampling of his serving men, tight-knit as he preferred these teams rework the mix though he did. If finally he was a man alone, if finally this was his quest, it should never be underestimated what a man like him took from those who had gone to some trouble to attach themselves, not least through recognition of their own comparative weaknesses. He, Pracha Wantana, he had his disciples, some with doting eyes, and though their attendance could have him tearing at himself in a fever of exasperation (who didn't disappoint him ultimately), it could also fill him with human might.

As he stepped up to the water's edge, this thirty-five year old Chinese man who was possessed of the courage for vast responsibility, and who equally burst with an absolute need of these things, trembled at the thought of the physical test awaiting him if he was at last to claim his victory and reach this offshore landmark that had risen up in his vision with something like his first steps in life. An island they called it, its high walls of ash-coloured stone ascending to one of those summits seen but never visited.

Richard Marshall, sombre-faced, slave to a contagion of recklessness, went in first amongst the floundering ribs of surf.